"This isn't about sex, Susannah," Remy said irritably.

Then, when she gave him a skeptical, raised-brow look, he grudgingly grinned. "Well, of course it's about that, too, but not *just* that. I'm talking about a relationship, about a future, about making something together, something that lasts."

Pain, emotional in origin but very real all the same, twisted deep in her stomach. "But I don't want those things—not with you, not with anybody, not ever."

"I don't believe you."

She forced herself to shrug casually. "You have that right."

"Yes, I do," he agreed softly. "And I have the right to want you anyway. I have the right to try to change your mind. And now that you've been warned, I have the right to try to seduce you."

Dear Reader,

This month it's my pleasure to bring you one of the most-requested books we've ever published: *Loving Evangeline* by Linda Howard. This story features Robert Cannon, first seen in her tremendously popular *Duncan's Bride,* and in Evangeline Shaw he meets a woman who is his perfect match—and then some! Don't miss it!

Don't miss the rest of this month's books, either, or you'll end up regretting it. We've also got *A Very Convenient Marriage* by Dallas Schulze, and the next in Marilyn Pappano's "Southern Knights" miniseries, *Regarding Remy.* And then there's *Surrogate Dad* by Marion Smith Collins, as well as *Not His Wife* by Sally Tyler Hayes and *Georgia on My Mind* by Clara Wimberly. In short, a stellar lineup by some of the best authors going, and they're all yours—courtesy of Silhouette Intimate Moments.

Enjoy!

Leslie Wainger
Senior Editor and Editorial Coordinator

Please address questions and book requests to:
Silhouette Reader Service
U.S.: 3010 Walden Ave., P.O. Box 1325, Buffalo, NY 14269
Canadian: P.O. Box 609, Fort Erie, Ont. L2A 5X3

REGARDING REMY

MARILYN PAPPANO

Silhouette®
INTIMATE™MOMENTS®
Published by Silhouette Books
America's Publisher of Contemporary Romance

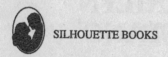 SILHOUETTE BOOKS

ISBN 0-373-07609-6

REGARDING REMY

Books by Marilyn Pappano

MARILYN PAPPANO

has been writing as long as she can remember, just for the fun of it, but a few years ago she decided to take her lifelong hobby seriously. She was encouraging a friend to write a romance novel and ended up writing one herself. It was accepted, and she plans to continue as an author for a long time. When she's not involved in writing, she enjoys camping, quilting, sewing and, most of all, reading. Not surprisingly, her favorite books are romance novels.

Her husband is in the navy, and in the course of her marriage she has lived all over the U.S. Currently, she lives in North Carolina with her husband and son.

Prologue

In his twelve years as an FBI agent, Remy Sinclair had lived a charmed life, but on a chilly New Orleans Saturday night, it almost came to an end. Lying facedown on the ground, he felt his clothing grow damp. From the puddles that dotted the ground? he wondered. Or from blood?

He knew he'd been hit, had been hit bad. He'd heard Michael's shout and Valery's scream.... Funny. Michael was part of his backup, but his cousin wasn't supposed to be here. She was supposed to be safe and under armed guard back at Michael's apartment. She wasn't supposed to see this, wasn't supposed ...

Oh, God, the pain was so intense, burning and tearing, that it was hard to sort out exactly where it was coming from. His arm, he thought, and his leg and chest. The Kevlar fibers of his bulletproof vest had protected his chest ... unless the bullet had been armor-piercing. But wouldn't he be hurting a hell of a lot worse if it had pierced the vest? Or was it even possible to hurt much worse?

He didn't want to find out.

He shifted, just a slight tensing of his muscles, and gritted his teeth on a curse. Oh, hell, yeah, his leg had been hit. It was useless. The only way he was going anywhere was on a stretcher. Please let it be an ambulance stretcher, he silently prayed, and not the coroner's. There were arteries in the leg, weren't there? A man could bleed to death getting shot there, couldn't he? Oh, God, he didn't want to die here. He didn't want to get Falcone badly enough to die for him. He didn't want to leave Michael . . . Smith . . . Valery . . . his parents . . .

The sounds around him—a few last gunshots, shouted commands, the clatter of metal against concrete—faded, came back, faded again. He hurt so badly that his throat clogged with tears. Every breath was painful, every sensation agony, every nerve raw. Maybe Falcone's men *had* been using armor-piercing ammo. Maybe that was why he couldn't breathe.

Maybe he was dying.

No, damn it. He wouldn't die. He couldn't. There was too much left to do. He had to see Falcone in prison. To make up the last fifteen years with Valery. To resolve the problems between him and his parents. God, there were so many things he'd never done. He had never fallen in love, had never gotten married, had never settled down and had kids. He had always thought there would be plenty of time for that later.

But maybe there wouldn't be.

Maybe not now.

"Remy!"

The voice sounded distant, although he sensed it came from somewhere nearby. Forcing his eyes open, he saw that he was right. Michael was kneeling beside him, bent low to see his face in the dim light—and damn it, yes, that was Valery right behind him.

Michael reached out and touched him, Remy knew, but he couldn't feel it. There was too much pain.

"The ambulance is on its way. You're going to be all right."

Now Michael had his hand. Remy could see it, could feel the tremors—his own? Or his friend's? This had to be bad for Michael—a replay of the night nearly a year ago when his partner had been killed—and he tried to reassure him. "I'm okay," he whispered, the effort to speak making his chest hurt even more. He even managed a faint grin. "I guess I'm slowing down a bit."

"Don't worry about it. Just be quiet until the ambulance gets here."

"Val… Tell Mom—" He broke off and squeezed his eyes shut on a new wave of pain.

Valery was crying. It was Michael who answered. "You'll have plenty of time to talk to her yourself. I'll call your folks as soon as we get to the hospital." He gripped his hand tighter. "You're going to be all right, Remy. Damn it, you're going to be all right."

The fierceness of his tone brought Remy another faint smile. Who was he trying to convince? Remy… or himself?

Far off in the distance he heard sirens. He wished he could roll over, wished he could ask Michael to check his vest, to make sure that the slug was embedded in the Kevlar and not in his chest, but he couldn't find the breath to give voice to the request. He couldn't find the strength to withstand the pain of movement.

All he could do was hold on tight to Michael's hand and pray.

Oh, God, yes, he could pray.

Chapter 1

It was funny how quickly things could change.

Only this morning Susannah Duncan had awakened in her own slightly lumpy bed in the slightly shabby apartment she shared with her brother, and tonight she was going to sleep in an elegantly beautiful, straight out of *Gone with the Wind* Southern mansion.

Only last week she had been a perfectly average, perfectly unremarkable woman, a nurse whose life was noticeably lacking in many things but not decency, pride or honor. Today there was nothing average or unremarkable about her. Nothing decent or proud. Nothing honorable.

Funny.

But she felt no urge to laugh.

She might never laugh again.

She stood underneath a live oak so massive that a number of its limbs required man-made support where their sheer weight pulled them back toward the ground. She knew how that must feel to the tree. Sometimes she thought *she* would bend and break under the weight of her own burdens. Her guilt. Her shame.

Resting her arms on one thick branch that dipped low, she cushioned her chin on her hands and studied the house before her. Belle Ste. Claire. The name was beautiful, the house even more so. It was Greek Revival in style, white, with eight square columns on each side and across the front, with forest green doors and shutters, a herringbone-patterned brick gallery encircling the first floor and a matching balcony upstairs painted pale gray on the floor and paler blue on the ceiling.

It had been in the Sinclair family for nearly two hundred years, had been built by the first Sinclair to come to Louisiana from France. It faced the Mississippi River, where that Sinclair and those who followed had built their fortunes in shipping and sugarcane. They weren't in the shipping industry any longer—or sugar, either, for that matter—and hadn't been in this century, but they still held their fortunes. Generations of prudent investments had seen to that.

She had driven up to Belle Ste. Claire this morning with Valery Navarre. Although a native of New Orleans, Valery had spent much of her life at this gracious old home halfway between New Orleans and Baton Rouge—had lived nine years of it here. She loved the place and had been more than willing to share her memories and knowledge of it. It had taken only a few questions from Susannah to keep the conversation flowing for miles. By the time Valery had realized that they'd talked about nothing but Belle Ste. Claire and Belclaire, the tiny nearby town named for it, they were only a few miles from their destination. She had sheepishly apologized, had lamented the loss of an opportunity to get to know Susannah better.

Which was exactly what Susannah had wanted. She had enough to do in her four weeks here. Making friends wasn't part of her job description. It was a complication she couldn't afford.

With a sudden shiver, she realized that the sun was setting on the far side of the river. It was time to go inside. Time to start dinner. Time to return to work.

It was time to face Remy Sinclair again.

Straightening, she ducked under the branch and started toward the gallery. The grounds spread for acres in all directions—yellowing grass, flower and shrub beds, plantings of fragrant vines, and all of it shadowed by hundred-foot-tall pines, magnolias and giant live oaks. The house sat square in the center, strong for all its grace, built to last an eternity. It had provided shelter and comfort for two hundred years and, with a little care, would continue to do so for the next two hundred.

And right now it was providing shelter to Remy Sinclair, the man who had hired her as his nurse, cook and driver for the next month. The man who was her only reason for being there. The man who was the key to her, and her brother's, future.

Thoughts of her brother—named Lewis for their father, but called Skip since he was a baby—and his future, if he even had one, brought her another chill, one that settled way down inside her, one that she feared she would never be completely free of. She hadn't seen him in nearly a week, not since she'd gotten a call from some lawyer who'd told her about a job she was going to apply for—who had told her in chilling detail what would happen to Skip if she didn't get it. Three months ago, fresh from Nebraska and naive as hell, she would have found the call totally unbelievable, would have shrugged it off as some prank in terribly bad taste.

But three months ago she hadn't known the extent of the trouble Skip had gotten himself into.

Now she knew, and the lawyer had made it perfectly clear exactly what she had to do to get him out of it. It wouldn't be such a hardship, he had told her. Belclaire was a lovely little town, Belle Ste. Claire a beautiful house. The salary was generous for only four weeks' work. It would be a nice break from the stress of her job as an emergency room nurse, a nice break from the city and from worrying over her brother. *He* would take responsibility for her brother for the next few weeks, he had ominously promised.

No, living here and working for a recuperating FBI agent wouldn't be such a hardship, she agreed silently, bleakly, as she climbed the seven steps to the gallery.

It only meant selling her soul.

And that wasn't such a high price, was it? Not when she would be getting her brother's life in return.

And so she had applied for the position, and she had gotten it. If only Remy had refused to hire her. If only he had looked at her the way her ex-husband had, the way other men often had, and found her lacking. Then she could have called the lawyer, could have said, "I did my best, but it wasn't enough." Surely, if he knew anything at all about her, he would have believed her. Never being enough—pretty enough, smart enough, ambitious enough, talented enough—had been the story of her life. Surely he wouldn't have allowed any harm to come to Skip when she had *tried* to comply with his orders. Surely he wouldn't have punished her brother for her failure.

But Remy *had* hired her. After interviewing a half dozen other nurses, he had asked her a few questions, then offered her the job, just like that. She had never gotten any job so easily.

She had never needed any job so desperately.

She had never wanted to be rejected so desperately.

The steps she had climbed led straight to ornate double doors, and she stood there a moment. Generations of Sinclairs had greeted their guests at this formal entrance. Standing there now in the quiet dusk, she could easily imagine herself into the past, watching carriages turn in the gate down by the river, passing between brick columns and along the shell driveway to discharge their passengers at the foot of these steps. It all would have been very genteel, very gracious, very Southern.

But she no more would have belonged here at any time in the past than she did today...except possibly during the Civil War, she mused, when traitors and betrayers had insinuated themselves into all sorts of places where they had no rights.

The guilt she'd been living with the past week settled heavier on her shoulders. Betraying the trust placed in her and endangering the life of a patient under her care—that was what Skip and his problems had brought her to. God help her.

God forgive her.

Turning abruptly, she started around the house to the side entrance near where her car was parked. More than an hour had passed since Remy had fallen asleep on the sofa; if he wasn't awake yet, he likely would be soon. She should have stayed inside, close at hand, but she'd felt the need to be up and about. She had needed a moment's fresh air. A moment's escape.

She had needed a moment away from him.

She opened the screen door, then the door, and closed them both quietly behind her. With any luck she could slip past the open door of the parlor where she'd left Remy. With any luck she could delay further contact with him until it was absolutely necessary. She could—

"Susannah."

She started guiltily, her muscles tightening, her face flushing. Forcing in a deep breath, she turned toward the voice, toward the softly lit parlor.

He was standing beside the sofa, leaning on his crutches in exactly the way he'd been shown not to. He hadn't been awake long—he still had a childlike, drowsy air about him. She wondered if he had called her, if he had been annoyed that she hadn't been available to cater to his needs. She regretted spending the last hour outside, regretted that she hadn't started dinner sooner, that she hadn't taken advantage of his nap to unpack his bags. She should be better at this servant role, she silently chastised herself. After all, she'd played it often enough for her father and Skip, especially after her mother's death, and she had lived it through her entire four-year marriage to Guy Duncan.

And she couldn't afford to lose this job. Whatever it took to please her employer was exactly what she had to do, including being at his beck and call.

Clasping her hands together, she moved into the doorway. "Tell me what you need and I'll get it for you," she offered, keeping her voice even and smooth, hiding her nervousness.

He gave her a crooked grin that was faintly abashed. "I believe I can handle this on my own."

Responding with a fading smile, she took a step back as he started toward her. It took him a few moments to navigate the parlor and the half dozen feet of hallway to the small bathroom. He wasn't particularly adept with the crutches yet. Yesterday was the first time he'd been allowed to use them and, according to Valery, after sixteen days of bed rest, he'd been so delighted to be mobile again that he had overdone it. His wince with each step supported his cousin's conclusion.

Susannah sympathized with him as she continued down the hall to the kitchen. Depending on the injury, using crutches could be more painful than the injury itself. The strain on the hands, arms, shoulders and back was tremendous, and only a few weeks ago, Remy's left arm had been subjected to a gunshot wound. The bullet had left a relatively clean trail with nothing more than soft tissue damage that was healing nicely, but the wound was still tender.

His other injuries had been both less and more serious: a fist-size contusion on his chest, where his bulletproof vest had saved his life, and a through-and-through gunshot wound of the right thigh. There had been no internal damage from the contusion, but the bullet in his leg had torn through the femur. The resulting compound comminuted fracture had required open reduction with internal fixation—opening his leg in surgery and putting the bone back together with a titanium plate and screws. Now he wore a hip-to-toe cast and was under strict orders for absolutely no weight-bearing on that leg for at least two weeks. If he wanted a full recovery, the strict use of crutches was mandatory.

Which was why *she* was here. He could have managed his convalescence with the other two injuries. They probably wouldn't even have slowed him down. But the severity of the leg wound, the cast and the crutches made him less than agile. They made her services necessary.

After washing her hands, she turned her attention to the contents of the refrigerator. Remy's parents, the current owners and residents of Belle Ste. Claire, had left only three days ago on a long-awaited trip to Europe. They were celebrating their fortieth anniversary, Valery had told her, and would be gone for a month. They, too, had made Susannah's services necessary. They had wanted to cancel the trip, again according to Valery—had wanted to stay here and look after their son themselves, but Remy had refused. They had been planning this trip for a long time; rescheduling, especially on such short notice, would have been a travel agent's nightmare.

Marie Sinclair had been a busy woman in the past week, Susannah thought as she began removing items from the refrigerator. Not only had she packed and gotten ready for a month abroad, but she had also prepared the house for Remy and Susannah's arrival—had seen to it that the unused servants' quarters were cleaned and aired out and the refrigerator well stocked. She had left Susannah notes explaining where any given item she might need in the next month was located, along with names and phone numbers for their housekeeper, local repairmen and neighbors and a detailed copy of their itinerary. And that was all in addition to spending the majority of her time at her son's side in the hospital.

Down the hall the sound of the bathroom door opening was followed by the slow shuffle and squeak of rubber-tipped crutches on the highly polished wood floor. Still hidden behind the refrigerator door, Susannah hoped Remy was going in the opposite direction, back toward the parlor, but it was a futile hope. The steps were definitely coming closer. Her fingers tightening into a fist, she waited until he stopped before she finally straightened and closed the refrigerator door.

"What's for dinner?"

She glanced at what she'd gathered on the counter: lettuce, cucumbers, carrots and an onion, along with a neatly labeled foil packet of chicken from the freezer and a handful of the potatoes piled nearby in a metal colander. "Fried chicken, mashed potatoes and gravy and salad...unless you don't eat fried food."

"Of course I eat fried food. Don't you know the first rule of Southern cooking? If it ain't fried, it ain't done."

Smiling faintly, she placed the chicken in a sink of cold water to thaw, then started opening drawers, looking for a knife and a vegetable peeler. With a backward glance over her shoulder, she made a suggestion for her own good as well as his. "Why don't you go back into the parlor where you'll be comfortable? I'll bring you some tea, and you can watch television, and when dinner's ready—"

"I've seen more television in the last two weeks than in the last two months combined. I'll be comfortable here." Balancing on his crutches, Remy pulled a chair from the table. Once he was seated, he used his good foot to maneuver a second chair into place in front of him, then raised his right leg to the seat. That done, he closed his eyes for just a moment, letting weariness wash over him, soaking into his muscles, claiming his entire body. All those days lying on his back in the hospital, he had anticipated the time he could be up and about whenever the mood struck him. Well, the time had arrived and, frankly, he couldn't think of anything more appealing than lying on his back in bed. He moved so clumsily that his thigh throbbed, and the cast chafed around his toes. His left upper arm twinged from time to time around both the entrance and the exit wounds, and the crutches hurt his shoulders, arms and hands.

Added to all that was his wounded ego. He wasn't used to being so awkward and graceless. He wasn't accustomed to revealing his helplessness and weakness to anyone.

Especially to anyone as cool, quiet and controlled as Susannah Duncan.

He had first seen her over two weeks ago in the emergency room the night he'd been shot. He remembered how

calm she'd been even though chaos surrounded them. He
remembered how gently she had touched him. Mostly,
though, he remembered her eyes. Other than a doctor's
blinding look with a penlight, no one else in the ER had met
his gaze; no one but Susannah had made that small human
contact with him. He had known when she did that he was
going to be all right, had known it with a certainty that had
eluded him until then.

They hadn't actually met until she'd come to his room a
week ago for the job interview. Michael, who'd been visiting, had wanted time to check out her background and her
references, but Remy had offered her the job on the spot. It
had taken him maybe a moment to make up his mind; from
the time she'd walked into the room and he had recognized
her, he'd known she was the one he wanted. The few questions he'd asked her had been for Michael's benefit. Impulse had told him that she was the one, and instinct had
backed it up.

Like any good cop, he trusted his instincts.

Settling his crutches against the table, he focused his attention on Susannah, rinsing vegetables at the sink. In spite
of their few meetings and spending the better part of today
here together, he hadn't yet learned much about her. She
was thirty-one—that nugget had come from Valery—and
had been living in New Orleans only a few months. She was
single and had nearly ten years nursing experience. She was
pretty, although no great beauty. She wasn't the sort of
woman to turn a man's head ... unless he was looking for
more than just a pretty face, unless he was intuitive enough
to understand that what she could offer was far more important than beauty that would fade with age.

What else did he know about her? That she had lovely
auburn hair and the gentlest hazel eyes he'd ever looked
into. That she wasn't too tall, wasn't too thin. That she carried about her a comforting air that said this was a woman
who could make everything all right—like a mother, he
thought, although there was nothing motherly about her. He

knew that she had a healing touch. That she was usually calm, serene and unflustered.

And he knew that she was troubled. There was a wariness and something more—a dispiritedness—in her eyes that hadn't been there two weeks ago.

Maybe it was just the strange situation they found themselves in—two strangers suddenly living together in very close quarters. Belle Ste. Claire was a large house, but she had to remain accessible to him, which meant staying nearby. It meant sleeping in the servants' wing, just off the kitchen and right across a narrow hallway from his own room, and sharing a bathroom with him. And while the house wasn't exactly isolated, it was a little remote. The nearest neighbors in either direction were more than a half mile away, and Belclaire, three miles east, was no more than the proverbial wide spot in the road: a gas station, a post office, a mom-and-pop grocery and a nothing-special café.

Or maybe that look had to do with her reason for leaving New Orleans to come here. Maybe whatever had driven her to take a leave of absence from the hospital, to temporarily give up her job, her home and her friends in the city and come here to live a quiet, dull life alone with him had put the sadness in her eyes. Maybe the end of a relationship? A breakup with someone important?

He could consider the possibilities all night—puzzles and mysteries fascinated him—but he would save the guessing games, he decided, for later. For when she wasn't around. For when he wasn't more interested in talking to her than in speculating about her.

"What do you think of the house?" he asked her.

She tested the sharpness of the knife blade with the tip of her thumb before glancing not at him but in his general vicinity. "It must have been a wonderful place to grow up."

"It was...for the most part." He had plenty of good memories of his childhood here at Belle Ste. Claire, but none at all of his teen years, and after that... He'd been barely twenty-two the night his father had told him to leave their home and to not return until he had become someone his parents could be proud of. He had stayed away for fifteen years. Until today. "Valery says you come from up north."

"Except for Florida and Texas, everything is 'up north' from here."

"Where in particular up north is home for you?"

"Nebraska."

She was a long way from home, he acknowledged—longer, even, than the miles accounted for. From the Great Plains to the Big Easy. From dry, dusty farm and ranch land to heat, humidity and pure decadence. Thinking back to an old favorite childhood movie, he murmured, " 'Gee, Toto, I don't think we're in Nebraska anymore.' "

"Wrong state." She turned from the counter to face him, her expression coming dangerously close to a smile. "It's 'I don't think we're in Kansas anymore.' "

"Oh, pardon me," he said dryly. "So what brought you to New Orleans?"

The hint of a smile disappeared, and he could see more than a little tension in the way she clasped her hands together. "I always wanted to live there."

"Why?"

"It's a beautiful city." Once again she was looking only vaguely in his direction. Except for that one brief moment when she'd corrected him, she hadn't gotten close to making eye contact with him this evening.

"Did you have friends there?"

"No."

"Had you ever visited there before?"

She shook her head.

Getting information out of her was like trying to interrogate a suspect who knew his lawyers were going to get him out before you even finished the paperwork. Luckily for him, he was patient. He could get to know her one piece of reluctantly offered information at a time. "So you woke up one morning back home in Nebraska and said, 'I think I'll get dressed, have some coffee and move to New Orleans.' "

She sighed softly—he saw the movement rather than heard it—then began the task of making ice tea. "Actually,

I ran into my ex-husband and his new wife one time too many and said, 'I think I'll move to New Orleans.'"

"You were married." Why did that surprise him? Most people did get married. He had always planned to do it himself someday... although after getting shot, he'd decided that someday was going to come soon. There would be no more putting things off until tomorrow, as he'd done all too often in his personal affairs. Not when he knew too painfully well that tomorrow didn't always come.

But it wasn't Susannah's having been married that surprised him. It was her being divorced. What man in his right mind, once he had her, would let her go?

"How does the joke go? I was married... but my husband wasn't." This time her sigh was audible.

"I'm sorry."

"So was I, for a very long time."

"And now?"

She didn't answer. She simply went on with her work.

He didn't ask the question again. He didn't have the right to probe into an area so obviously painful, at least, not until he knew her better. Much better.

And he had no doubt that day would come.

"So..." He returned to their earlier conversation. "You moved to New Orleans, found a place to live, found a job. Is it everything you thought it would be?"

"Absolutely," she replied with a smile—nothing dazzling, just a sweet smile of pleasure that brought such life to her face that, on second thought, Remy decided, it was pretty damned dazzling after all. Her ex-husband must have been a fool to let her get away.

"Before you came here, had you always lived in Nebraska?"

She nodded.

"I've never been there. What's it like?"

"Kansas," she replied immediately.

He laughed. "I wasn't too far off then on my misquote, was I?"

Slowly she ventured across the room, taking a seat across from him. "Nebraska's a nice place. The northwestern part of the state, where our farm is located, is pretty sparsely populated. We have cold winters, hot summers and beautiful springs that are much too short."

"Do you miss it?"

"No." As if she immediately regretted the answer, she made an impatient gesture. "It's my home, and my family and friends still live there. For those reasons, I do miss it. But I left there with the intention of never going back for more than occasional visits."

He wondered if he was putting her answers together properly, if he was reaching the correct conclusion. She had left her home, family and friends and intended never to return. She had traveled hundreds of miles to a strange city in a place where she knew no one, and she'd done it because of her ex-husband. Was *he* the reason for the despair in her eyes? Had she come here hoping to put him behind her, hoping to start a new life? Had she reached the conclusion after a few months of trying that it wasn't working?

Was she still in love with the guy?

Sometime he would find out—not tonight, not next week or probably even the week after that—but sometime.

Before she left here, he intended to know everything there was to know about Susannah Duncan.

It was nearly ten o'clock that evening when Susannah finally escaped to the privacy of her bedroom. She wasn't used to going to bed so early—she ordinarily worked the three-to-eleven shift, went to bed around two or three and got up about eleven in the morning—but she had to adapt her hours to match Remy's, and he, after refusing any help from her, was settled in his room.

Closing the door quietly behind her, she kicked her shoes off, pushed them underneath the bed, then sat down to remove her socks. These servants' rooms were nothing compared to the family bedrooms upstairs, but she had lived in worse. The room was a nice size and furnished with mismatched pieces: an iron bed painted white and made up with plain cotton sheets, a scarred oak dresser with an oval mirror that reflected a wavy image, an armoire that had seen better days and a small writing desk and straight-back chair in some dark wood she couldn't identify. The walls were painted white, the woodwork stained dark and there were two windows on the south wall, wide and covered with simple white curtains that hung café-style from wide-spaced tabs.

In her half day here, she had already left her mark on the room. There was a basket of bath supplies on the dresser, a twig wreath decorated with silk flowers and ribbons hanging from a nail in the wall, scented candles in brass holders on various pieces of furniture and a free-form sculpture she'd picked up of bubbles suspended in glass.

She'd brought two other things from the apartment she shared with Skip, but they weren't for display: a family photograph to remind her why she was here and the phone number, already memorized, for the lawyer in New Orleans who had sent her here. They were hidden away, wrapped inside a dark plastic bag and tucked at the back of the armoire behind her other shoes.

Leaning across the bed, she turned on the bedside lamp, then shut off the overhead light. She was tired—she'd been up late last night, packing for this move and dreading it—but she didn't think she could sleep, not yet. Still, she undressed, draping her jeans over the desk chair, tossing everything else into the wicker laundry basket in the corner, brushed out her hair, then pulled on a pale green nightgown. Sliding into bed and beneath the covers, she shut off the lamp and settled in, pretending that this was the end of a normal day, that nothing was wrong. She pretended that she wasn't in a strange house with a strange man, that she wasn't taking advantage of his misfortune, taking his money and betraying him and herself at the same time.

She pretended that she didn't hate herself for what she was doing.

The moon was bright tonight, giving the white curtains a ghostly luminance. She wished she had opened them, wished she could see whatever was outside her window. When she had first moved to New Orleans, it had taken a while to adjust to the city lights and noises after years on the Crouse family farm. Now here she was, back out in the country, where the only light was moonlight, where the only sounds, other than an occasional car on the road, were nature.

And Remy. Across the hall his bed squeaked. When she looked toward the door, she could see the thin line of light that came from his room. Had he gone to bed early this evening merely so she could, or was he in the habit of reading or working in bed? She imagined that in the next few weeks, she would find out. After all, that was part of what she was here for—to learn his habits. His routine.

It was harmless information. What would it hurt if she passed on to the lawyer what time he got up and what time he went to bed? What time he ate his meals and how he spent his afternoons? Whether he had company and when and who?

Harmless information, she insisted to herself. Believing it was the only way she could live with herself.

But she didn't believe it.

Not for a minute.

Again, his bed squeaked, and there was a muffled thud, followed by a curse. Crutches hitting the wooden floor. It was becoming a familiar sound. It would serve him right if she put them someplace out of reach until morning, but of course she couldn't do that. What if he had to get up during the night? He had to have access to them, clumsy though he was with them.

There came another quiet curse, and she pushed the covers back and reached for her robe, hanging over the iron headboard. Tugging it on, she tied the belt at her waist, then opened the bedroom door.

His door was open. His bed was placed the same as hers: in front of the door. All told, less than fifteen feet separated them—a fact that didn't make her comfortable.

He was sitting up in bed, pillows behind his back, the sheet pulled to his waist. Seeing her, he smiled ruefully. It was sweet and charming, and she couldn't begin to deal with it. "Sorry I disturbed you."

He had righted one of the crutches, but the other had fallen out of reach. She bent to pick it up, leaning it against the first one. "That's what I'm here for. Do you need anything? Medication, a snack, something to drink?"

"No, thanks." He closed the book that had been open on his lap. "You don't normally go to bed so early, do you?"

When he fixed his gaze on her, she wished she had pretended not to hear the disruption in here.

She wished she had pretended to be asleep.

God help her, she wished he wouldn't look at her that way.

Brushing her fingers nervously through her hair, she answered his question with one of her own. "Why do you ask?"

"You were working evenings the night we met. If you were back in New Orleans, you wouldn't even be home yet."

That was true. Back in the city, she would leave the hospital a little after eleven. She would go home to an empty apartment, and she would wonder where Skip was, would worry over what he was up to. Most nights she would be asleep before he finally wandered in, and if he did come home while she was awake, they would argue about his friends, his activities, the aimlessness of his life.

Thoughts of her brother inevitably led to thoughts of that damnable lawyer, so she put him out of her mind and concentrated instead on the first part of Remy's comment. "We didn't exactly meet that night in the ER."

"Yes, we did."

"Do you know how many patients we get in the emergency room on a typical Saturday night?"

He grinned. "You remember me whether you want to admit it or not."

Guiltily, she looked away. He was too appealing, damn it, and too willing to trust her when she didn't deserve it.

Moving away from the door, she picked up the clothing he'd worn earlier, a pair of black sweatpants roomy enough to accommodate his cast and a red T-shirt. She folded them carelessly and left them on the bureau top, then placed his single tennis shoe in the armoire with the others. "What makes you so sure of that?" she finally asked when there was nothing left to do.

"Women tend to remember me," he replied confidently.

No doubt they did. He was tall, nicely muscled, had blond hair and gorgeous blue eyes, was too handsome for his own good, and he knew it. But that brash self-assurance was part of his charm—that, and the certainty that he was a good guy. Decent. Fair. Nice.

Returning to lean against the door frame, she folded her arms across her chest. "You're right. I do remember you. You were the third gunshot wound we'd gotten that night, and you bled all over my scrubs."

"How inconsiderate of me."

She studied the bruise, in healing shades of yellow-gray and green, on his chest, then hesitantly asked, "Do you always wear a bulletproof vest when you're working?"

"Not in the office. But if I'm going out in the field, you can bet I've got my Second Chance on."

"It certainly gave you one." The bruise was dead center in his chest. Without the vest, he surely would have died. If she had seen him at all at the hospital, it would have been too late. She would have regretted it, would have thought it sad that the patient had died so young, would have thought it unjust that one of the cops had died when so many criminals lived. She would have grieved for him for a moment or two.

Then, when the next patient arrived, she would have forgotten him.

"Why the ER?"

"Why the FBI?"

"I like arresting people."

People like Jimmy Falcone. Trying to arrest him had almost gotten Remy killed.

People like Skip.

Oh, God, people like *her*.

"I answered. Now it's your turn."

She shrugged restlessly. "I used to believe I could make a difference."

"You don't believe that anymore?"

She shook her head. "Innocent people keep dying. Drunks keep driving drunk. Punks keep robbing for drug money. Crooks keep shooting and stabbing and beating and maiming their victims. Users keep overdosing." Again, she shrugged; then, changing the subject, she gestured toward the nightstand. "If you'll turn on the lamp, I'll shut the light off so you don't have to get up later."

He did as she suggested, and she flipped the switch, then turned away. She made it to her door before he spoke.

"Susannah."

She swallowed hard. A million people had called her by her first name, but no one had ever made it sound quite the same way he did. Soft. Sweet. Gentle. Slowly, blinking hard against the tears that threatened, she looked back.

"You shouldn't stop believing," he said quietly, intensely. "That night... You made a hell of a difference for me."

Before any of the warnings swirling around in her brain could tumble out, she slipped into the quiet, dark safety of her own room. There, chilled once again all the way to the bone, she lay underneath the covers, staring dry-eyed and empty into the night, and whispered three silent, desperate pleas.

Don't trust me, Remy.

Don't be grateful to me.

Please don't take me on faith.

Because doing any of the three would be a mistake on his part.

A mistake he might not live to regret.

Chapter 2

Remy awoke early Wednesday morning, before the rising sun had brought more than a touch of color to the eastern sky. Despite the less-than-familiar surroundings, he was immediately alert, immediately aware of where he was.

Home. He had lived in a variety of places over the last fifteen years—a college dorm room and an apartment shared with the three best friends a guy could ask for. He had lived in Virginia while attending the FBI Academy and had called a number of apartments and condos his own after returning to New Orleans for assignment. But none of those places—whether temporary or, like the place he was in now, relatively permanent, whether cozy or cramped, shared or solitary, Spartan or luxurious—had ever been home. That name, that feeling, was forever reserved for Belle Ste. Claire.

He had loved the house for as long as he could remember, had missed it during his fifteen-year exile as much as he had ever missed any person in his life. Sometimes it had haunted him, along with the fear that he would die without ever seeing it again.

Two and a half weeks ago, lying on the wet pavement in more pain than he'd believed possible to endure, he had thought he'd come close.

But now here he was, back home again. This servant's room, unoccupied for as long as he could remember—while his mother had always had help around the house, it had never been of the live-in variety—was a far cry from the elegance and grace of the bedroom upstairs that had been his for the better part of twenty-two years, but it was still home. It was part of Belle Ste. Claire, and it was his for the next month.

His and, to some extent, Susannah's. She would finish his unpacking later today, would be cleaning in here and generally helping him out. She would have as much access to his room as he would.

As if cued by the thought of her, from across the hall came the beeping of her alarm. He wondered why she was getting up at six forty-five. They hadn't discussed a schedule yet, but apparently they needed to. When she was already accustomed to working the evening shift and would, when she finished here, return to those hours, there was no reason for her to make major changes in her schedule just for him.

Although he could think of a few other changes he wouldn't mind her making just for him...such as becoming softer again, regaining the serenity the last few weeks had taken from her and losing the wariness that kept her at arm's length.

Her alarm went off again, this time followed by the sounds of movement filtering through her closed door. He thought of her as she had looked last night here in his room—her hair falling in loose waves to her shoulders, the plain white terry-cloth robe so long that it had practically covered her bare feet, the bit of drab green nightgown showing at the neck of the robe. With her coloring, he wouldn't dress her in white or pastels; he would choose jewel tones—emeralds and rubies, sapphires and deep, rich amethysts. He would also do away with the ponytails and braids

she showed such fondness for—perfectly reasonable hair-
styles, he acknowledged, when you wore a uniform and
worked in an emergency room, but just as perfectly unnec-
essary here.

Especially when Susannah with her hair down was so
much softer. So much more appealing.

When her door opened, he grew still. He slept with his
own bedroom door open—the better for the cop in him to
hear any out-of-the-ordinary sounds—but she didn't glance
his way. She glided down the hall, a wicker basket over one
arm, her long white robe and soundless passage giving her
an otherworldly quality so fitting in the ancient house.

A moment later the gurgle and splash of water filling the
tub reached his ears, and he felt a stab of longing sharp
enough to hurt. The longing wasn't for Susannah—although that was coming; it wouldn't take many more hours
in her company to turn interest into desire and desire into
need—but for the bath she would soon be indulging in. Ever
since he had awakened after his surgery to find himself
wearing a bulky, itchy, scratchy cast, he'd had visions of
soaking away all his aches and pains in a long, relaxing bath.
Every time he'd endured a sponge bath given by someone
entirely too young—and entirely too female—to suit him,
he'd entertained fantasies about a big, deep tub, a locked
door and water hot enough to steam.

Maybe in four weeks. If his leg had healed enough, if the
cast could be removed, then he could take the longest, hot-
test, steamiest bath ever. Then he could do a lot of things.

Then he would no longer need Susannah.

Maybe.

While she was occupied, he sat up and carefully swung his
legs off the mattress. The wood floor was cold beneath his
bare foot, but Susannah had insisted on removing the bright
braided rugs his mother had scattered around, deeming
them a threat to his less-than-stable gait. Taking his crutches
from their niche, he used one to nudge the door shut, then
slowly pushed himself to his feet. For a moment he simply
stood there next to the bed, stretching, tensing and easing

muscles. He was a little stiff, a little sore, but all in all, he felt fine.

His first steps, from the bed to the dresser where a few of his clothes had been unpacked and put away, were easy, almost smooth. There, balancing carefully, he stripped off the gym shorts he had slept in as a concession to Susannah and pulled on the sweatpants he'd discarded the night before. When he moved from there to the armoire for a T-shirt, he felt the discomfort begin—mild twinges in his shoulders and upper arms, tenderness across his palms. His mouth formed a grim line as he stuffed the shirt between one hand and the crutch's grip and limped his way back to the bed.

After more than two weeks of bed rest, boredom and pain, he had thought that being allowed the mobility of crutches and getting discharged from the hospital he so disliked were the answers to his prayers. He hadn't realized there would still be so much pain. He hadn't understood that these first few days on crutches weren't going to be easy—or particularly mobile. He hadn't quite understood that being discharged from the hospital didn't mean he was well again, didn't mean everything was back to normal.

He was disappointed, he admitted as he sat down, his breathing a little heavier for the exertion. Until he grew used to the crutches and his palms callused over, until his body adjusted to compensating for his bad leg, life was going to remain tough. He was going to continue being clumsy and awkward. His body was going to continue to let him down, putting his weaknesses on display for the world to see. He was going to continue to need Susannah's help more than any grown man should.

As he pulled the T-shirt over his head, that last thought almost made him smile. Some clouds truly did have silver linings, and Susannah, it seemed, just might be his.

The house was quiet as he hobbled out of his room and down the hall to the kitchen. He didn't bother with any lights but took a seat at the table, facing the bay window and the lightening sky. He hadn't seen a sunrise or paid attention to a sunset in longer than he could remember. They were both on the mental list he'd compiled in the hospital of things he wanted to do now that he'd been given a second chance. It wasn't a long list, and some of the items on it, like those two, were simple, easily fulfilled and crossed off.

Some were major.

He had wanted to bring an end to his estrangement from his parents, and that had been accomplished. They had spent much of the past few weeks at the hospital with him. While nothing could ever replace the fifteen years they had lost in their feud, while there were still some awkward moments, some resentment and leftover anger, at least they were speaking. At least they were all willing to work at resolving the problems that had driven them apart in the first place.

He wanted to make things right with Valery. His cousin had been one of the most important people in his life, and he had missed her friendship, her love. He wasn't sure he would ever earn those things from her again—he had hurt her badly, maybe too badly to be forgiven—but at least she was no longer afraid of him. She was willing to get to know him again, willing to explore whatever relationship they might manage after all these years.

And the big one, the one that would surprise everyone who thought they knew him, the one that would astonish every single woman he had ever gone out with, every woman to whom the only commitment he'd ever made was no commitment at all: he wanted to get married. He wanted a wife, a family, a house with a mortgage, a big yard, bikes in the driveway and dogs underfoot. He wanted the kind of normal, everyday home life that most people took for granted. He wanted someone who would be happy to see him when he came home at night, someone who would miss him and worry over him when he was gone. He wanted to know that someone's life was richer, happier, because of him.

He wanted to love someone and be loved in return. Like his parents. Like Valery and Michael.

He had come too close to death. He wanted to make the most of the life he'd been given, and love, a wife and kids were the best, the surest, way to do that.

Way down deep in his gut, he suspected Susannah was the place to start.

He wasn't young enough, romantic enough or foolish enough to believe in love at first sight. He knew all too well that most relationships grew from friendship or were stirred by lust. He knew there had to be something beyond desire, knew respect, understanding and genuine caring had to develop.

And he knew to trust his instincts. Whenever he met a woman, he usually figured out pretty quickly what, if any, role she would play in his life—whether they would remain acquaintances, become friends or lovers. He could generally predict the course of a relationship right up front. He usually knew who was going to be important to him and who wasn't.

That Saturday night in the emergency room, he had known that Susannah would be important. She had touched him, had connected with him, at a time when he had desperately needed such contact. Even if he had never seen her again, he had known intuitively that he would never forget her face, her touch, her serenity.

Had her applying for this job been fate or sheer luck? He didn't know and didn't much care. Maybe if she hadn't applied, he would have continued to find fault with all those who did. According to Michael, he'd turned down some highly qualified nurses. Maybe eventually he would have sought out Susannah, would have offered the job to her and no one else.

But, for whatever reason of her own, she *had* applied. Call it fate. Luck. Destiny.

He smiled faintly. He was sitting here in an unlit room, watching the sun rise and contemplating his future with a woman he barely knew.

Who said he wasn't young enough, romantic enough or just plain foolish enough?

* * *

Susannah dried the mirror with a towel, then drew a comb through her hair, pulling it straight back from her forehead. This morning's long bath had been a luxury, one that she wouldn't be able to indulge in most days because of time limitations, but she'd felt the need this morning to get herself into the best frame of mind possible before facing Remy. After a less than restful night, she needed all the relaxation, all the soothing, she could get.

After slipping into her robe and belting it, she gathered her bath things, replacing them in the wicker basket. There was plenty of room in the bathroom to store them—a long counter, shelves on the wall, a cabinet underneath the sink—but she felt uncomfortable leaving her toiletries behind. There was something too intimate about placing her shampoo and conditioner on the counter beside Remy's, something too personal about her razor and shaving cream sharing shelf space with his. Maybe she was being silly, but transporting everything back and forth in the long-handled basket allowed her to maintain some sense of distance between Remy and herself.

And she desperately needed that distance.

When she opened the door, the steamy warmth of the bathroom quickly dissipated in the chill air. She shivered but didn't move immediately. Instead, for a moment she simply stood quietly and listened. There were no windows in the hallway or the bathroom, but morning light filtered in from Remy's room and, at the opposite end of the hall, the kitchen. She wondered if he was awake yet, wondered how much solitude she had left before he claimed her time.

Then she heard the noise in the kitchen—she thought it was an impatient sigh. Was he already up and waiting for her, eager for his coffee and hungry for his breakfast? Did he normally get up early, or had she awakened him with her bath?

She hurried to her room, dressing quickly in jeans and a thin cotton sweater. After taking a moment to apply a little blush and eye shadow and another to pull her hair back and secure it with a tortoiseshell clasp, she slipped on her shoes, then headed for the kitchen with a none-too-quiet—and none-too-eager—sigh of her own.

He was sitting at the kitchen table. Last night he had watched her from there while she fixed dinner, had insisted on eating there, too, the two of them together, and he had watched while she cleaned up afterward. Sharing meals was one thing—one of many, she was afraid—that she hadn't quite been prepared for. She had hoped to keep their relationship strictly professional, employer to employee. Growing up in a house this grand, he was surely accustomed to having servants, or a full-time housekeeper at the very least. He had to know how to treat them, how to keep them in their proper places, how to be friendly but never familiar. She had counted on that treatment to make the next few weeks bearable.

But if last night was any indication, he had no intention of treating her like an employee. Not once had he been aloof or distant. When she had tried to inject some professionalism—in politely trying to usher him out of the kitchen or in assuming that he would take his meal in the family dining room while she ate in the kitchen—he had simply, naturally overruled her.

And now here he was, waiting once again. Watching once again.

"Good morning," she greeted him as she crossed to the sink. The first order of the day was coffee—as if she wasn't already jumpy enough—and breakfast, for an already-nervous stomach.

He murmured a response, but didn't turn to face her. She glanced over her shoulder once to see what held his attention outside, but saw nothing other than a dilapidated barn and the sun breaking above the tree line to the east. She'd seen plenty of sunrises back in Nebraska. At home on the farm, she had been up, dressed and cooking breakfast by four-thirty most mornings. During the four years of her marriage, she had continued to rise early, simply because Guy had. That was part of the reason she had requested the evening shift when she'd started at the hospital in New Orleans. There was a whole other world out there, one that she had missed for the better part of her life, and she had wanted to know what it was like.

After three months, the best thing she could say about nightlife was that it gave her an excuse for her nonexistent social life. When she worked five nights a week, including most Saturdays and Sundays, no one was surprised at her lack of dates. It was just as likely that she didn't have time, the reasoning went, as that there was simply no one interested.

Not that she was looking. If she had finally learned one thing from her marriage to Guy, it was that she didn't need a man in her life. She didn't need the criticism, the sly taunts, the snubs and subtle insults. The best sex in the world wasn't worth being made to feel inadequate the rest of the time. It wasn't worth hurt after tiny hurt. Sharing her life with a man who had no respect and little fondness for her wasn't better than being alone.

At this point, she wasn't sure if she ever wanted to get married again, wasn't sure if she ever wanted children. That had been one of her goals since she was a child herself—to be the sort of loving and giving mother that her own mother had been. To have at least three kids, maybe four or even five, and help them grow from cuddly babies to mature, responsible adults who could make any parent proud. But right now she wasn't sure she wanted that. She had helped raise Skip after their mother had died, and look how immature, how irresponsible, he had turned out. He was twenty-three years old and still relying on big sister to get him out of trouble. She wasn't sure she had any mothering left in her to give. She wasn't sure she had the strength to be responsible for another life, to shoulder the obligations and demands of marriage and motherhood.

She wasn't sure, but she thought she might be completely satisfied spending the rest of her life alone.

Even if it did sound like an awfully lonely way to live.

Once the coffeemaker was filled and running, she turned to Remy. Sunlight was reaching through the window now, turning the blond of his hair to gold, a rich, burnished shade that reminded her of the wheat fields back home under the strong plains sun. He was a handsome man, if a person cared about that sort of thing. She noticed, but she didn't care. Guy was a handsome man, too—all tanned and chiseled and perfect on the outside, all empty, weak and petty inside. Skip was also handsome, in a softer, younger, less formed sort of way. Like her ex-husband, her brother lacked all the stronger qualities that made looks unimportant.

But Remy didn't.

Just as she started to look away, he twisted in the chair and their gazes met for the span of a second, maybe less. It was enough to see that his expression, while not including a smile, was pleasant enough. Harmless enough. But looks could be deceiving. Remy was strong, tough. Even temporarily impaired as he was, he could be dangerous.

Her own looks were deceptive. When he gazed at her, he surely saw what most everyone else did: a plain, uninteresting, modest little mouse of a person. He saw no cause to worry for his safety. He certainly didn't see a woman capable of bringing him harm, of fooling him, of betraying him.

He didn't see a woman who just might destroy him.

"How did you sleep last night?"

She opened the refrigerator and removed a package of bacon and a carton of eggs. "Fine, thank you," she lied. She had lain awake most of the night, looking at her future and at herself and hating what she saw. "How do you like your eggs?"

"Scrambled is fine. It didn't bother you—being in a strange place?"

"No, not at all." After taking a bowl from the cabinet, she cracked a half dozen eggs into it, added a little milk and seasoning, then whisked them until the yolks broke and blended. She put them aside and set the first strips of bacon to sizzle in a skillet before forcing herself to speak, to step into her nurse's role and deal with her patient. "How do you feel today?"

"Sore" came his immediate response.

"That's to be expected."

"Not by me. I thought getting out of the hospital meant all the pain would be gone."

"It doesn't go away that easily." Leaving the stove, she crossed the few feet of tile to the table. "Let me see your hands."

He obediently offered them to her, palms up. If he'd been any other patient—if he'd been *just* a patient—she would have had no qualms about taking them, about holding them in her own hands while she examined them. As it was, her hands were less than steady as she reached for first his left hand, then his right.

His skin was smooth, unblemished except for the small, raw places across the middle. These hands had never done any physical labor, had probably never done anything more arduous than grip a tennis racquet—or a gun. She had more calluses from her years of helping out on the farm than he would ever see.

The smell of bacon on the verge of burning gave her an excuse to abruptly drop his hands and return to the stove. "You're going to get blisters on your palms," she stated matter-of-factly. "They'll make using the crutches even harder. I'll add another layer of foam to the handgrips, and I'll pick up some gloves while I'm in town today."

"Why do you want to go to town?"

"Because we need milk and a few other groceries. If there's anything in particular you'd like to eat in the next few days, let me know and I'll get it."

"I'll come with you," he announced.

She risked a look at him over her shoulder. "That's not a good idea."

"You don't know your way around Belclaire."

Her look grew a few degrees drier. "Your cousin drove through town with me yesterday. There are a few blocks of houses and one block of businesses. I don't think I'll get lost." After she'd turned back to the stove, she casually added, "Anyway, I wasn't planning to go to Belclaire. I thought I would drive back to New Orleans."

"Why? You can get all the groceries you need right there in town."

"But I can't get foam rubber and biking gloves there." And she couldn't go unnoticed there. She knew towns like Belclaire. Nebraska was full of them—little places where a stranger in town was worthy of scrutiny, even if he was simply buying gas and passing on through. If there hadn't already been rumors about the Sinclair son coming home to recuperate from his wounds and bringing a live-in nurse with him, it wouldn't take long for them to start. It wouldn't take long at all for her to be identified as the nurse.

And today she needed to go unnoticed. She needed to make a phone call. She needed to check in with the lawyer.

With Jimmy Falcone's lawyer.

"Baton Rouge is closer."

"But I don't know my way around Baton Rouge."

Remy's smile held more than a hint of triumph. "That's why I need to go with you." After a moment, his smile shifted, becoming a charming grin. "Come on, Susannah, I've been cooped up inside for two and a half weeks. It's about to drive me nuts. I won't insist on going in the store with you and slowing you down. I'll just go along for the ride." Sensing that she was weakening, he saved his best appeal for last. "What if I stayed here alone and something happened? What if I needed you and you weren't here?"

After a long silence, she faced him again, coming to set a platter of crispy bacon on the table in front of him. "You don't need my permission," she said quietly, meeting his gaze fully, unwaveringly, for the first time that morning. "You're in charge here."

Meaning she would let him accompany her because she had no choice, because he was, after all, paying her salary. His victory was hollow . . . but it was still a victory. He was going along—and he was going to enjoy it. He was even going to accept the challenge of making *her* enjoy it.

He munched on bacon while she cooked the eggs. When she brought them, disproportionately divided between two plates, to the table, he ate heartily while she picked at her own food. She hadn't had much of an appetite last night, either, he had noticed. Nerves, he decided. She wasn't yet comfortable with him. If she didn't settle down soon, he might have to reconsider her suggestion of last evening— that they take their meals separately, the way an employer and his employee should—just to keep her from wasting away.

Or he would have to help her settle down.

"You drink too much coffee," he remarked as he finished off the last strip of bacon. He was still on his first cup, heavily sweetened and diluted with cream to disguise the taste, while she was finishing her third.

"I like coffee. It keeps me going."

"You'd do better to get your energy from food rather than caffeine."

The look she gave him was steady enough to make a lesser man back down.

Not so Remy. "Let's talk, Susannah."

"I thought we were."

"Let's talk about business." As he watched, she stiffened and withdrew a little inside herself. He went on, keeping his voice level, his tone casual. "We never really discussed what this job would entail, beyond the basics. I don't expect you to stay quietly in the background until I snap my fingers. I don't expect you to keep to a schedule or to get up early and have breakfast waiting when I awaken. I don't expect you to behave like a servant, and I don't intend to treat you like one."

"So what exactly do you expect?"

He ran his fingers through his hair, remembering as he did so that he had forgotten to comb it this morning. That reminded him that he hadn't shaved yet, either, or subjected himself to the dubious pleasure of a bath—a sponge bath, at least until he was able to stand long enough without his crutches to manage a shower. He must look pretty scruffy, not a bad accomplishment for someone who'd been buttoned-down and spit-polished for the better part of his professional life.

"I don't know," he responded with a shrug. "Someone to make the days easier and the nights warmer?"

That brought a flare of color to her cheeks and made her gaze snap up to meet his. Before she could speak, though, he raised his hand to silence her. "Since you obviously don't like that idea, how about just keeping me company? Take care of the things I can't handle, help me out when I need it and be a friend when I need that."

"You're looking for a companion."

He didn't like the way she said the word. He didn't need to know exactly what it meant to her to know that it wasn't quite what he wanted. Her inflection made that clear. Of course, "friend" also fell far short of describing what he wanted from her, but it was the only word he could think of right now that wouldn't scare her back to New Orleans. "A friend," he argued.

When she responded, her tone was both prim and disdainful. "You don't *hire* friends."

She had him there. He had plenty of friends—had been lucky enough to have three of the best friends in the world, friends of the sort that money could never buy. There was Michael, the Arkansas farm boy turned New Orleans cop. Funny... with his small-town, agricultural background, he and Susannah shared more in common with each other than either of them did with Remy, but Michael hadn't wanted him to hire her, at least not without thoroughly checking her background, and Susannah had seemed even more uneasy with Michael than she was with *him*.

There was also Smith Kendricks, an assistant U.S. Attorney based in New Orleans. He was a little more distant than Michael or Remy, a little less demonstrative, but no less important in their small family. There was nothing he wouldn't do for one of them, nothing he wouldn't give if only they asked.

And there had been Evan Montez. Ten months had passed since Evan's death, but a small, vicious wrench of pain still accompanied every thought of him. A detective with the New Orleans Police Department and Michael's partner, he had died doing the job he'd loved—upholding the law, catching the bad guys and making the world safe for innocent little girls and wounded partners. It was small consolation that the man who killed him, the man who had kidnapped that one innocent little girl in particular, had also died. It hadn't comforted Evan's widow. It hadn't lessened Michael's guilt over surviving when his partner had died. It hadn't eased Smith's or Remy's grief.

No, Susannah was right. You didn't hire friends, particularly not of the quality he was used to.

But you also didn't tell a skittish woman with shadowy hazel eyes, a bad marriage behind her and a serious case of nerves that you were looking for a wife and you thought maybe—just maybe—she was the one.

"All right," he said, giving in. "You can be my companion." Just as she started to visibly relax, though, he added, "And I'll be your friend."

She stacked their dishes together, laying the silverware across the top plate, then got to her feet. "Thank you, but I have friends already. I'm not in the market for more."

Her rejection had been polite, even gentle, but firm. Remy listened to it, considered it and decided to disregard it. It was entirely possible that his instincts were wrong this time—rare, but possible. Hadn't he been way off on the Falcone case? Hadn't he thoroughly misjudged his partner on that case? Hadn't he damn near paid for it with his life? It was possible he was wrong about Susannah, too. Maybe he had simply gotten fixated on her because he had been so very frightened and she had been so very reassuring. Maybe fate, luck or destiny had never intended the connection between them to extend beyond those few moments in the emergency room. Maybe this link he felt with her was all one-sided, born of his gratitude for her cool composure when his world had been turned inside out.

And then he looked at her and rejected all of his logical arguments. There was something between them. Maybe he was reading it wrong. Maybe it wasn't the forever-and-ever something, but it was there just the same. It was worth exploring.

In the awkward way that he was coming to hate, he pushed his chair back and maneuvered up and onto his crutches. "I'm going to clean up and change, and then we'll head into the city. Okay?"

Susannah simply shrugged. He could see she wasn't happy about it. Did she want to escape his company so badly? But she obviously wasn't going to argue with him. He wished she would. Giving in as easily and as completely as she had hinted too unpleasantly at submissiveness, and while he wanted a great many things from her, that wasn't one of them.

He hobbled to the door, then abruptly turned toward her again. "I told you what I wanted from our arrangement. What about you? What were you expecting?"

"I expected to do the job I was hired for," she replied in a curiously flat tone. "To provide whatever assistance and care you need over the next month. As far as specific details, I assumed you would fill me in on those as they came up."

She wasn't being entirely truthful—his cop's instinct told him that—but that was all right. One of these days she would come to trust him.

He could wait.

As soon as the breakfast dishes were done, Susannah retreated to her room, closed the door behind her and exhaled heavily. The muscles in her neck ached, and there was a throbbing starting somewhere deep behind her eyes that threatened to become a first-class tension headache. If she hoped to survive her time here in reasonably decent physical condition, she was going to have to find an outlet for this stress. She had to find a way to deal with Remy without making herself sick.

He was still in the bathroom down the hall. While she was cleaning the kitchen, she'd heard occasional splashes, muttering and curses, but she hadn't knocked at the door, hadn't asked if he needed assistance.

She had been afraid he just might say yes.

Removing the clasp from her hair, she got her hair dryer and brush from a drawer and set about drying her hair. It was thick, dry on top, still heavy with dampness underneath. Someday she would cut it, she promised herself, would choose some short, sleek, carefree style, something like Valery Navarre wore, something better suited to New Orleans and its heat and humidi—

Abruptly she cut off the thought. She didn't need to worry about finding a hairstyle more suitable for New Orleans' climate. She couldn't possibly return there when she completed her job here. She couldn't continue to live in Remy's city, in Jimmy Falcone's territory. She couldn't go back to the job she loved at the hospital, couldn't return to the apartment she shared with Skip, other than to pack up their belongings. She would take him home to Nebraska, she decided. Back home on the farm, he would have to look longer and harder to find trouble to get into. Back home, he would have their father, their uncle, cousins and friends to help keep him in line.

And once he was safe there, away from the city's temptations of easy money, glamour and excitement, she would find someplace new for herself. Someplace where she didn't know a soul. Someplace where no one could ever make a connection between her and New Orleans, where no one had ever heard of Remy Sinclair or Jimmy Falcone. Someplace where she could lie to everyone, including herself, and try to create a new Susannah Duncan, one she could live with.

Once her hair was dry, she went to the mirror sitting atop the dresser to brush it. The image that greeted her there made her stand motionless for a moment. The mirror was old, probably a hundred years or more, and the reflection looking back at her was distorted, full of ripples and waves,

a carnival fun-house version of herself that was both familiar and alien.

Since coming to this house, since taking on these two
similar but very different jobs, since agreeing to sell out
every principle she'd ever held, she had found a stranger, a
Susannah she didn't know at all, taking over her life. It
seemed fitting, she thought with a choked-back laugh, that
she now faced an image of herself that she barely recognized. So fitting.

And so damning.

"Hey, Susannah." Remy's call was followed by a tap on
the door. "Can you come over in a few minutes and see if
you can find where Valery hid my shoes?"

Shaken out of her stillness, she slowly drew the brush
through her hair. "All right," she replied, her voice little
more than a whisper. He heard her, though. The sound of
his unbalanced gait withdrawing was proof.

She gave him his few minutes, plus an extra or two while
she pulled her hair back, before slowly opening her door.
His door was already open, and he was sitting on his un-
made bed, fastening a watch around his wrist. He had
changed from black sweatpants to red, from a plain white
T-shirt to one advertising a ten-kilometer run last fall. His
hair was damp and combed carelessly back, and his jaw was
clean-shaven, with a small bloody nick on one side.

Already he looked tired.

Her first impulse was to suggest again that he remain
here—not so that she would have the freedom to make her
phone call in complete privacy, but because he obviously
needed rest. Sixteen days was a long time to stay in bed; his
body needed time to adjust to the demands of being up and
about again. He needed to take things a little slower, a little
easier.

But he would merely overrule her again, and she couldn't
even convincingly argue the point. She knew how tedious
bed rest could be, especially to a man as active as Remy. She
completely understood how anxious he was to be in control
again, to make his own choices again.

He'd been digging through the bags she hadn't yet unpacked and had located a pile of socks. Valery had packed
for him; Susannah had met her yesterday morning at his
apartment to pick up both her and the bags for the trip up
here. His neighborhood was old and gracious, the apartments also old, sprawling, situated on lush grounds. She had
gotten a glimpse inside the door of gleaming wood floors
and high ceilings, of elaborate woodwork and a polished
stair rail curving toward the second floor, and she'd been
impressed.

Then she'd seen Belle Ste. Claire.

The two homes had encouraged her hopes that she could
keep things on a strictly professional level between them. A
man who had grown up here in what was nothing less than
a mansion, who now lived in a place so dramatically different from the small apartment *she* could afford, surely had
to have at least one snobbish, smugly superior bone in his
body.

But if he did, it was the one he'd broken. He'd already
made it clear, both with his words and, more importantly,
with his behavior, that he intended to treat her not as a servant or employee, but as an equal. As a companion. As a
prospective friend.

That knowledge hurt Susannah, somewhere way down
inside. He didn't deserve her deceit, and she didn't deserve
his friendship.

Even though some small part of her wanted it.

Pulling a tissue from the box on the night table, she offered it to him. "You're still bleeding," she said, releasing
the small froth of white as soon as he took it.

"I haven't cut myself shaving since I was seventeen," he
grumbled as he pressed the tissue to his jaw.

"You haven't tried to do it balanced on one leg and a
wooden stick before . . . have you?"

His laughter erased the sourness from his expression.
"No, I can't say I was ever that dumb. If you could just find
a shoe for me . . ."

She bypassed the suitcases he had already rummaged through and moved on to a nylon duffel. It was filled with magazines and books, notebooks, stationery and pens.

"I told Valery to bring whatever I might need in the next month," he remarked from the bed where he was watching her. "It looks as if she didn't leave much behind."

The last bag, pushed half under the bed on the opposite side, was also a duffel and, judging from the variety, was the last one his cousin had packed, the one that had gotten all the last-minute choices. Lifting it to the bed, Susannah pulled out a pile of mail that had accumulated during his hospital stay, a couple of jackets, three single left shoes and, from the very bottom, a leather holster and a zippered nylon case. The case was triangular, black and surprisingly heavy for its size, and for a moment she simply stared at it.

For a time Skip had had the same thing at home: a gun rug, he'd called it when she had confronted him with it. Finding it in his room—complete with a semiautomatic pistol and an extra clip of ammunition inside—when she was putting away the clean laundry had frightened her more than she'd ever been frightened before. It was one thing for Remy Sinclair, a responsible adult and FBI agent, to have a gun at home, but another entirely for her immature baby brother. She had caused such a commotion that Skip had promised to take the gun back to wherever he'd gotten it that same day. She didn't know if he had or if he had simply found a better hiding place.

He'd made so many promises.

And he hadn't kept a single one.

Well, she had made a promise, too—to their mother, only minutes before she died. To their father the day she'd set out from Nebraska for New Orleans. To her brother and to herself. She had promised that she would look out for Skip, had promised that she would help him and take care of him, had promised that she would protect him from harm, even when the greatest harm that threatened him was of his own making. She had promised, and she would keep it.

No matter what it did to Remy.

He was watching her now with an absorbed look, a curious sort of scrutiny, that reminded her uncomfortably that he was a cop. After a moment, he leaned across the bed and pulled the case from her hand. "Do you know what's in here?"

She didn't answer, didn't look at him.

He unzipped the case and opened it flat for her inspection. She risked only a quick glance, only enough to see that there was, indeed, a pistol inside, very similar to but somehow even deadlier-seeming than the one Skip had had. Nestled on the corduroy lining beside it was an extra clip. "This is a ten-millimeter semiautomatic," he said quietly. "I keep it fully loaded, with one round chambered. When we go out, I'll carry it. The rest of the time, it'll stay in the nightstand drawer. You leave it alone, all right?"

She nodded dumbly.

He withdrew the pistol and rezipped the case, then claimed the holster from her. "I'd think, growing up in the country the way you did, you'd have at least a passing familiarity with guns."

"I have a healthy respect for them," she corrected him as she turned away, folding the empty duffel and laying it on top of the dresser.

"Good." In the mirror she caught a fractured glimpse of his wry smile as he rubbed the bruised area on his chest. "I wish more people did."

While he began the task of putting on one sock and shoe, Susannah started neatly refolding some of the clothing scattered around the bed. She had unpacked the smallest of his bags last night after dinner and should have completed the job, but he'd insisted it could wait until today. As soon as they got back from town, she promised herself.

When he was ready, she followed him from the room, confirming with a quick glance back that the pistol was gone from where he'd laid it on the bed. Tucked somewhere underneath the T-shirt and fleece jacket he wore? "Are you expecting trouble here?" she asked, pausing in the hallway before ducking into her own room for her purse.

He glanced back at her over his shoulder. "Trouble?" he echoed, sounding too innocent and surprised to be believed. "At Belle Ste. Claire?"

The idea, she thought, seemed somehow obscene. According to Valery, the house had survived the Civil War unscathed. It had withstood the Mississippi's flooding and the occasional hurricanes and tornadoes that happened along. It was a safe place, a secure place.

At least, it had been until yesterday. Until they had opened the doors to *her*.

She got her things from her room, then caught up with him at the side door, where he offered her a set of keys. As she locked up, he gestured toward the back of the house. "The garage is back there. The round key unlocks the side door. You'll have to try the keys. I don't know which set goes to which car. You can take your pick."

Susannah's nerves tightened fractionally. "Why can't we take my car?"

"Because I don't think both the cast and I can fit in your front seat—at least, not comfortably. Besides, I told you when I hired you that a car would be provided for you. There's no reason for you to use your car to run my errands."

Although she would have liked to argue the point, she didn't, because he was right. Her car was a good little car—with the emphasis on little. To get the kind of mileage she'd wanted and the price she'd needed, she'd had to compromise on something, and size had been it. "Wait here," she instructed, starting down the steps and across the driveway.

The lock on the side door turned easily. There was a light switch right inside, along with a button for the automatic garage door. She pressed both, then circled the Cadillac for the Buick on the other side. The color was a rich burgundy outside, a subdued shade inside. The seats were leather, luxurious and soft, and the interior smelled of a woman's fragrance, something unfamiliar to Susannah, rich and appealing.

She started the engine, adjusted the driver's seat for more leg room and the mirrors for better visibility, then slowly backed out of the garage. The car was a far cry from the '63 Chevy truck that she'd learned to drive in or even from her own little blue sedan parked outside. How nice it must be, she thought without any real twinge of envy, to have money. It was an experience she would probably never know. She had finally finished paying off her school loans, only to find that her income could barely keep even with Guy's outgo. The year following the divorce had been better for her, but then she had come to New Orleans and had found herself providing the majority of Skip's support.

Someday she would be responsible only for herself and only to herself. That was a promise.

And Susannah Duncan kept her promises.

She pulled up close to the house to save Remy as many steps as possible. Although she got out of the car to help him down the steps, he ignored her and started down by himself. Hovering nearby in case he slipped or lost his balance, she silently counted each of the steps—five, six, seven—until he reached the bottom. A fine layer of sweat glistened across his forehead, and pain-etched lines crinkled the corners of his mouth as he drew a deep, frustrated breath. After a moment to catch his breath, he glanced at her, almost smiled and faintly murmured, "Damn."

In another few minutes, he was settled as comfortably as the cast would allow and they were on their way. Other than giving directions to the interstate, he remained silent for the first portion of the trip. Maybe this wouldn't be so bad, she thought, concentrating on traffic and the soft sounds of jazz flowing from the speakers.

Then he broke the silence. "Tell me about your family."

Her fingers tightened around the steering wheel. "My family?"

"You know—mother, father, sister, brother. You do have a family, don't you?"

"Yes, I do."

"So...?"

"So I have a family back home in Nebraska, running the
farm."

"You're not very good at this small-talk stuff, are you?"
he asked, his tone mildly amused. "It works like this. I ask
you questions and you answer them, and then you ask me
questions and I answer. That way we learn something about
each other so we're not strangers anymore."

She resisted the natural urge to smile at his teasingly patient explanation. "All right. What about your family?"

"It's not your turn, but I'll answer anyway to show you
how it's done." He paused, glancing out the window for a
moment, then began. "My father is a lawyer, like me, and
my mother is involved in every charity within a hundred
miles. They've been married forty years next month. I'm
their only child, and I've been a great disappointment to
them in one way or another more than half my life."

His words made Susannah uncomfortable. That was more
than she'd wanted to know... and yet she wanted to hear
more. She wanted to know how a man as bright and accomplished as he seemed to be—a lawyer, for heaven's sake,
and a federal agent in addition to that—could possibly be a
disappointment to anyone, most especially his parents. She
wanted to know how a man as damn near perfect as he
seemed to be could have even a vague acquaintance with the
feelings of inadequacy that she'd lived with most of her life.

But he was staring once more at the scenery passing by,
saying nothing. Feeling compelled to respond, she lamely
murmured, "I'm sure you're mistaken about that."

He looked at her, catching her gaze for an instant before
she hastily turned back to the road. The expression in his
blue eyes was grim and unforgiving. Of his parents? she
wondered. Or of himself? "They asked me to leave their
home. They told me not to come back until I had become a
son they could be proud of. We didn't speak for fifteen
years." A hint of self-directed bitterness crept into his voice.
"No, I don't think I misunderstood."

She'd heard enough, she silently warned herself. That lit
tle pang of sympathy that clutched at her meant she'd hear
too much. She didn't want to continue this conversation
She didn't want to hear one more word for the rest of thi
trip.

So why did she find herself, only a moment later, quietl
saying, ''Tell me what happened''?

Chapter 3

Remy continued to gaze out the window. He liked wintertime in the south. There were always blasts of cold weather, enough to remind you that it was winter, but nothing cold or interminable enough to prompt vows of moving to a warmer climate. A number of trees lost their leaves, so there were the new buds of spring to look forward to, but just as many stayed green so that they avoided the starkness of barren forests. You could even find flowers in bloom, if you looked, every month of the year.

Tell me what happened. Was she interested or simply making conversation? He could turn to his left, could study her face and her eyes, but he wouldn't find any more of an answer there than he did in the scenery outside the window. For a woman with such expressive eyes, she was good at revealing next to nothing.

Tell me what happened. Drawing in a slow breath, he did just that. "I assume Valery told you that she had once lived at Belle Ste. Claire." From the corner of his eye, he saw her hair swing with her nod. "Her father is my mother's brother. When his wife left him, she left Valery, too. She

didn't want…I don't know—didn't want to be a wife, didn't
want to be a mother, didn't want to make any more sacri-
fices. I guess she assumed that my uncle would take over,
would fill the void she left in Valery's life, but he didn't. If
she wasn't going to be responsible anymore, then damn it,
neither was he. Since he couldn't just abandon Valery, he
brought her to Belle Ste. Claire. He just showed up one day
with her, with everything she owned packed in a couple of
cardboard boxes, and he left her there without apologies,
without any promises, without even a goodbye.''

More than twenty-three years had passed since that day—
a lifetime, Remy thought—but his memories were vivid. He
remembered how surprised he'd been to come home from
school in the middle of the week and find his cousin there.
He remembered how the matter of her parents' divorce
hadn't struck him as important at all. His parents were
happily married; so were his grandparents, his other aunts
and uncles and all the other adults he'd known. He hadn't
understood the ramifications of a divorce, hadn't realized
that it meant anything at all to him beyond the fact that he
wouldn't be seeing his aunt Trish anymore, which had been
fine with him because she'd never been one of his favorites
anyway.

His parents had explained over dinner that evening that
Valery would now be living with them, and he remembered
how intensely and how immediately he had disliked the idea.
He and Valery had been good friends, even if she was three
years younger and something of a pest. She could throw as
good as any eleven-year-old boy, could slide into base better than most and could trade wisecracks and insults with the
best of them. All in all, for a girl, she wasn't half bad, and
he liked it when she came to visit or when he spent time with
her in the city.

But he hadn't wanted her living in his house. He hadn't
wanted her to be a closer part of his family. He hadn't
wanted to share his parents, his home or his life with her, not
on a full-time basis.

"I wasn't particularly happy about having her move in." That was an understatement. He had been so dismayed by his parents' announcement that he had argued the matter with them right there in front of Valery. Already teary-eyed and distraught over the upheaval in her life, at his display of temper, she had burst into tears and run from the room, and he had been sent to bed without dinner.

That had been the first time his refusal to accept and welcome his cousin into the Sinclair family had gotten him punished, but it hadn't been the last. The last time had cost him, and the price had been dear: he had lost the very family he'd been trying in his own selfish way to hold on to. He had lost fifteen years of his parents' love and respect. Fifteen years of being able to go home. Fifteen years of birthdays and holidays, of having a place he belonged and people he belonged with.

"As far as I was concerned, we didn't need her. We didn't have room for her. We'd gotten along perfectly fine as a family for fourteen years without her. If she needed a place to live...well, hell, that was *her* parents' responsibility, not mine. Let them provide for her." His laughter was short and sour. "I was a selfish kid."

Susannah glanced briefly in his direction. "You liked your life the way it was, and you didn't want it to change. That's not so selfish."

She spoke with the sort of knowledge that came from experience, which raised about a dozen questions in his mind. What was it about her life that had been changed against her will? Her marital status? Had she been happy with her marriage, unaware that there were problems until they could no longer be surmounted? Or had she known the problems were there but opted to ignore or tolerate them rather than give up the life she had become comfortable with?

Rather than ask questions that he suspected she wouldn't answer, he went on with his story. "My parents thought that because Valery and I had gotten along well before the divorce, eventually I would welcome her into the family and we would go back to being friends, that we would become . . . I don't know, pseudosiblings. Valery thought so, too, and she tried to make it happen, but I refused. I resented every bit of attention, every ounce of affection, Mom and Dad gave her. I hated that they treated her exactly the same way they treated me—as if she were their own child and not some niece whose own parents hadn't wanted her. I devoted most of my energy in the next eight years to shutting her out, to never letting her forget that she wasn't a Sinclair, that she didn't really belong.

"And then I found out something that my parents, and most of the adults in the family, had known all along, something that they'd kept hidden from all of the kids but especially from Valery and me—that she really wasn't part of our family. Her mother had already been pregnant when she met and married my uncle. And during one particularly angry argument with my parents, I brought that fact up, not knowing that Valery was standing outside the door listening."

He knew Susannah was smart and compassionate, knew that she would understand exactly what effect such knowledge had had on his cousin, but he continued anyway, sparing himself nothing. He didn't shy away from letting her see exactly how selfish, how jealous and immature and bitter he had been. He wanted her to know. He wanted to be honest about his biggest shame.

"Both of her parents had abandoned her, and her best friend—that was what she always called me—had turned his back on her when she was only eleven. For all those years the only constant in her life was the family—my parents and all the Navarres. They meant everything to her. And I took that away from her."

"And so your parents asked you to leave."

He still remembered the sick feeling inside when he realized that Valery had overheard, when she had walked into his father's study and he'd seen the hurt and disillusionment on her face. He still remembered the deep gutwrenching fear that his father's anger had stirred. He and George Sinclair had had more than their share of father-son disagreements—most of them over Valery and Remy's treatment of her—but he had never faced such rage. He had turned to his mother—disappointment was her specialty; it seemed so often he had disappointed her—and he had known then, in one brief moment of emotionless clarity, that his relationship with them wasn't going to survive. For eight years he had been pushing, fighting, trying to force them to choose between him and Valery, between their only child and this girl who was no relation to them at all, and finally they had made their choice.

They had chosen her.

He had gone away, feeling as hurt and abandoned as Valery must have when her parents had left her. He had been angry with himself for being so careless, for hurting Valery, for repeating something he'd never intended her to know, for forcing the issue and losing. He had berated himself for being unable to get past his jealousy, for being unable to make even a token acceptance of her, for being so selfish and so immature and so stubborn.

But, somewhere deep inside, he had still blamed Valery herself. If only she hadn't done whatever she'd done to cause both her parents to not want her, if only she had never come to live with *his* family, if only she hadn't been so damn needy...

If only his parents hadn't preferred her to him.

It said something for the man he was, Susannah thought grimly, that something he'd done half a lifetime ago still held such power over him. The fact was there was nothing so out of the ordinary about his resentment toward Valery. It seemed to her, in fact, that his parents had gotten just what they'd asked for: they had wanted Remy to treat Valery like a sister. Well, sibling rivalry seemed as accurate a description for the behavior he was describing as anything else.

Even that last part was worthy only of a little regret. So he'd blurted out something Valery wasn't supposed to know. It was a fact of life—people lost their tempers and said things they were later sorry for—but it was rarely a great tragedy. It wasn't worth an estrangement between parents and son. It certainly didn't call for a fifteen-year exile.

Besides, wasn't there an old saying, something about eavesdroppers never hearing anything good about themselves?

No, if Remy wanted to know shame, guilt and regret—*real* shame, the unforgivable kind, guilt you never recovered from—he should step into her life for a few hours. He should make this phone call she would soon be making.

"So..." He sounded more cheerful, but his expression didn't match. "Your turn now. What about your family back home on the farm in Nebraska?"

Silently she apologized—to her father, her brother and to Remy himself—for the lies she was about to tell. Then she shrugged and told them anyway. "There's just my father. My mother died when I was fifteen."

"Are you an only child, too?"

"Yes."

"Were you lonely growing up?"

"Not at all. Daddy farms with my uncle. Richard and his family have a house there, too, so I had my cousins around. The oldest two boys work with Daddy and Uncle Richard now and have places, and families, of their own on the farm."

"What was the best thing about growing up on a farm?"

She considered the question for a mile or two. There was much to recommend farm life, if you didn't mind hard work and gambling your livelihood on the whims of the weather. She'd been given more responsibility and at an earlier age than most of her friends in town. She'd been driving a tractor and that old Chevy truck for years before her friends were finally able to get behind the wheel. She had learned a respect for the land and the people who worked it, had learned a respect for life. She'd grown up with good, hardworking people, had grown up with a work ethic and a value system that she had thought would stay with her forever.

"I miss the innocence," she said at last. "Life was simpler in that time in that place. We worked hard, but we still had time to play. We took care of the land, and it took care of us. We treated people and their property with respect, and they did the same in return. We never had a lot of money, but we never went hungry and we never had to worry about being homeless. We had family, friends and good neighbors. There was never any trouble you could get into that you couldn't get out of, and there was always someone there to lend a hand.''

''And yet you left with the intention of never going back for more than occasional visits. Why?''

Because Skip, who had come south to New Orleans to go to school and to work, was doing neither. Because he wasn't mature enough to be completely on his own. Because he needed someone looking after him, someone to gently nudge him back into school, to help him stick with a job.

And because, as she had admitted last night, in the past year she'd seen way too much of Guy Duncan and the woman he had left her for, the woman he'd been having an affair with months before he'd finally moved out. Because he had taken such delight in his snide little put-downs, in his public snubs and deliberate little cruelties. Because she had needed to put him and what he had done to her pride—to her ego—behind her before she could face whatever might be ahead.

''It was time,'' she said simply. That was as true as any of her other reasons. Nebraska was a perfectly fine place for people who wanted to be there, but she had been searching for something else. She had needed a new life, new confidence, a new start. She had needed to see other places, to do other things, to experience other walks of life.

She had needed to be more than the woman she could be in Homestead, Nebraska.

The answer seemed to satisfy him—or, at least, to give him something to think about—because he remained silent until they reached the outskirts of Baton Rouge. There he advised her to take the next exit, then directed her to a shopping center where she could find the items she needed.

She parked a fair distance from the front door of the busy variety store. "Do you need anything?" she asked as she unbuckled her seat belt.

"I suppose coming in with you is out of the question."

"I suppose so."

"Let me give you some money—"

"We'll settle up later. I'll make it quick." Before he could say anything else, she left the car, slinging her purse strap over her shoulder, and set off across the parking lot, weaving between parked cars until she could no longer feel his gaze on her back. That one small freedom brought her a sigh of relief.

The strip shopping center was nearly a block long. She could probably find both the gloves and the foam rubber in the variety store, but she wasn't wasting time looking. She would get the gloves there, she decided as she approached the main door, and then walk to the fabric shop for the foam. It was at the opposite end, behind Remy, and there were at least three pay phones that she could see between here and there.

She took only a few moments to select a pair of gloves, then got a roll of adhesive tape on the way out. Not sparing even a glance for Remy a few aisles over in the car, she headed for the fabric store, where she bought a length of one-inch-thick foam. As she started back, though, her steps slowed and grew less purposeful, especially as she approached, then passed, the first pay phone. And the second.

It was now or never, she thought as she drew even with the third phone. Stopping, she fumbled in her purse for a quarter, then silently ran through the number she had memorized a week ago. Still, for a time she just stood there, numb and cold, before taking the first of the steps that would carry her to the phone. The second step was harder, the third damn near impossible.

Oh, God, she couldn't do this! She couldn't call that slimy lawyer, couldn't tell him any of the things he wanted to know. She couldn't help him or his sleazy boss in what they were trying to do. She couldn't betray herself this way. She couldn't betray Remy.

And then she thought of Skip, safely in the care of the lawyer and, therefore, his boss—safe as long as she cooperated. As long as she did what they had instructed her to do. Safe as long as she didn't let him down.

Going cold inside, she took the last step. She picked up the receiver, dropped the coin into the slot, dialed the number and listened to the rings, followed by a greeting.

"This is Susannah Duncan," she said, her voice steady and unrecognizable. "I'd like to speak to Mr. Carlucci."

Across the parking lot, Remy was slumped in the passenger seat, which he had reclined to a reasonably comfortable position, and using the outside mirror to follow the progress of a blonde two aisles behind him. "You're easily bored, Sinclair," he mumbled as he adjusted the mirror for a better look. "Lucky for you *and* Susannah, you're also easily amused."

The blonde was just his type—pretty, petite and oh, so consciously feminine. The first thing she'd done after parking her car was check her hair and makeup in the rearview mirror; first thing after exiting the car, she had adjusted her slim skirt and snug sweater, then brushed her fingertips across her hair. She walked with a slow, deliberate grace, and he would bet she talked that way, too—a lazy, honeyed southern drawl that could turn a man to stone. She was a beautiful woman, and she made the most of it.

In contrast, Susannah seemed hardly even aware of her appearance. If asked the color of her eyes, she would probably say mostly brown and drop it at that, leaving out all the subtle shadings, the soft browns, dark golds and muted greens. If pressed for an opinion on her own prettiness, she would likely reply acceptable. If asked to judge her effect on men—on this man in particular—she would probably say negligible.

And, oh, how wrong she would be.

The blonde reached the sidewalk that ran in front of the shops and turned away from the variety store. Tilting the mirror as far as it would go to follow her progress, Remy found the rear view as interesting as the other angles . . . at least, until she passed a pay phone, a pay phone where Susannah was making a call.

Slowly he straightened in the seat, returning it to its upright position, and twisted around until he had an unimpeded view. The woman's back was to him, but it was definitely Susannah. He recognized the faded jeans, the pale pink sweater and the rich auburn hair. He recognized the sense of familiarity that struck him each time he saw her anew.

Who was she calling, and why was she calling him or her from a pay phone? He had explained when he hired her that she should consider Belle Ste. Claire her home. She was welcome to have her mail delivered there, to give the phone number to her family and friends and to have visitors, and she had accepted his offer with a solemn nod. Only now that he knew her a little better, he suspected that nod hadn't been acceptance, but simply acknowledgment. She had understood his offer, but hadn't been sure she would take him up on it.

So who *was* she calling? A friend? He knew she'd made friends—other hospital employees—in her short time in New Orleans because Valery had talked to a few of them after he had hired her. Maybe a boyfriend? He had asked a few questions about her marriage, but he hadn't asked if she was involved with another man. He hadn't even considered it. He had simply assumed that any single, attractive young woman who was willing to leave New Orleans to live with him at Belle Ste. Claire for an entire month had to be unattached. After all, what kind of man would quietly accept such a separation from the woman he was seeing?

Or maybe it was simply business. Maybe there'd been some loose end she hadn't been able to tie up before leaving the city yesterday.

But why couldn't she make a simple business call from the house? In fact, why couldn't any of those calls be made from home? There were at least a half dozen telephones in the house, and he would gladly give her the privacy—well, not gladly; he was too nosy for that, but at least without suspicion—to make whatever calls she needed.

Her call lasted only a minute longer. After she hung up, she simply stood there for a moment, her head bowed, her shoulders rounded. Bad news? Remy wondered. A less-than-pleasant conversation with a disagreeable boyfriend? Whatever the cause, she looked even wearier than he'd been feeling lately.

Then the moment passed. She straightened her shoulders, raised her head and started toward the car. Slowly he turned around, resettling in the seat, and waited for her to reach him.

The air inside the car cooled a few degrees when she opened the door. She tossed her purse and one bag in the back seat, then offered the second bag to him as she fastened her seat belt. "Try those on for size."

Inside the small plastic bag was a pair of black biking gloves. He looked at them skeptically. "I'm barely walking. It'll be a while before I feel like getting out the old twenty-one speed."

She simply looked at him, not even tempted to smile.

He opened the package and removed both gloves. Even those small movements made his hands ache. His fingers were sore and swollen, and in addition to the places where his palms were blistering, small bruises were forming, he noted as he cautiously wriggled one hand into the fingerless glove. The fit was snug, the nylon and suede soft—and the thick padding across the palms was heavenly.

"When you ride a bike," she explained, "depending on your position, you can put a good deal of weight on your hands. You grip the handlebars in pretty much the same way that you hold onto your crutches, so the glove's padding is already in the right place. It won't stop your hands from hurting, especially these first few days, but it *will* help."

He pulled on the second glove, then adjusted the Velcro closures across the back. "Not bad," he remarked, flexing both hands before grinning at her. "They teach you this in nursing school?"

Darned if she didn't smile back. "No. I learned that at home when my—" Her words stopped abruptly, her smile disappeared and she looked at him with an expression that, after twelve years with the FBI, he recognized all too well: guilt. He could see it in her eyes, could feel it in the car— hell, he could damn near smell it. She felt guilty about something, but what? Something she had done or hadn't done? Something she had said, something she had tried and failed at?

Like marriage? *I learned that at home....* Her ex-husband was back home, with his new wife, and he was part of the reason Susannah was here. Had she learned the trick with the gloves from him? Was she trying to avoid talking about him? Did it still hurt to even think about him?

"Susannah? Are you all right?"

She looked away then, turning to stare straight ahead. "Of course." Her voice was chilly, tautly controlled, and her jaw was clenched tightly enough to hurt.

"Are you sure?" When she didn't respond, he hesitantly reached across the seat, touching his fingertips to her jaw, intending to turn her gently toward him. But the instant he made contact, she cringed—*cringed,* for God's sake, as if his touch was unbearable—and shrank away from him.

He drew back, fastened his seat belt, then folded his fingers loosely together in his lap. His right hand rested on his cast, and for a moment he simply stared down. It was stupid to take her rejection so personally, but, damn it, it *felt* personal. He wouldn't have hurt her. He had never been rough with any woman except an occasional suspect who interfered or resisted arrest. He had just wanted to touch her, had just wanted her to look at him.

For a long time she sat without moving; then, peripherally, he saw her reach for her seat belt. A moment later the engine purred to life, and she pulled out of the parking space. The only errand left to run was the grocery store. He didn't bother pointing out to her that they had passed two in the last couple of blocks before reaching the shopping center. He trusted that she had noticed them.

Neither of them spoke until they were at the grocery store. Then she finally faced him, her expression remote and as wary as ever. Now there was something else, too: regret. "What kinds of food do you like?"

"I don't eat liver or fish except catfish. Other than that, I'm easy to please." As an afterthought, he added, "I'd like some orange juice."

She nodded.

"And strawberry ice cream."

Another nod.

"And rice. Spicy foods. Barbecue. And I don't like pork."

"Not even bacon?"

"Of course I like bacon. It's hardly the same as pork chops or ham. And I like sausage."

"Spicy sausage?"

This time it was Remy who nodded.

"What about sweets besides ice cream? Do you like cakes, pies, cookies, candy?"

"Carrot, pecan, chocolate chip and pralines." He hesitated, then offered, "It'll be easier if I go with you."

She patted his hand, an awkward little touch where the black nylon stretched across his skin, then hastily left, closing the door with a muted thud behind her. This time he didn't watch her go.

Instead he reached down and, although it was too late, he slowly peeled off each of the gloves and stuffed them inside his jacket pockets.

By seven-thirty that evening they had eaten dinner, Remy had returned to the parlor to watch television and Susannah was just finishing up in the kitchen. She glanced around as she dried her hands on a towel, thinking about what she had accomplished that day. She had finished unpacking all of Remy's things and carried in and put away all the groceries. She had baked a carrot cake and frosted it with real cream cheese frosting, had cooked dinner and talked with Remy and had even stolen away for fifteen minutes for a solitary walk around the grounds at dusk.

And she had talked with Nicholas Carlucci.

She shared the national prejudice against lawyers in general, and she disliked this lawyer in particular. He was one of those people who cared nothing about the law, about the courts or justice. His decision to earn a law degree had been motivated by financial gain and a seriously undeveloped sense of ethics. He had learned to manipulate the system to benefit his clients and himself, and justice be damned.

He was polite. Smooth. Polished. He hadn't hesitated in telling her right up front that he was enormously successful at whatever he set out to do. In her case, what he was doing—for the time being at least—was watching out for her brother. But if she failed, if she let them down, he could destroy Skip as easily as he was now protecting him.

She hadn't had much information to offer him today, but he had insisted on regular calls. He had asked a few questions about the house, about Michael Bennett and Valery Navarre's visit yesterday—while Valery had ridden up from New Orleans with Susannah, Michael had picked up Remy at the hospital and brought him—and about Remy's parents' vacation plans. He had told her that Skip was fine, that her brother was enjoying his stay at Mr. Falcone's house and that he wanted to hear from her again in three days' time.

She hadn't told him anything important, she reminded herself.

Not a single thing.

Laying the towel aside, she thought longingly about her bedroom, only a few feet down the hall and the only place in the entire house that—so far, at least—offered any measure of privacy from Remy. But when she moved away from the counter, she turned toward the parlor instead.

Of all the rooms in the house, the parlor was her favorite. The others, even the bedrooms upstairs, were decorated with an eye toward history, with antique furniture, silk wall coverings and valuable old rugs, but the parlor was meant for comfort. It smelled of furniture polish and hothouse flowers, of rich old leather and cinnamon potpourri. The furnishings were inviting: overstuffed pieces with tons of pillows, tables that didn't mind a scratch or two, footstools that you weren't afraid to put your feet on. There was a big leather recliner that had definitely seen better days— Mr. Sinclair's, she wagered—and a barrel chair that looked just about perfect for curling up in with a book or needlework.

Remy was sitting on the sofa watching television, a newspaper open but ignored in his lap, his cast propped on the coffee table. As she passed the recliner, she took a pillow, then lifted his foot and placed the pillow underneath to protect the tabletop from fiberglass scratches. He gave her a sleepy sort of smile of thanks, one that made her stomach flutter all out of proportion to the deed.

Sleepy was not sexy, she sternly admonished herself as she settled in the barrel chair. Oh, but in his case, it was—hair tousled, body relaxed, eyes hazy and soft and mouth softer. A sleepy Remy was more appealing than any other man she'd ever seen.

But she couldn't afford to find him appealing. If she couldn't afford to be his friend, she certainly couldn't afford to even think about being anything else.

God help her, she hated this job. She hated Carlucci and Falcone. She hated herself, and sometimes—she whispered a silent, shameful prayer for forgiveness—sometimes she even hated Skip.

"Anything in particular you want to watch?" Remy asked, offering her the remote control.

She shook her head.

"I don't guess you see much evening television with your schedule." He laid the remote aside. "You're not missing a lot."

"Your job's not usually nine to five, is it?"

"That depends on my caseload."

"Do you do the same kind of stuff all the time, like narcotics or vice?" She knew little about law enforcement, and what she knew was probably inaccurate, since it came from television and movies. Back home, Homestead was too small and too quiet to have a police department of its own; whatever crimes committed there were few and far between, were rarely more serious than teenage mischief making and were investigated by the sheriff's department.

"I work organized crime, which these days can include a little bit of everything."

Organized crime. It sounded so ominous, so threatening. The first time she had heard Jimmy Falcone's name, she hadn't known that he *was* organized crime in New Orleans. Law and order and criminal justice hadn't held much interest for her. She rarely watched the local news, and although she read the newspaper each day, she merely skimmed or skipped those sorts of stories completely. It was just coincidence, she supposed, that she had read or heard something about Jimmy Falcone and the corruption that was his business only a day or two before Skip had mentioned his new job and his boss, Mr. Falcone.

She had asked Skip about Falcone, and he had brushed her off. The man's reputation was undeserved. Yeah, some of the people who had once worked for him had taken some less-than-legal shortcuts, but it had been without Mr. Falcone's knowledge, and once he had found out, he'd gotten rid of them, had fired them right away. Skip had talked his way out of it and she had let him, because she'd had other things on her mind. Because, deep in her heart, she had remained convinced that her brother—while a little wild, a little reckless and a whole lot irresponsible—would never do anything really bad. He might drink a little too much, might pick a fight with the wrong guy, might create a public disturbance, but he was just a high-spirited kid. He would never do anything *really* illegal. He wasn't a crook, wasn't a thief or a thug or worse.

Good Lord, she had been naive.

Even now she didn't know exactly how Skip was involved in Falcone's business. All she knew was that her little brother, the brother she had practically raised, the brother she had promised to always take care of, to always protect, had become someone she hardly knew. He had become someone who would carry an illegal weapon. He had become someone who saw nothing wrong with earning large sums of money for doing very little work for a man who controlled half the money-making crime in the city.

All she knew was that Nicholas Carlucci was promising one of two outcomes to Skip's situation. If she cooperated, sometime within the next month, her brother would be allowed to leave New Orleans, with no threats hanging over his head, free for her to take home to Nebraska. But if she didn't cooperate, Carlucci would see to it that Skip went to prison for a very long time . . . or worse.

Susannah always kept her promises.

Nicholas Carlucci had assured her in a voice that had left her shaking with fear that he, too, always kept his promises.

Realizing that Remy was watching her, waiting for her to continue their conversation, she gestured toward his cast. "Why did you get shot?"

His mouth thinned, and his eyes turned hard. "Because I trusted the wrong person."

A shiver rippled through her, and she moved uncomfortably, trying to contain it. When she responded, it was in a thin, small voice. "I don't imagine you make that mistake often."

"No, I don't. It won't happen again."

You're wrong, she wanted to warn him. *It's already happening again. You're trusting me when you should lock me away with all the rest of the criminals.* But she simply clasped her hands tightly together to hide their trembling, and she quietly asked, "What happened?"

Remy studied the remote for a moment before pressing the button to mute the sound. Where should he start? How much did she want to know? More importantly, how much did he want her to know? Anything that might boost her interest. Nothing that might give her cause for concern. Everything that could help her come to trust him.

He turned on the couch so that he was facing her, then leaned forward to slide a pillow underneath his foot. Before he managed, though, Susannah left her chair and arranged the pillows so his cast was at just the right elevation for comfort. He could have done it himself, he thought with a faint smile.

But there was something awfully sweet about her doing it for him.

"Do you remember the Simmons murder in the Quarter last month?"

She was back in her chair again, her feet tucked beneath her. "I remember hearing about it. I didn't pay a lot of attention."

"The guy was walking down the street, talking to a woman he'd just met, when two of his buddies drove up, got out of their car and blew him away. The dead guy was one of my informants, and the woman who witnessed his murder was my cousin, Valery."

"Interesting coincidence," she murmured.

"We, the FBI, thought it *was* just coincidence at first. Valery worked in the Quarter. She always left work at the same time every afternoon, always walked the same route to her car every day. It was just bad luck and timing, we thought, that she was there the day Nate Simmons got killed."

"But you were wrong."

"We were wrong. Simmons knew he was part of a scam— he was a con artist by trade; he could smell a game a mile away. He was supposed to meet Valery that day, was supposed to walk down the street with her, was supposed to run into his buddies. Unfortunately he didn't know the rest of the plan. These guys killed Simmons but left Valery unharmed, the best witness the police could ever ask for. She was standing only a few feet from the two men. She got a good look at them, could describe them perfectly. She even heard them mention the name of the man who had hired them to kill Nate, and she had a damned good reason to repeat the information to the police. But she didn't.''

"You," Susannah guessed. "They said you were the one who had hired them.''

Nodding, he thought back to that Monday afternoon last month. It hadn't been so long ago, but it seemed like forever. He hadn't been hobbling around in a cast then. He hadn't had any contact with his parents or Valery in years. He hadn't known that someone he trusted was going to betray him. He hadn't known he would soon come too terrifyingly close to dying.

He hadn't known Susannah even existed.

Or maybe he had. Maybe he hadn't known her face or her name, but had known the woman, the spirit, the soul. Maybe that was why he'd felt such an immediate connection to her a few weeks later in the emergency room.

Putting those thoughts aside, he continued with his story. "It was a setup from the start. I was conducting an investigation into Simmons's boss's activities, and I was getting close. All it would take to get me pulled off was even a hint of impropriety. Being implicated in the murder of my own informant could have ended my career. The bastard figured that if he could get rid of me, the case would be turned over to my partner, who just happened to be on his payroll. He assumed that, with our history, Valery would be more than happy to bring me down, but he didn't count on family loyalty. She wasn't convinced that I was guilty, and she wasn't going to ruin my reputation until she *was* convinced.''

He broke off for a moment to study Susannah. She seemed more distressed by his tale than the facts warranted. Concern for *him* certainly wasn't responsible for that look in her eyes. Maybe innocence was. Growing up on a farm and living a small-town Nebraska life weren't enough to prepare her for the crime, the lack of caring and the violence that were part of life in a big city. No doubt she'd heard plenty about violence before leaving the prairies behind, but what was it she'd said today? *I miss the inno-*

*cence. There was never any trouble you could get into that
you couldn't get out of...*

"Once we figured out what was going on, we made a deal
with my partner. He'd get me hooked up with Jimmy Falcone—his boss—and he wouldn't spend the rest of his life
in prison. He arranged the meeting, but it turned out that he
was more afraid of Falcone than he was of us. He warned
the bastard away, and he shot me." He shook his head, still
disbelieving even after all this time. "My own partner shot
me."

"So Nate Simmons was a sacrifice to Jimmy Falcone's
ambition and greed." Her voice was flat, as if she found the
very words too repulsive to say with any degree of comfort.
"What happened to your partner?"

"He's in jail, awaiting trial. He's considered too big a
flight risk to allow bail."

"Is he going to testify against Falcone?"

Remy shook his head again. "He's afraid. People like
Falcone...their influence extends everywhere. Even into the
jails."

"What about Falcone? Did you arrest him?"

His grin was rueful. "We're working on it—or, at least,
the agents who replaced my partner and me are. The man's
slippery, and he's smart, and he inspires tremendous loyalty. The night I got shot, we made eight arrests, but not one
of them will implicate their boss in any way. Plus, he's
bought himself one of the best damn lawyers in the state of
Louisiana. Nick Carlucci knows the law inside and out. He's
as slick and as sly as the best of them."

"What about Valery? Will she testify against Falcone?"

"She'll testify against the men who killed Simmons, unless they cut a deal first, but she doesn't know anything
firsthand about Falcone."

Susannah picked up a needlepoint pillow that his mother
had made and signed and stroked her fingertips lightly
across the textured surface. "It must have been terrible for
her...seeing someone murdered."

"Yes," he agreed grimly, thinking back to the only time in his career when he had watched someone die. "It was. But—if it's not wrong to look on the bright side—because of it she met Michael, and they're getting married as soon as my parents get back from vacation."

"Considering your…" Still studying the needlepoint, she borrowed his earlier word. "History, does that bother you?"

He did consider it for a moment. He'd grown up a lot since that last angry night here, a lot more than the passage of time could account for. Much of his maturing had come in the last ten months, starting with Evan's death. In less than a year, he had lost one of his three best friends. He had watched Michael damn near drink himself to death in a futile effort to ease the pain, the sorrow and the guilt. He had gone through the Simmons case, had coped with his concern for Valery's life and with his partner's betrayal. He had faced his own mortality.

Did it bother him that, after taking his place in his parents' affections, Valery had now taken precedence over him with his best friend? "No, not at all. She's good for Michael. She brings him peace, a reason to believe, and he makes her feel loved. They're both happier than I've ever seen them."

No, far from being bothered, if anything, he was envious of Michael and Valery. He wanted what they had, wanted to share that same sort of love, devotion and commitment with someone. He wanted the future they were facing together: the family, the promises, the years and the undeniable assurance of a lifetime of love.

And he had no doubt that he would find it. Maybe with Susannah, maybe not.

But he *would* find it.

Chapter 4

Sunday was a beautiful day, sunny and warm, a late-winter reminder that spring was coming. Back home spring was Susannah's favorite season because it meant the long, harsh winter was over. She had loved the weeks of snow and ice when she was a kid, but found them less than enthralling as an adult. The hard weather and slick roads had bothered her so much more each year that, last November, she had said a prayer of thanks as she'd driven away from Homestead that she wouldn't be enduring them again. She had refused to even bring her heavy winter clothing with her. Sweaters and a jacket or two had gone into her bags, but the down-filled coats, the gloves and scarves and the warm boots had stayed behind, boxed up in the attic at the farm.

Down here, she speculated, spring couldn't be too different from winter. The temperatures would be warmer—although they'd had plenty of December and January days that were shirtsleeve weather—and there would be more flowers in bloom, although she had already spotted the delicate blooms of wood violets and yellow jasmine, and the honeysuckle was fragrant outside her bedroom window. The change in seasons here would be subtler, more gradual, lacking Nebraska's drama. The world would slowly become greener and warmer, and then one day they would wake and it would be summer.

She regretted with a deep sigh that she wouldn't experience a Louisiana summer.

"If you're bored, you don't have to stay out here."

Rolling her head to the side, she looked at Remy. It had been his idea to come outside this afternoon, to find a sunny spot on the lawn and soak up a few rays. They had brought books—his a murder mystery that Valery had brought from home, hers a history of Mardi Gras from his parents' library—and he had made his way with more grace and assurance than any man on crutches ought to have to one of the few places in the side yard where the giant oaks and pines allowed the sun to reach the ground. It had taken her only a moment to bring chairs from the gallery, wooden ones painted hunter green, along with a small table he could use as a hassock, and they had settled in to read.

"I'm not bored. I'm reading," she replied, fully aware that the book had slipped halfway off her lap at least thirty minutes ago while she had contemplated any number of lazy thoughts.

"You can't learn about Mardi Gras from a book. You have to experience it."

She didn't point out that if she were back in New Orleans instead of here with him, sometime in the next few weeks, she would be doing just that—would catch at least one of the parades, would spend at least a few hours in the Quarter soaking up the atmosphere and being generally overwhelmed. "I didn't realize that technically Mardi Gras refers only to Shrove Tuesday and that all the festivities leading up to it are actually part of Carnival instead." She gave him a smug look. "So I *can* learn from a book."

"Yeah, but being there is a lot more fun." He paused, then offered, "You can go back for the last couple days of Carnival if you want. That's when they have the big parades, and you'll probably be ready for some time away by then.''

His suggestion held a certain appeal, Susannah silently acknowledged. But if she got away from him and Belle Ste. Claire for a few days, if she was out of Nicholas Carlucci's reach for forty-eight hours... Who knew? She just might give in to her cowardice—or would it be courage?—and run away and hide. She might abandon Skip to his fate. She might save Remy from his.

She smiled faintly, politely, in rejection of his offer. ''It'll come around again next year.'' But she wouldn't be there to see it. She would be in a quiet corner of some anonymous city, someplace where it didn't get cold in winter, where a person didn't know her neighbors and didn't make friends. In a place where she could forget—no, not forget, but could live with who she was and what she had done.

She would never forget.

Closing the book, she stretched her legs straight out in front of her, then let them dangle over the broad arm of the chair. ''You don't seem particularly fascinated with your book, either.''

''I figured out who done it and how by the end of Chapter One.''

''Must be an occupational hazard. I think cops would find mysteries too easy and would read something totally unrelated to work.''

''My reading material usually *is* work—reports, investigative notes, criminal histories. I don't have much time for fiction.''

Her next question slipped out before she realized it. ''Why did you join the FBI?''

''Didn't we have this conversation before?'' he asked with a wry grin. ''Because I like to arrest people.''

''You didn't have to go to college and law school to do that. You could have just gotten a job with the local county sheriff's department.''

''Parish,'' he corrected her. ''Down here we have parishes instead of counties.''

She didn't miss a beat. "With the local parish sheriff's department. Why spend seven years in school, only to become a cop?"

"I didn't plan it that way," he admitted. "I went to college because all Sinclairs go to college, and I went on to law school with the intention of becoming a lawyer like my dad. By the time I started my last year, Michael and Evan—he was one of our roommates in college—were already working for the NOPD, and Smith, our other roommate who was also in law school, already knew he was going to be a prosecutor somewhere. They got me interested enough to follow along, only I didn't want to be a city cop and I sure as hell didn't want to spend my life in courtrooms, so I went with the bureau instead."

"Do you ever regret it?"

"No."

"Not even the night you got shot?"

He shook his head.

It must be nice, she thought, to be so certain. She'd made few choices in her life that she hadn't had doubts and regrets about. Going to school, being a nurse, getting married—even the divorce had been a major indecision for her. Even though it had been Guy's choice, she could have made it difficult for him, and a part of her had been tempted. A part of her had actually wondered, back in those bleak days, if maybe a bad marriage was better than no marriage at all, if maybe a husband who felt little liking and no respect for her was better than no husband at all. She had wanted to be rid of him as much as he wanted to be gone, but she had been afraid—of admitting failure, of being alone, of facing their families and friends on her own, no longer as one half of a couple, no longer Guy's wife, but the woman he had left. The woman he had been so publicly unfaithful to. The woman who couldn't hold on to a man.

Thank God she had regained her sanity—and her dignity—and had let the divorce proceed without objection.

"So you're never going to practice law, like your father," she said, getting her thoughts back in line.

"I can't say never. I don't know what might happen in another ten or twenty years. I *can* say I don't plan to. What about you? Are you ever going to quit nursing?"

"I don't plan to."

"Not even when you get married again and have kids to raise?"

"I don't plan to do that, either."

He studied her for a moment, his gaze steady and intense enough to make her want to squirm. When he finally broke his silence, his voice was quiet and edged with sympathy. "Was it that bad?"

She pretended ignorance. "What?"

"Your marriage. Was it bad enough to scare you away from trying again?"

She didn't have to answer. She could ignore his question or simply tell him that she didn't want to discuss it, and he would let it drop. He was too polite, his manners too deeply ingrained, to insist.

But he was also curious—he'd made that clear their first evening here. And wasn't it only fair, since she was the one who had turned the conversation to a personal level, that he be allowed to ask questions, too?

"I consider my marriage a learning experience," she said at last.

"And what did you learn?"

"That the institution of marriage is largely overrated. That people you think you know can surprise you. That, while it may be true that someone else can't be responsible for your happiness, he can sure as hell be blamed for your misery."

The words hung between them, caught in the ensuing silence, spoken without overt anger or cynicism but brushed with bitterness at the end, Remy thought. He had lived with the feeling for so long himself that he would always recognize it, and he would always remember the other emotions it encompassed: resentment, animosity, hopelessness and pain. Always pain.

After a moment, he responded, keeping his voice carefully neutral. "Those are some interesting lessons."

She simply shrugged.

"They raise a hell of a lot more questions than they answer."

"I get the impression everything raises questions with you."

He acknowledged that with a nod. "But to show you how considerate I can be, I'm not going to ask you to go into it further. Just tell me one thing." He looked away, following the progress of a car as it traveled along the highway out front. When it had rounded a curve and disappeared from sight, he returned his gaze to her. "Do you have regrets?"

"About the marriage?"

"About the divorce."

"Do you mean am I sorry he left me?" She drew a deep breath, then blew it out. "I would like to have been the one doing the leaving and not the one left behind. For the sake of my ego, I would like to have been the one who initiated the divorce. But would I undo it if I could? Would I go back if he'd have me? No." For a moment she looked as if she wanted to say something more, but she settled for repeating and qualifying her answer. "No, I wouldn't. Not ever."

He had assumed, upon learning their first night here that she had been married before, that ending the marriage had been her decision. What man in his right mind, he had wondered, would be fool enough to let her go? Only Duncan hadn't *let* her go; he had pushed her away with both hands. *He* had walked away from *her*.

Why? What had there been about this quiet, pretty, intelligent, gentle and capable woman that he hadn't liked? Exactly what had he been looking for that Susannah couldn't provide? Maybe Duncan had liked his women dumb, brassy and flashy. Maybe he resented a woman who was brighter than he was.

Or maybe he had taken whatever it was he wanted from her, and then had discarded her for someone else. Hadn't she said that part of her reason for moving to New Orleans had to do with seeing too much of her ex-husband and his new wife?

"I plan to get married," he announced, tilting his head back and studying the thin, stringy clouds in the sky.

"You've never been married?" She sounded as if she were asking against her will. Because she was asking only to be polite? Because she disliked the subject? Because she wasn't interested?

Or maybe because she didn't want to be interested but was?

He preferred that last possibility himself. "No. First there was law school to get through, then starting the job with the bureau. After that...I always thought there would be plenty of time to find someone and settle down. There wasn't any rush. I could always do it next year."

"And then you got shot in the chest and realized that next year might not come." The cynicism that had been missing from her voice earlier was there now. "So now you want to do all the things you'd been putting off until later. Life offers no guarantees, so you'll go for whatever you can get."

"You're too young to be so cynical, Susannah," he said, his tone a mild rebuke.

"Marriage is too important to be taken so lightly," she retorted. "You don't wake up in a hospital bed and say, 'Gee, I may not live to see forty-five, so if I want to get married, I'd better do it now.' You don't get married for the sake of having done it. You do it because you've fallen in love, because you can't imagine living without this person, because she completes who you are, because there's an emptiness to your life that no one can fill but her."

"So you do have a romantic streak hidden somewhere inside. I was beginning to wonder," he teased. After a moment, though, his smile faded. "I'm thirty-seven years old, and I've never married. It's not because I haven't had the opportunity. There have been women, but none that I want to wake up with five years down the line, and certainly none I can imagine spending the rest of my life with. You know those pictures you see sometimes in the newspaper of little old gray-haired couples who have been together fifty and sixty and even seventy years? *That's* what I'm looking for. Getting shot didn't make me decide to get married for the sake of being married, but it did make me rethink my priorities. It made me reconsider what's important in life."

"And you consider marriage important." She shrugged as if the conversation now bored her. "Well, good luck. Because you know those little old gray-haired couples who have been together fifty, sixty and seventy years? They're getting harder and harder to find. Marriage is no longer a commitment in our society. It's a short-term affair."

"Not to everyone." But, no doubt, he thought grimly, that was all it had meant to her ex-husband. She had wanted the fifty or sixty years, the commitment, but he had only been interested in the affair. Now she was determined not to give anyone else the chance to change her mind.

She didn't yet know how persuasive *he* could be.

Knowing instinctively that they had covered the subject as thoroughly as Susannah intended to at the present time, he let his attention drift from her to the grounds. His mother had always had help with the house, but the yard had been a family job. The azaleas, numbering well into the hundreds and some of them taller now than Remy, were his father's pride and joy, and the flower beds and vines—wisteria, honeysuckle and jasmine—were his mother's responsibility. He supposed that now they hired someone to help with the acres of mowing that had once been *his* job. At his apartment in town, he had a handkerchief-size patch of lawn with an azalea or two, a dogwood, a crape myrtle and the kind of lush, thick grass that couldn't be grown underneath the shade that covered most of this lawn, and the management company hired someone to come in and take care of everything so all he had to do was admire it.

He had hated the mowing when he was sixteen and eager to be off with his friends. Now he kind of missed it.

"How does it feel to be home?"

He glanced at Susannah and grinned. "A little strange with Mom and Dad gone."

"Valery said they wanted to cancel their trip and stay here, but you refused."

"They'd been planning it for a long time. After all, how often does a fortieth anniversary come along? Besides, we had two weeks in the hospital to get caught up on the last fifteen years, and we'll have plenty of time to visit when they get back."

And, he had to admit, he'd had other, more selfish reasons for encouraging them to continue with their vacation as planned. He hadn't wanted to share his first visit home with anyone else. Susannah didn't quite count; after all, the place was new to her. She didn't have any memories of it, good or bad. It didn't represent anything to her. He had wanted the house to himself, had wanted to indulge only his own memories.

And then there had been Susannah. With his parents here, he would have no need of her care. He would have missed out on the long hours they'd spent together, on the conversations and the simple pleasure of sharing her company. He would have missed out on getting to know her. He would have missed out on starting to care about her.

A car on the highway drew his gaze as the driver slowed, then pulled to the shoulder of the road. Tourists, he thought, as the woman in the passenger's seat raised a camera and snapped off a few pictures from inside the car. "Belle Ste. Claire has never been open to the public," he remarked, "except for an occasional fund-raiser for one of Mom's charities. But that's never stopped people from pulling off the road and taking pictures. When I was a kid, we used to find strangers wandering around the grounds, and I remember coming home from school one day and there were people up on the gallery, peeking through the windows."

She lazily turned her head to glance at the couple before they drove on. "It's an impressive place," she murmured. "You grew up here. It's all very familiar to you. It's *home*. But most people will never know what it's like to live in a house like this. It's so gracious and elegant and grand. They like to look. They like to wonder, to pretend, to fantasize."

To fantasize. Over the past few days he'd been developing a few fantasies of his own, but they had nothing to do with the house. No, his fantasies could take place anywhere or nowhere. They didn't involve elegance or grandeur, but in a sense—spiritual almost—they had a great deal to do with *home.*

They had a very great deal to do with Susannah.

With a sigh that sounded like regret, she got to her feet. "I need to start dinner and run a few loads of laundry. Do you want to stay out here a while longer?"

Of course not. He wanted to follow wherever she went. Laundry, cooking, cleaning—he'd discovered a fascination in the most mundane of chores when she was the one doing them. He could watch her do nothing for hours and never be bored. He could do nothing with her for hours or, better yet, he could do with her all the things his fantasies were built on. Like touching. Looking. Undressing. Getting familiar.

Getting intimate.

"I'll come in. It's going to get cooler as the sun starts going down." His voice was huskier than it should be, but she didn't seem to notice.

Standing up from the low, slanted seat had been so easy for her, a smooth, graceful flow of movement. Damn this cast, it was awkward as hell for him...at least until she took his hands in hers and pulled.

Susannah almost always regretted acting on impulse, and she knew the instant she touched him that she would regret this. But there was no way to help him up without touching him, no way without getting much too close.

By the time he was on his feet, they were indeed close. So close that to see his face, she would have to tilt her head back and look up. So close that she could smell the fabric softener that scented his T-shirt. So close that she could feel his heat and imagined that she could hear his heartbeat, although it was really probably her own, erratic and rapid, echoing in her ears.

Once he was steady on his feet, she would let go, would back away and retrieve his crutches. She told herself that. But once he was steady on his feet, *he* let go and instead skimmed his hands along her arms until they rested on her shoulders.

"Susannah."

She swallowed hard. She couldn't pretend the huskiness in his voice was normal.

"You know I'd like to kiss you."

Her response was little more than a frightened plea. "No."

"No, you don't know? No, I wouldn't like to? Or no, I can't?"

"You don't... I... You can't."

Bit by slow bit, his hands moved, sliding across the thin cotton of her shirt, inching up until his palms cupped her cheeks, until his fingers were gently stroking her jaw, raising her head, lifting her face to his. "You have to know that I would never hurt you."

She forced a deep breath, then another. Feigning the calmness that had long since forsaken her, she met his gaze. "Is this part of the job, Remy?" she asked in a soft, blunt voice. "Is this part of what you expect from a companion?"

She saw the surprise in his eyes, saw the denial and the faint flare of hurt that she had even asked; then his expression subtly shifted, emotions taking cover behind shadows. "What if it is? What if keeping your job here means accepting this? What if this is one of those specific details you thought I would fill you in on as they come up?"

He was bluffing. She knew it as surely as she knew anything. Remy Sinclair was a handsome man. He was charming, sexy, came from a genteel background, had an advancing career and the promise of fortune in his future. With everything he could offer a woman, he had no reason to resort to blackmail. All he had to do was pick up the phone, make a call or two, and he could have his choice of women up here from New Orleans within the hour.

He had no reason to resort to *her*.

"I'd say one of us got a bad deal," she said, her voice even, her tone noncommittal. "Either I hired out cheap...or you're not getting what you paid for."

His smile was grudging. "Any price you might ask would be too cheap."

"Any price you might pay would be too much."

He chuckled. "You're a hard woman, Susannah."

That was one of the insults Guy had thrown at her from time to time. She was hardheaded when she was too stubborn to give in to him on some minor issue, hard-hearted when she wouldn't let him sweet-talk his way out of trouble, and just plain hard when he was looking to undermine her self-esteem. Men liked their women soft and sweet, he would remind her. They liked women who knew how to act like women, women who were feminine and seductive, tenderhearted and malleable. They didn't much care for hard, tough bitches.

But, search as she might, she couldn't find any insult in Remy's use of the word. He just seemed amused, but kindly so—not in the cruel, calculating way that Guy had always found her amusing.

She raised her hands to his forearms, intending to push his hands away, slip free and get his crutches for him before fleeing to the house. But her focus was so fully on her own intention that she overlooked his...until his mouth touched hers.

The kiss lasted only a moment, only long enough to stun her, to make her go utterly still, barely breathing, her heart barely beating. It was a moment of surprise, unexpected and brief. It was a moment that never should have happened. A moment that ended way too soon.

Then he released her, taking a hobbling step back, reaching for his crutches while she stood motionless. His gloves were fastened around the foam-padded grips; she was vaguely aware of the ripping sound as he pulled the Velcro apart, then tugged each glove on and refastened the hook-and-loop closures. When that was done, he looked at her again. This time there wasn't a hint of amusement or teasing in his expression. "I don't know whether you prefer games or seduction or honesty, Susannah, but I prefer the honest approach myself. I'm a patient man, and I'll give you all the time you need. I'll also give you a fair warning. That kiss was just the first. I want a lot more from you than that. I want more than companionship, more than friendship. I want intimacy. I want whatever you have to give. I want it all."

Feeling as if the ground were slipping beneath her feet, she took a few awkward steps away until she bumped into her chair. She took cover behind it, holding tightly to the curved wooden back for support. If he had given her a chance to choose between games, seduction and honesty, she would have told him that she, too, preferred honesty.

But his next words still would have knocked her for a loop.

She had no right to speak of honesty, not when her very presence in his life was the worst of deceptions. Not when her every word or action was a lie. Not when her lies were likely to cost him his life.

And she had no right to want his kisses, his companionship or his friendship. She had no right to even think—as some small, buried part of her was doing right now—about intimacy with him. She had no right to want whatever he might give before she destroyed him.

"You don't ask for much," she said, her voice small and cold because the place it came from, her heart, was small, tight and cold.

His smile was faint and crooked as he shook his head. "I'm asking for everything."

"Which amounts to just about nothing. I don't have anything to give, Remy."

"I think you do." He lifted one hand as if to touch her again, but the distance between them was too great. With obvious regret, he let his hand fall to rest again on the crutches. "I have a better opinion of you than you have of yourself."

"That's because I know myself. You don't."

"You're wrong. I know enough to know that I want you."

She smiled at that, striving for disbelieving but achieving something more along the lines of thin and hurtful. "Call your girlfriends in the city. Get one of them to drive up for the night. She'll take care of you more willingly and more capably than I ever could."

"This isn't about sex, Susannah," he said irritably. Then, when she gave him a skeptical, raised-brow look, he grudgingly grinned. "Well, of course it's about that, too, but not *just* that. I'm talking about a relationship, about a future, about making something together, something that lasts."

Pain, emotional in origin but very real all the same, twisted deep in her stomach. "But *I* don't want those things—not with you, not with anybody, not ever."

"I don't believe you."

She forced herself to shrug casually. "You have that right."

"Yes, I do," he agreed softly. "And I have the right to want you anyway. I have the right to try to change your mind. And now that you've been warned, I have the right to try to seduce you."

"And *I* have the right to say no." She tried to sound forceful and strong, but in her own ears, her words sounded more like a plea.

"Of course. Always." He started toward the house, but when he was about even with her, he stopped and faced her again, delivering his final warning in a husky voice with a sweetly confident smile. "*If* you can."

Susannah remained where she was long after he was gone, her fingers clenching the wood so tightly that they went numb. God help her, this was a complication she didn't need, one she couldn't even begin to afford. For all her talk, she knew she was a weak woman. She knew she could be seduced by sweet kisses and sweeter words. She knew she would sacrifice pride, resolve and dignity for an hour or two of believing that she was loved. Guy had taught her those lessons on a humiliatingly regular basis.

He had also taught her how easily she could be shattered by sweet lies.

And every feminine instinct in her said that Remy's lies would be the sweetest—and most devastating—of all.

Forcing her hands to release their grip on the chair, she picked up their books, then slowly turned toward the house. Remy was already inside, their conversation probably already put aside, his thoughts directed elsewhere. And why shouldn't they be? After nearly three weeks of recuperation, he was well enough to crave activity but not quite well enough to seek it out. He was bored, restless and looking for some entertainment. For all his talk of honesty, of a future and something that would last, he was simply looking for someone to fill his hours, to—how had he put it?—to make the days easier and the nights warmer.

He was looking for a good time.

She had already been Guy's good time. She couldn't go through that again.

It was funny. As different as Remy and Guy were, their approaches were unnervingly similar. She had first seen Guy at a party, had noticed time and again that he was watching her from across the room, until finally he had come over and introduced himself. It had been a charming introduction, one that had mentioned honesty, destiny and marriage all in the same line.

And she had fallen for it. Innocent, naive and incredibly flattered by his attention, she had believed everything he'd told her. She had believed him for the five months they'd dated and the four years they were married. She had believed that he was interested in a future together, one that would last. That he loved her. That he intended to keep the vows he made to her in church. She had believed his apologies every time he'd hurt her, every time he'd spoken carelessly or cruelly, every time he had treated her without consideration. She had believed that the first affair she knew about truly was the first, had believed his promises that it would never happen again, and when it had happened again—and again—she had believed those apologies, those promises, too.

She had been a trusting fool. But, as she'd told Remy, she considered her marriage a learning experience.

And the best lesson she had learned was not to be so trusting.

Oh, she believed Remy when he said he wouldn't hurt her—at least, not unless he discovered her real reason for being here. He wouldn't deliberately hurt her, but he didn't know, in spite of his protests, who he was dealing with. He didn't know that Guy had already destroyed whatever defenses and protections she'd ever had. He didn't know how easily he could destroy whatever was left. He didn't know that *she* was here to help destroy him.

The parlor was empty when she passed it on her way down the hall, but she could hear Remy's voice from one of the more distant rooms—Mr. Sinclair's study, she thought, one of three rooms on the first floor that had a phone. She wondered if he was taking her advice and making a date with one of his lady friends in New Orleans. She hoped he was.

Even if the mere thought made her ache inside.

Leaving the books on the kitchen table, she gathered the dirty clothes from their rooms and carried the two baskets to the laundry room. It was located off the kitchen and past the pantry in a small room that had once been a screened-in porch. The screens had been replaced by tall windows, but the same white boards that sided the house formed the interior walls, and the original floor of dusty red brick remained.

After sorting the laundry and starting the first load, she returned to the kitchen to make dinner. Remy's voice still filtered down the broad hallway, a low murmur, the words indistinguishable from this distance. If she were doing her job the way Nicholas Carlucci wanted, she would sneak down the hall and hover outside the study. Remy was still slow, still noisy, with his crutches. She would have no prob-

lem, once his call ended, in retreating to the kitchen before
he made it to the study door, none the wiser.

But she didn't slip down the hall. She continued chop-
ping vegetables for a quick-cooking stew, listening to his
voice and the occasional sounds of his laughter and wishing that she could simply disappear off the face of the earth.

She browned chunks of beef in a deep pot, added cans of
broth and water, tossed in the vegetables and seasoned them.
Then, with one quick check on the laundry, instead of returning to the kitchen, she slipped out the door and started
across the lawn.

Her usual work schedule kept her on her feet for such
long hours that regular exercise was the farthest thing from
her mind, but in her days here, she had developed a fondness for late-afternoon strolls around the grounds. It was
time away from Remy, time to relax and regain a little of the
equilibrium that she always lost around him. It was a chance
to appreciate being in the country—to hear the birds' songs,
to watch the small changes each day as winter gave way to
spring and daffodils sent up new shoots and barren trees
began forming buds, and to listen to the traffic on the Mississippi River, unseen on the opposite side of the tall levee
that fronted the road.

It was an opportunity to escape.

The grounds were enormous, measurable in acres rather
than footage. Across the front a tall iron fence separated the
lawn from the shoulder of the road. The spikes were eight
feet tall and were broken up every twelve feet with a tall,
square column of brick. She found the fence itself and the
sheer length of it impressive, but it was the wooden fence
across the back that captured her fancy. Once upon a time
it had been painted white, possibly when Remy was a child,
and been maintained in a long, straight row. In recent years,
though, it had been allowed to begin a slow and graceful
decline into disuse. Boards had fallen to the ground, posts
leaned at precarious angles and vines overgrew entire sec-
tions. Such disrepair would never be tolerated on the farms

she knew back home, but she found something soft and appealing about it here.

She had completed one circuit of the grounds and was beginning another, approaching the stately front fence again, when she noticed the car sitting on the shoulder a few yards down. It was an unremarkable car—a year or two old, four doors, a dusty shade of gray, with a man behind the wheel and a woman in the passenger seat. It looked like any of a hundred other cars that might pass this way every day, someone going to evening church services or returning home from work at one of the riverside factories, locals on their way to town or a relative's house, tourists seeking one last look before dusk....

Tourists. *Belle Ste. Claire has never been open to the public... but that's never stopped people from pulling off the road and taking pictures.* She'd had only a glimpse of the people and the car that had prompted Remy's comment earlier this afternoon, but that glimpse certainly seemed to match this car. That woman had been blond, too, and Susannah distinctly remembered the bright red of her jacket.

What kind of tourists, she wondered, feeling the evening's chill for the first time, would still be hanging around? Why would they be parked a short distance down the road, apparently just watching the house? And why, as she watched them, did they finally decide it was time to go, to start the engine, make a U-turn and head downriver toward New Orleans?

Maybe the sort who worked for sleazy lawyers. Maybe Carlucci didn't trust her. Maybe he had someone keeping an eye on her while *she* kept an eye on Remy.

She walked right up to the fence, curling her fingers around one rusty bar, staring hard after the car until it was gone from sight, its brake lights a hazy red glow in the gathering dark. Carlucci—if he was, indeed, responsible—needn't worry. She had made promises, and she would keep them. While she wasn't one hundred percent certain that he and his boss would keep their promise—that when she was finished here, she could take Skip away from Louisiana with no threat or danger hanging over him—she *was* certain of something else.

They *would* keep the other promise they'd made if she failed.

They *would* see to it that her brother faced prison for the rest of his life.

Prison . . . or worse.

"So everything's okay up there?" Michael made a question out of something he was trying to present as a simple statement and making Remy grin in the process.

"I'm fine. Susannah's fine," Remy replied, swiveling his father's chair so he could see out the window. He had seen Susannah pass by a while ago on her evening walk, strolling along at a leisurely pace, occasionally stopping to examine something more closely. It had been many long years since he'd taken the time to enjoy a simple walk . . . but he intended to do just that soon. In another week or so, if his leg had healed enough, the doctors would let him trade the crutches for a cane. Then all he would have to do was persuade her to let him join her.

He could manage that.

"So we'll see you Tuesday," Michael was saying. "Do you need anything from here?"

"A muffuletta, maybe, or a little shrimp Lafitte," he replied with a wry smile. Whatever Susannah was fixing for dinner smelled wonderful, but the mere mention of his two favorite dishes could still make his mouth water. "No, I don't need anything. Listen, you guys come by the house and we'll go out for lunch before you head on up to Arkansas."

After settling on an approximate time, they said their goodbyes, and he turned his attention fully outside. Susannah was in sight again, this time at the southernmost corner of the yard. She was standing still, gazing at something outside the fence. All he could see there was a flash of silver. A car, he realized as the driver turned across the road and headed in the opposite direction. A neighbor stopped to say hello, maybe, or a tourist asking for directions.

She stood there by the fence for what seemed like forever before finally turning and heading straight back toward the house. She moved so gracefully, so naturally. Although she had chosen city life over the country, she was obviously very much at home out here. He could easily see her on a farm— competent, efficient, serene and in control...and breaking all the farm boys' hearts.

Except it was *her* heart that had gotten broken up there in Nebraska and, damn that ex-husband of hers, she was determined not to risk it happening again.

So somehow he would have to convince her that he was a better man than her ex. That—in this respect, at least—he shared her talent for healing. That one bad relationship didn't automatically condemn her to another. That mistakes she had learned from didn't have to be repeated.

He had to convince her to give him a chance. Just a chance.

Everything else would follow from there.

Her path to the back door took her past the study windows, then out of sight. For a moment he was content to remain where he was, to give her a few moments of peace without him. It wasn't long, though, before *she* sought *him* out.

She signaled her presence with a tap on the half-open door before pushing it back and stepping inside. "Dinner will be ready in about ten minutes."

Stretched out comfortably in the leather chair, he turned to face her, acknowledging her announcement with a nod, then waited for her to take flight right away. When she didn't, he gestured with one hand to the chairs opposite the desk in a silent invitation. Surprisingly she accepted it, venturing farther into the room, seating herself almost primly in the oldest and shabbiest of the three chairs. It was also, Remy knew from experience, the most comfortable.

"This is my father's room," he remarked. "When I was a kid, he spent hours in here every evening. When the door was open, anyone could come in. When it was closed, only an emergency or an act of God—or an occasional act of defiance—could get us in.''

"It's a comfortable room,'' she murmured, then frowned. "Not comfortable, exactly. Comforting.''

He nodded in agreement. There was a certain comfort, a coziness, to be found within these four walls. It wasn't the faded or, in some places, ragged air that said the room was well used, or the homey touches—family pictures, old heirlooms, small treasures. It was the feeling of life, of continuity, the connection between the past and the present. "This chair belonged to my grandfather. The desk was *his* grandfather's. Other than the phone, I don't think anything ever came in here new. It was all passed down from some relative or another.''

After a moment's silence, he picked up a framed photo and studied it. "When I was a kid, I used to come in and sit in that chair you're in and just watch my dad work. I admired him. I wanted to be just like him when I grew up. We used to fish from the levee out front, hunt in the woods out back and play football and baseball out in the yard. He was a busy man, but he almost always made time for me.''

At least, until Valery came.

He looked at the photograph a moment longer before leaning forward and offering it to Susannah. He was about seventeen in the picture, Valery around fourteen, and they were both scowling. His parents stood between them, his mother nearest him, his father beside Valery. *They* were both tense. "Somewhere around here Mom has an entire photo album of pictures like that. You didn't see too many smiles or displays of affection in the Sinclair family during those days.''

"I imagine you were pretty typical of families with teenagers,'' she replied, her gaze on the faded picture. "We have some pictures at home—'' Abruptly she broke off and leaned forward, passing the frame back to him. "Kids don't always get along,'' she went on at last. "With each other, their parents or anyone else. It's part of growing up.''

What did those last remarks have to do with her family pictures at home? he wondered. As far as that went, what did *her* family pictures have to do with *his* family problems? She was an only child, and her mother had died when she was fifteen. Her father was the only one left for her to not get along with, and somehow he couldn't imagine her ever showing the slightest disrespect to her father.

Setting the questions aside, he returned the picture to its place. "That was Michael on the phone earlier. He and Valery are going to Arkansas Tuesday—he's taking Valery home to meet his family—and they're stopping by here for lunch. Do you mind?"

She shrugged. "It's your house."

"And your time."

Another shrug. "Is there anything special you'd like me to fix?"

"No. We're going out. All four of us," he said, clarifying his answer, stalling the protest he knew she was about to make. "It'll only take an hour or two. You'll enjoy it." A break in routine wouldn't hurt either of them, and he really did think she would enjoy a little time with Valery. His cousin wasn't the most outgoing person in the world, but she had gotten on the phone long enough to inform him that she really liked Susannah. That was high praise from a woman who, in her entire adult life, hadn't gotten close to anyone other than Michael.

He was looking forward to the visit himself. Back in the city, he usually saw Michael and Smith three or four times a week; when their schedules interfered with that, they checked in regularly by phone. He missed his friends' company, missed their presence in his life. Of course, with Michael getting married soon, their friendship would change, would have to alter and adapt to include Valery.

It would be good practice for when *he* got married and brought his wife into the circle.

A glance across the desk at Susannah showed that she was none too anxious to be brought into anyone's circle of friends. "Don't fret over it, Susannah," he said, his tone deliberately mild. "I'm not asking you to make friends or anything vile like that. I'm just asking you to have lunch with my friends. Do you think you can survive that?"

She gave him a dry look. "I think so."

"Good. They'll be here around eleven o'clock Tuesday morning. That will give you more than—" he glanced at his watch and did some quick figuring "—forty hours to disguise that reluctance in your eyes."

After another long, steady look, she got up and started toward the door. "By the time you hobble into the kitchen, dinner will be on the table," she called over her shoulder. "Try not to let it get cold."

Chapter 5

As the clock down the hall struck the first of eleven chimes Tuesday morning, Susannah laid down the small sewing scissors she'd been using and studied her handiwork. The cut she'd made across the right leg of the jeans was crooked, and the hem hastily secured with a long, running stitch, but for short notice—and for someone who had never displayed much skill at sewing—it was satisfactory work.

On the fourth chime, she shook out the jeans and rose from the table, heading for Remy's room. When he had mentioned that he'd like to have a pair of the jeans Valery had packed for him altered to fit over his cast, she had offered, maybe with just the slightest bit of reluctance, to do it for him. She hadn't been thrilled by the idea of using scissors and a seam ripper to take out the long, double-stitched outer seam all the way from hip to hem, but she had learned at a very young age that every job included some tasks she didn't like.

But Remy had had other ideas—better ideas, she secretly thought. Don't waste time removing a seam that would later have to be replaced, he had advised. Just cut the leg off so he could get the jeans on. Then, when the cast came off in another month's time, he would get rid of the jeans along with the cast, the crutches and the cane.

So that was what she had done, somewhat inexpertly. It had taken a couple of efforts and a couple of fittings before she had cut away enough denim to allow the jeans to pass over the cast, and then a few minutes quick sewing to lessen the fraying. Now, just in time for his guests, she was finished.

He was waiting in his room, dressed in a sweater and gym shorts. The beautiful weather of the weekend was gone, replaced by a dreary, grim winter chill that had prompted his desire for jeans. The wind gusting outside would cut right through the cotton sweats he'd been living in. It was also going to turn his toes into cubes of ice, she thought as she handed the jeans over.

"If you don't mind sacrificing a pair of socks, I'll see what I can do for your foot," she volunteered.

"I'd sacrifice my best leather running shoes if it would keep me warm," he said, accompanied by a gesture toward the drawer where she'd stored his socks.

Crossing the room to the dresser, she tugged open the top drawer and removed a pair of thick, white socks. She was about to turn to leave again when she caught a glimpse of him in the mirror, balanced unsteadily against the bed, pulling his gym shorts down over his hips. Quickly—but not quickly enough to avoid a glimpse of narrow waist and slender hips or the blush that warmed her face—she averted her gaze.

This was silly, she chastised herself. She'd been a nurse for more than nine years. She had seen men in various stages of dress—more men than she cared to count. She saw men on television and in magazine photos wearing much less than Remy wore. It wasn't as if she had so little familiarity with the male form that she should be embarrassed by this particular male form.

But all those men she saw as a nurse had been patients, and Remy wasn't.

And all those men on television and in magazines were strangers. Remy wasn't.

And she wasn't embarrassed by what she'd seen. Heavens, no. She wanted to see more. Wanted to touch. Wanted to stroke, to caress, to explore.

No, she wasn't embarrassed.

She was intrigued. Fascinated.

Aroused.

Drawing a deep breath, she pulled one last sock from the drawer, then went to the armoire to pick out a shoe. She pretended she didn't hear the sounds of Remy dressing as she left the sock and shoe on the mattress, then turned toward the door. "I'll see what I can do with these," she announced, her voice insubstantial as she slipped out.

Back in the kitchen, she forced herself to concentrate on this new task. Curiously, the arrival of their guests—of Remy's guests, she reminded herself—made it easier. Remy insisted that she act as a friend, not an employee, but his real friends, especially Michael Bennett, expected her to act as an employee, a nurse and housekeeper. Susannah knew instinctively that Michael didn't accept her as Remy's friend. Because he was a cop and was suspicious by nature? Because his friend had almost died and Michael was protective of him now?

Or because whatever it was that made Michael a good cop—instinct, intuition, sixth sense—told him that she wasn't to be trusted?

Valery let herself and Michael into the house with her own key, calling out as they came down the hall. "Remy? Susannah? We're here."

Susannah heard Remy approaching from his room as the other couple approached from the hallway. She stayed at the table, her head down, now thankfully occupied with cutting the heavy sock just right... or so, she hoped, it appeared. In reality she was watching covertly as the three entered the room from opposite doors.

Valery released her fiancé's hand to hug her cousin. It wasn't an exuberant greeting, as Susannah might have expected, but a long, silent embrace that said more of her feelings than any words could have. When at last she stepped back, she turned to Susannah and offered her a smile. "It's been . . . what? A week? And you're still here. I figured Remy would have run you off by now."

The slight smile Susannah had been prepared to offer in return seemed to freeze, then dissolve. Did Valery know something she didn't, something Remy didn't? Had Michael uncovered something about her—maybe her relationship to Skip and his own ties to Jimmy Falcone—that he had passed on, or intended to pass on, to Remy?

Oh, God, had he come here for more than an innocent visit on his way home to see his family?

"That's an awkward remark, Val," Michael said dryly. "Why don't you explain it?"

The other woman laughed. "I guess it did sound kind of funny. I just meant because Remy's such a grouch. He was awfully ill-tempered in the hospital. He has this idea that he ought to be in control, you know. The day he checked out, the staff lined the halls to wish him farewell and to celebrate his release."

The knot in Susannah's stomach slowly started to loosen. "I've had a few patients like that myself."

"But I'm not one of them," Remy challenged, coming to sit beside her. "I've behaved, haven't I?"

If "behaving" meant watching her too often and too intensely, she thought privately. Or being too friendly. Or kissing her. Or bluntly announcing that he wanted to have an affair with her.

Instead of answering, Susannah held up the sock. "Let me see your foot."

"I can do it." He took the cut-down sock from her and bent forward, only to discover what she already knew: unable to bend his leg, he was also unable to reach his toes, at least not well enough to manage.

Slipping from her seat, she took the sock back and knelt in front of him. This was the first time she'd had to help him with any of his clothing since they'd moved in. It helped that they had company and that it was nothing more personal than a sock.

So why did it feel so damn personal?

Circling them to get to the next empty chair, Michael rested his hand briefly on Remy's shoulder. "How are you?"

"I'm fine."

Shifting his dark gaze to her, Michael repeated the question. "How is he?"

Glancing up, she met his eyes for less than a second before looking at Remy. "He *is* fine," she repeated. "His arm is healed, and the bruise from the bulletproof vest is almost faded. He's more or less used to the crutches, and he doesn't have any more bruises or blisters on his hands. If he could get around a little better, he wouldn't have any need for assistance, except for driving."

"So you could go back to your job at the hospital anytime."

There was a challenge in Michael's softly spoken words that made the muscles in Susannah's neck tighten. What did he know? she wondered. What did he see in her that Remy and Valery missed?

"But I can't get around a little better," Remy said, drawing Michael's attention away from Susannah and over to himself. "And I can't drive, I can't cook, my parents said I couldn't stay here alone, and Susannah promised me a full month. Don't give her the idea that I'd let her off so easily."

Keeping her gaze on her hands, she worked the sock into place over his toes, then carefully smoothed the excess fabric inside the opening of his cast. It was difficult to tell whether his foot was cold because her hands were. In fact, there were chills shivering all through her.

Once the sock was in place and she felt reasonably certain of it remaining there, she got to her feet. "I'll get your jacket," she murmured before escaping the kitchen. Down the hall she went first to Remy's room to get the heavier of the two leather jackets that hung in the armoire there, then she crossed to her own room. She was pulling on her coat when Valery joined her there.

"Hi," the other woman said softly.

Susannah straightened her collar, then pulled her hair free. "I hope you don't mind my tagging along. Remy insisted."

"I wouldn't dream of leaving you behind." Valery came a few steps farther into the room, glancing around. "You guys seem to be getting along okay."

"He's easy to work for."

Valery turned from the desk where she was sniffing a fat, vanilla-scented candle. "I bet you half the FBI agents in New Orleans would disagree with you. *I* think he's on his best behavior because he's sweet on you."

Steadfastly ignoring the last part of her comment, Susannah took a moment to run a brush through her hair. Lacking a scarf or cap, she had opted to leave her hair down today to provide some measure of warmth for her neck and ears. And that was the only reason it was down, she reminded herself. Not because, on the few occasions she'd worn it loose, Remy had given her such appreciative looks.

"Remy's a good guy."

Susannah laid the brush down and picked up the leather jacket again. "It says a lot that you think so."

"What do you mean?"

"He told me about when you came here to live and when his parents asked him to leave."

Valery looked surprised. "Did he?" she murmured. "Hmm. That says a lot, too."

She didn't want to ask, didn't want to know...but the question slipped out anyway. "In what way?"

"Remy, Michael and Smith Kendricks have been best friends since college, but until about a month ago, neither Michael nor Smith knew that I existed. You've been here a week, and he's already confided in you."

It wasn't that way, Susannah wanted to deny. There hadn't been anything special or important about Remy telling her his family history. It had just been small talk, an exchange of information, a little "I'll tell you this and you'll tell me that." It was nothing that merited examination.

"It was just conversation," she said at last. "You spend as much time together as we have, and you wind up looking for things to talk about."

Valery gave her a long, disbelieving look, then laughed. "Remy got a little bored, and so he hauled out his biggest secrets for your entertainment. Right, Susannah."

Clenching her fingers tightly together underneath the jacket, Susannah forced a faint smile. "Are you ready to go?"

The hamburgers at Belclaire's only café were thick and greasy, the french fries thin and crispy and the atmosphere undeniably small town. Remy figured he'd seen at least eighty percent of the town's residents in the last ninety minutes and that he remembered every single one of them from his years at home. He and Valery had spent half the meal introducing Michael and Susannah to everyone who had stopped by and fielding questions about his injuries, his stay at Belle Ste. Claire and his parents' trip to Europe.

Now Susannah had slipped off—for a trip to the post office, she had said—and Valery was sitting at the counter, visiting with a high school classmate. Now was his chance to talk, to *really* talk, with Michael. "You don't like her, do you?"

Michael spared him a moment's glance, then looked out the window again. "She seems like a nice woman."

Remy chuckled. "What's that old saying? Something about damning with faint praise?"

"It doesn't much matter what I think, does it? Because *you* like her."

"Of course it matters."

"No, it doesn't. It's gone beyond that for you."

"What do you mean?"

Michael glanced across the restaurant at Valery, and his expression softened. "In the first few days after I met Valery, I would have cared about your opinion of her. You probably could have influenced *my* opinion of her. But after a certain point . . . I wouldn't have given a damn if you hated her. Don't get me wrong. We've been friends a long time. Along with Evan, you and Smith have been the best part of my life for nearly half my life. It would matter to me if you didn't like Val . . . but it wouldn't stop me from marrying her next month. It wouldn't stop me from spending the rest of my life with her.'' He grinned. ''It wouldn't stop me from making you spend a good deal of the rest of *your* life with her.''

Remy understood exactly what Michael meant and knew, too, that his friend was right. He *had* already passed the point where he could be influenced against Susannah by anything less than hard and fast proof of wrongdoing on her part. Opinions were subjective. He didn't need Michael's or Smith's approval.

He just needed Susannah's.

Still . . .

''Out of curiosity, exactly what is it about her that bothers you?''

'' 'Bothers' is a little strong,'' Michael replied. ''It's just a feeling that something's not right.''

''An instinct feeling or a *feeling* feeling?'' Remy knew the question sounded silly, but it was an important distinction. His cousin and Michael shared more than love; they were both more than a little on the psychic side. For Valery, it was mostly minor things—foreknowledge or second sight. She sometimes knew the doorbell was going to ring before it did, knew who would be there before she opened the door. On occasion she knew what a person was going to say before they spoke, knew something was going to happen long before anyone else was aware of it.

She had known that Remy's partner on the Falcone case was going to betray him; unfortunately, she hadn't known in time to warn him.

For Michael, though, it was a lot more than that. He had visions—visual, auditory and sensory—and what he had visions of were people in trouble. His first contact with

Valery had been in a vision. Another of his visions had led him and Evan to the kidnapper who killed Evan. If he was having *those* kinds of feelings about Susannah...

"Instinct," Michael replied, easing the tightness in Remy's nerves. "I'm not saying there's something *wrong* with Susannah. There's just something not quite right."

"She got divorced not too long ago," Remy said. "Her husband left her and, apparently, married someone else pretty quickly. He left her thinking she doesn't have anything to offer anyone. She's convinced that she's never getting married again because it's safer that way. If you don't love or trust someone, then you can't get hurt."

"But you can get damn lonely." Michael finished the last of his coffee, then shook his head in dismay. "You never do anything the easy way, do you?"

"Oh, like you found Valery the easy way," Remy scoffed.

"Yeah, but—" Having no argument to offer, Michael broke off with a grin. "I hope she's worth it."

"Valery?"

"Susannah. I *know* Val is. So... is she aware that you've got plans for her?"

"I've warned her."

Michael raised one eyebrow. "Don't you think you'd have better luck romancing her or seducing her?"

"What do you think I was warning her about?"

"Well, the least you could do is make the woman feel enough at home to get her mail there, and maybe give her access to a telephone now and then. It's damn cold to be standing out in the wind while you chat."

Remy pushed back the gingham curtains that blocked his view of the street and followed the direction of Michael's gaze. Indeed, Susannah was standing across and down the street, at one of only two pay phones in town. The wind whipped her hair around her face, and when she turned once to impatiently wipe it away, he saw the stack of mail she held.

Interesting. He had given her the address for Belle Ste. Claire when he hired her, had told her to feel free to have her mail forwarded there. In the week since they'd moved in, he hadn't considered whether she'd done so. She picked up the mail each day—the walk from the side door to the box at the end of the driveway was still too far and, in silty sand and shell, too risky for him to make. She always left the mail on the kitchen table for him to tend to, to separate his from his parents' and to sort through theirs for anything that might require a response before their return. He had assumed that she took her own from the stack before leaving it for him.

But she was having hers delivered to a post office box in town. Was she really so intensely private?

Or was she getting mail that she didn't want him to see?

Right, Sinclair, he silently chastised himself. It wasn't as if he would ever even consider snooping through her mail. He would never do more than maybe glance at return addresses, and since they didn't know any of the same people, what would that tell him? The names of the people who wrote to her would mean nothing to him.

The names of the people—or the person—she was calling from pay phones would, though. Judging from his occasional glimpses of her face, it didn't seem that this call was pleasure. Even from this distance he could see that her expression was stony. He could read the tension in her body, in the way she held her shoulders back instead of huddling as any other person would have done against the wind. He could tell that her voice, if only he could hear it, would be that small, empty, chilling tone that she used on occasion with him.

Suddenly feeling as if he were invading her privacy, he let the curtain fall into place and settled back in his seat. Across from him, Michael had looked away, too, directing his gaze once again toward Valery.

I'm not saying there's something wrong *with Susannah. There's just something not quite right.*

Maybe Michael had more of a point than Remy wanted to admit. Maybe there was more in her background than just a marriage that had ended badly. Maybe her wariness was more than the distrust a woman would naturally feel when someone she loved hurt her. Maybe there was a reason other than her ex-husband for her claim that she had nothing to give *him*.

Maybe something else was going on.

The bell over the door tinkled, and cold air blasted in as Susannah came through the door. Her purse was over her shoulder, the mail she'd been holding a moment ago tucked away inside, Remy guessed. She took her seat beside him in the booth, her clothes cold, her cheeks red, her hair tousled, and reached for her coffee cup with both hands. She didn't drink from it, though, but simply warmed her hands on the heavy pottery.

"I'm sorry if I kept you waiting," she said, not looking at either of them.

"It's okay. We were just waiting for Valery to finish visiting with her friend." Remy turned on the bench so he was slightly facing her. "Did you get what you needed at the post office?"

"Yes. I just had to pick up some stamps and mail a few letters."

Michael's gaze met his over the table, then they both looked away again. After an awkward moment, his friend broke the silence. "I'm going to have to drag Val out of here if we're going to make it to Titusville today. Since you're having a little trouble getting around, why don't you head on out to the car, Remy, and I'll get her and pay the bill?"

Remy nodded and, as soon as Susannah slid out of the booth, got to his feet. She got his crutches from the corner, then held the door open wide for him. At his mother's car, she helped him get settled, then got behind the wheel, starting the engine, letting it warm up.

"Your friend doesn't like me much, does he?" she asked, shivering visibly as the heater blew cold air over their feet and up into the compartment.

"Does it matter?"

"I don't know." She stared straight ahead. "Does it?"

Instead of answering her question, he asked one of his own. "Who were you calling?"

Abruptly she swiveled around to look at him. Her face
was pale except for two bright circles of color on her cheeks.
That was a guilty look if ever he'd seen one ... and after
twelve years as a federal agent, he'd seen thousands of them.
But why should she feel guilty for making a phone call? At
the moment, he could think of only one reason: she'd been
calling a man.

A man she was involved with.

A man whom she was giving all the things he had arro-
gantly expected her to give *him.*

Arrogant. God, yes, he was that. He hadn't even bothered to find out if she was available before he'd announced
his intention of seducing and possibly—probably—marrying her. It was no surprise that she'd done nothing to en-
courage him. The only surprise, in fact, was that she was still
around, that she hadn't packed her bags and gone racing
back to New Orleans.

Back to *him,* whoever he was.

She hadn't yet found her voice when Michael and Valery
joined them. Still looking stricken—and so terribly guilty—
she at last looked away from him and turned her attention
to the driving.

It was a quiet few miles back to Belle Ste. Claire. There
Michael and Valery refused Remy's halfhearted invitation
to come inside. They had to be on their way, Michael insisted.

"Oh, before we go, Remy, I brought you something,"
Valery exclaimed. She waited impatiently for Michael to
unlock the trunk of his car, then pulled a heavy black gar-
bage bag from it. "A few years ago, Aunt Marie was doing
some housecleaning, and she gave me a stack of quilts. You
know the ones—they used to be four and five thick on the
guest room beds. They're family heirlooms and rightfully
belong to you, but since Aunt Marie gave them to me, I'm
keeping them anyway," she said with a confidence that
Remy knew she couldn't have managed too long ago. "Except for this one. I thought you might like it."

She offered the bag to Susannah with a smile that reminded him of the Valery he had loved like a sister when they were kids...before she had come to live with them and he had been expected to actually accept her as a sister.

"Thanks, Valery." Balancing on his crutches, he pressed a kiss to her forehead. "Feel free to enjoy the rest of them with my blessings."

"Thank you." She extended her hand to Susannah. "It was nice seeing you again."

Wrapping her arms around the bag, Susannah accepted her handshake and murmured something in response, then began edging toward the door. She wished she could go inside and go to bed. She wanted to shut the door, draw the curtains, pull the covers over her head and hibernate for the next three weeks. She didn't want to talk, to think or to feel. She didn't want to want, didn't even want to live for the next twenty-one days.

But there was little chance of Remy granting her wish.

Little chance. The phrase described her life and her future. There was little chance of getting what she wanted. Little chance of escaping the guilt. Little chance of being happy again.

There was no chance at all that Remy would ever forgive what she was doing.

She unlocked the door, then held the screen for him. He didn't glance her way as he swung expertly over the raised threshold, then turned into the parlor. Shrugging out of his jacket, he tossed it onto a nearby chair, dropped onto the sofa and let his crutches fall to the floor nearby as he reached for the TV remote.

Susannah hesitated in the doorway, then, using the heavy bag as an excuse, she said, "I'll put this quilt in your room."

She hadn't done more than pivot when he suddenly spoke. "You never answered my question."

Stubbornly she asked, "What question was that?"

"Who were you calling from the pay phone?"

She hugged the bag tighter, making it crinkle. "You sound like my ex-husband," she said flatly. "He thought he had the right to question every part of my life, and because he always lied to me, he believed that *I* lied, too.''

"I'm not accusing you of lying."

"But you're suspicious."

"I was curious the first time I asked," he replied, clarifying his answer.

"And now, because I didn't answer right away, you're suspicious."

"Because your reaction when I asked was as guilty as any I've ever seen, and, honey, I've seen a lot." The hostility slowly faded from his expression, from his voice. "If you're involved with another man, Susannah, just say so. I won't fire you. I won't cause problems for you. And I won't come on to you again."

She stared down at the wooden floor. Could it be that simple? Could she lie and say yes, she was seeing someone else? Could she really put an end to his looks and his sweet smiles and the soft seductiveness that accompanied his mere presence with one simple, single three-letter reply?

Could she banish her own yearnings so easily?

It was an easy lie. She said nothing at all, and Remy found his own answer in her silence. "So... tell me about him."

She supposed he was trying for casual interest, but she heard disappointment instead. Dismay. A little bit of wounded ego. She opened her mouth for more lies—damn, she hated dishonesty! "There's nothing to tell. That call was business. It wasn't important, and it's something that I prefer not to discuss. I can handle it myself. I made it from the pay phone because I wanted privacy and because it was long distance and because that's the way I wanted to do it. I wasn't aware that you expected to be keyed in on every aspect of my life while I work here. I wasn't aware—'' Breaking off, she drew a deep breath. What she was about to say was unfair, and she had to swallow hard first. "I wasn't aware that you were so much like my ex-husband in that regard."

After a moment to let that sink in, she quietly asked, "Are there any other questions you'd like to ask, or am I free to go now?"

He didn't say anything...oh, but he wanted to. She could see it in his eyes, just as she could read his determination to say nothing in the set of his jaw. What other suspicions was he harboring? she wondered.

And then she remembered: if he had seen her on the phone, then he had likely seen the mail she was holding. She had been nervous when she had opened the creamy white envelope with no return address, had been chilled when she had seen the photographs inside—pictures of her and Remy, sitting in the sun Sunday afternoon. There had been no note, nothing but that little photographic message—warning—that they were being watched. Her name and address had been typed, and the envelope had been mailed locally, postmarked yesterday and delivered to her box today.

So, if he had seen the mail, then he knew she was getting it delivered elsewhere, just as she was making her phone calls elsewhere. He knew she was being secretive and evasive.

And he knew she had lied in the café when she'd told him that her business at the post office had consisted of buying stamps and mailing letters.

He *knew* she had lied to him.

Feeling sick deep inside, she slowly crossed the room to the chair where his coat was. She picked it up, tucking it under her arm with the quilt, and sat down. "You say I should feel at home here, that for this month, Belle Ste. Claire *is* my home. But I don't feel at home here, Remy. I'm here to work. I'm here because it's a condition of my employment. But it's *not* home. That's why I'm having my mail delivered in town. That's why I make my phone calls from pay phones. If you think that's silly or secretive or suspicious, I'm sorry, but it's what I'm comfortable with."

She waited for some response from him. When none came, she tiredly got to her feet again. "I'll put these in your room now."

After leaving her things in her own room, she went to his and hung up his jacket. She had made the bed earlier this morning, but it was wrinkled again from when he'd waited while she fixed his jeans. She smoothed out the wrinkles, then tore open the plastic bag and slid the quilt free.

Having grown up with hand-pieced quilts by the dozen, she had never placed much value in them, as so many people did. They were special because they had been made by her mother and grandmother and other relatives she had never known, but at the same time, they had been common and undeserving of special attention because she'd had them from the time she was in a crib. To her they had been functional, same as the dresses, rompers and playsuits her mother had sewn for her or the tables, chairs and cradles her father had put together in winter when farm life was slow. They were something for everyday use, not works of art.

Only one quilt held any real sentimental value for her, and that was the one she had brought with her from Nebraska. It was the last one her mother had completed before she died. It was pieced of three fabrics: squares of a tiny lavender floral print, squares and triangles in unbleached muslin and trapezoids in solid lavender. It had been a gift from a mother to her only daughter, a gift chosen for reasons as sentimental as could be.

This quilt of Remy's, the one Valery had thought, of all those given to her, that he might like, was pieced in the same pattern.

With a soft sigh, she traced over the straight seams. Although the patterns were identical, the differences between her quilt and Remy's were readily apparent. Hers in its soft shades was as feminine as his was masculine. It was done in a rich cranberry, a deep blue that was almost black and a print mixing the two colors with subdued gold. Whoever had crafted his was more of a perfectionist than her mother had been—a corner that didn't quite line up or stitches that rarely came close to uniformity in size had never been of great importance to her mother—and the fabric was undoubtedly of better quality. The three layers of her quilt—

front, batting and back—were secured in a simple and easy cross-hatch pattern, while his had been quilted together in an elaborate, time-consuming system of swirls, curlicues and interlocking diamonds.

But hers provided as much as comfort to her as his would to him.

She unfolded it carefully, unsure of its age, and smoothed it across the bed, settling it accordion-style at the foot.

When that was done, she returned to her own room, pushing the door up until it almost closed, then kicking off her shoes and taking a seat on the bed. Her purse was there where she'd left it. Removing the mail, she settled back to thumb through it.

There was nothing of interest to anyone but her—and Remy, who seemed to be interested in everything. A few bills, a piece or two of junk mail, a letter from her father and those pictures. Those damnable pictures. With a sigh, she swept everything aside and turned her attention to her father's letter.

Lew Crouse wasn't much of a writer—had never had the practice, he'd written to her in his first letter. Except for a brief stint in the army before she was born, he had lived his entire life in the same little corner of Nebraska, within shouting distance of his brother Richard and only a few miles down the road from both of their sisters. He'd known his friends and neighbors for a lifetime, had been best friends with the same man for fifty-one years.

But, while he wasn't overly comfortable with putting his thoughts and feelings down on paper, he was reliable. His letters came every two weeks without fail. If there was anything new—a rarity, it seemed to Susannah—it came first, followed by a mention of the weather that was so important to a farmer, a few lines about Uncle Richard's family and a hello from some friend or another in town. He always asked after Skip, always remarked how grateful he was that Susannah was looking after "their boy" and always ended with the same somewhat stiff closing. *Love, Your Dad.*

Susannah's smile was teary. Her father wasn't comfortable putting feelings into words, either. She supposed there must have been a time, maybe when she was a little girl, when he had told her straight out that he loved her, but she couldn't remember it. Not that she'd ever had any doubts. He had shown her in every way possible. He'd been the best father a girl could ask for.

But he'd been an even better father to Skip.

She didn't begrudge Skip his favored place in the family. She remembered how desperately her parents had wanted more children, remembered her mother's three pregnancies—two that had ended in miscarriage mere weeks after they'd begun and the third one that had resulted in a premature stillborn daughter. She remembered her mother's hopes as each pregnancy progressed and her father's grief as each one ended. Even though Susannah hadn't fully understood their sorrow, she had shared it.

And then, after they had given up hope, after they had accepted that the daughter they had was the only child they would ever have, Skip had come along. If her mother had been thrilled, her father had been ecstatic. Finally he'd had the child he had always longed for, the son who would follow in his footsteps, who would carry on the Crouse name.

The entire family had adored Skip, had pampered and treasured him. Infractions that had earned Susannah and her cousins suitable punishment went ignored when Skip committed them. His temper tantrums were indulged, his whims catered to. Because his presence in their lives seemed nothing less than a miracle, he'd been treated with too much love and too little discipline.

Would Skip be different today, she wondered, if he had been held to the same standards of behavior that her parents had imposed on her? Would he be more responsible, more reliable, more honest and trustworthy?

Not that she was sure that the person she had become was of any more value than the person Skip was. After all, look at her: she'd had rules, limits and guidelines. She'd been taught the difference between right and wrong, had learned to respect others and the law, had developed values and morals and ethics, and look at what she was willing to do for her beloved brother: she was putting a man's life in danger. She was trading Remy's life for her brother's.

She was going to be responsible for Remy's death.

A soft, choked cry escaped her as she curled into a tight ball and pressed her fist to her mouth. God help her, she couldn't do it.

There had to be some other way, some way to free Skip and protect Remy. Maybe if she confided in him... But he was an FBI agent. He would have no interest in saving, of all the people who worked for Jimmy Falcone, her brother. He would find Skip guilty by association and would direct his energies toward punishing him right along with Falcone.

He would find *her* guilty, too. What was the penalty, she wondered with a shudder, for what she'd done so far? Prison, most likely. The end of life as she knew it.

But she had faced that two weeks ago when Nicholas Carlucci had called her the first time.

Maybe there was some way she could outsmart Carlucci and Falcone. Maybe she could give them inaccurate information, just for the duration of her time here. Once the month was up, it was up, and there was nothing either of them could do to change that. They couldn't expect any further help from her. They couldn't place any further demands on her.

But who was she, a nurse from Homestead, Nebraska, to think she could outsmart one of the best damn lawyers in the state, according to Remy, and the biggest crook in southern Louisiana? Who was she to succeed where others far more capable, far more skilled at that sort of thing—including Remy himself—had repeatedly failed?

She stood little chance at getting away with passing on lies to Carlucci...and very likely might get her brother killed for her efforts.

She could go to the authorities, could talk to Michael Bennett. But he'd made little effort to disguise the fact that he didn't approve of her presence in Remy's life, that he didn't approve of *her*. She might get as far as mentioning Carlucci's or Falcone's names before he hauled her off. She wasn't likely to find any sympathy for Skip or herself from him.

Her best bet, she thought hopelessly, was to quit thinking about it and to do exactly what the lawyer had told her to do. To answer his questions and pass on her little bits of information. To go back to pretending that it was harmless information, that knowing Remy's schedule, activities and movements couldn't possibly be of major importance to anyone. To hiding from the truth and trying to create a version of it that she could live with.

At least until she found a better option.

Remy lay on the couch, the television on but ignored, his gaze fixed on the white cylinder of his cast and his thoughts on the other side of the house in the servants' quarters. Susannah hadn't come back after taking the quilt to his room, but he hadn't really expected her to. It wasn't as if he couldn't get around fine on his own, and if he needed her, he could call. In fact, she would be perfectly within her rights to avoid him the rest of the day. She didn't have to sit down to dinner with him, didn't have to spend the long evening hours with him. She didn't have to have any real contact with him for the next three weeks, even though he had succeeded at badgering her into it for the past week.

You never do anything the easy way, do you? Michael had asked. Sometimes it seemed that was, indeed, the way of his life. Unlike Michael and Evan, he'd had no natural flair for investigative work; he had become the good agent he was through damned hard work, endless patience and never giving up. After fifteen years of stubbornness and foolish pride, it had taken getting shot for him to resolve his problems with his parents. And instead of falling for any number of willing women down in New Orleans, he'd picked the one woman in the state least likely to surrender to his charms.

Had she told the truth when she'd denied being involved with another man?

He couldn't say, because the truth was she hadn't actually denied it. "Tell me about him," he had invited, and she had replied, "There's nothing to tell." She had explained the telephone call and had come clean about her mail, but she had never actually said, "No, I'm not seeing anyone else." He had accepted it as a denial because that was what he'd wanted to hear.

Maybe he had been wrong.

Maybe he should give up, leave her alone and make the next few weeks as easy and uncomplicated as possible for them both.

You never do anything the easy way, do you?

And maybe he shouldn't.

Maybe he couldn't.

He wasn't afraid of hard work. He had immeasurable patience. He was stubborn as hell. And he knew what he wanted.

He knew something else, too: if he accepted that Susannah felt nothing for him, that she didn't share his attraction, if he gave up after so little effort, he would always wonder what might have been. He would always wonder if she had, indeed, been the right woman for him.

He would always regret giving in.

Reaching for his crutches, he got to his feet and headed toward their rooms. His was quiet, the door open, the quilt Valery had brought folded across the bed. Susannah's room was also quiet, the door open a few inches. Through that small bit he could see the corner of the dresser, the desk against one wall and the foot of the bed. He could also see Susannah's feet, tucked underneath the edge of the coverlet. She was asleep, he guessed, judging from her stillness and the utter silence in the room.

As a kid he had sometimes slept in this room when one family get-together or another had filled the upstairs bedrooms with out-of-town relatives, but he hadn't been inside in years longer than he could remember. Since he and Su-

sannah had moved in, it was the only place in the house—in
a house where she didn't feel at home—that she could consider her own; she hadn't invited him in, and he hadn't in-
truded.

He wished he could go in now, wished he could push the
door open and sit down on the bed beside her. He wished he
could lie down with her, wished he could simply hold her
while she slept. For now that would be enough.

For now.

Turning, he made his way back through the kitchen before taking a left down the long, central hallway. The ceiling there soared more than twenty-four feet to the second
floor, where a massive chandelier hung centered in a plaster
medallion of rosettes, curling leaves and flowing vines. The
hall was as wide as the first floor rooms, wide enough to require its own furniture: a sofa and tables in a niche over
here, two chairs flanking a gracefully turned table over there
and a pair of vases, blue and white, slender and nearly five
feet tall, standing one on each side of the front doors.

He loved this house, but he understood Susannah's refusal to think of it as home. It was beautiful, grand and intimidating as hell. Everything about it was just so perfect—
the architecture, the construction, the symmetry, the furnishings. He could well understand how someone who
hadn't grown up in such surroundings could be made uncomfortable by them. His own mother had felt out of place
when she had moved here with his father forty years ago.
Marie Navarre had grown up in a perfectly normal family in
a perfectly middle-class home. She had known that one day
George, as the oldest Sinclair son, would take over Belle Ste.
Claire, just as one day Remy would, but she hadn't expected that day to come for years.

Instead it had immediately followed the wedding. Remy's
grandparents had retired to a smaller property they owned
upriver, leaving Belle Ste. Claire to George and Marie and
the family they were expected to start.

As luck—or choice, Remy had preferred to think—would
have it, their family had consisted of only the three of them.

There would have been plenty of room for his grandparents to live with them at Belle Ste. Claire. He had never questioned why he was an only child, although, as kids, Valery had often teased him that it was because he'd been more than enough. His parents had gotten a taste of what life with him was like and had sworn off having any more kids for fear of getting another just like him.

He wondered now as he rubbed the gleaming stair rail why they hadn't had more children. *Had* it been by choice? Considering the willingness, even eagerness, with which they had taken responsibility for Valery, he didn't think so. How different would he be if he'd had brothers and sisters? Would he be less selfish if he'd had to share his home and his parents with others whose claim on their time, attention and love was as strong as his? Would he be less arrogant if he hadn't lived the first fourteen years of his life as the center of their lives?

Would Susannah find him more appealing, less threatening?

Maybe.

Maybe not.

For a moment he stood at the foot of the stairs, gazing around. It was colder in this part of the house, both in temperature and in nature. The rooms here at the front were rarely used even when his parents were home. The furnishings were more formal, every piece an antique. The chairs weren't comfortable for sitting, the rugs too fragile for everyday traffic. The walls were hung with tapestries, the windows with heavy draperies that puddled on the floor, and over each fireplace were imposing portraits of long-dead Sinclair relatives, a stern-looking, grim-faced bunch if ever he'd seen one.

He hardly even considered the rooms a part of the house. They were always on the tour for new visitors—Valery had taken Susannah through them their first day here—but, other than being opened up and decorated for holiday celebrations, they were otherwise ignored. The housekeeper dusted them once a week and did a serious cleaning peri-

odically, but for all of Remy's life, at least, the living at Belle
Ste. Claire had been done in the parlor, the library, his
father's study and the kitchen.

And the bedrooms, of course. There had originally been
seven of them, but two had been sacrificed in the early part
of the century for the addition of modern bathrooms. Of the
five that remained, one belonged to his parents, of course,
and two were guest rooms. One was kept ready for Valery's
visits, and the fifth one... The fifth one had been his.

He wondered how his mother had changed it in the years
he'd been gone. What had she done with the things he'd left
behind and never reclaimed, all the things he hadn't been
ready to part with and yet had had no need, or space, for in
school? Knowing his mother, everything was probably
packed up in boxes and stored somewhere in the attic, just
in case he ever decided he wanted it badly enough to ask for
it.

Still, he wouldn't mind seeing for himself.

He gazed up the stairs. They were pretty straightfor-
ward—no spirals, no turns, just one long shot from here to
the next floor. The day Michael had brought him here from
the hospital, he had looked forward to seeing his old room,
to sleeping in it. Over the years he had forgotten that this
was no ordinary staircase, that it climbed for forever, and
he had overestimated his ability with the crutches.

But his mother had planned ahead. She had prepared the
servants' quarters for him and Susannah. She had even left
a note warning him to avoid these stairs as long as he required crutches. There would be time for reminiscing up
there later, she had written.

Listening for and hearing no sound from the back of the
house, he carefully swung onto the first step. It wasn't bad.
He managed the steps leading to the gallery every time they
went out someplace, and he hadn't had a problem yet. These
were exactly the same.

There were just more of them.

By the tenth step he was starting to breathe hard.

By the twentieth, the muscles in his good leg were starting to ache.

By the time he reached the top, he needed a moment to sit
down and recover from the effort. Fortunately there was a
petit-point divan at the top for just that.

Within a few minutes, he was hobbling down the hall toward his room. More recent family portraits were hung on
this floor. Here were his grandparents, only weeks after their
wedding, and there they were, celebrating their fiftieth anniversary. Next was his own family, the occasion his first
birthday. After that, oils and canvas were traded for the ease
of cameras and film. The formality was still there, though,
as their close-knit family of three became a fractured group
of four. The only decent shots from that point on were
individual ones—his high school graduation photo, his
parents on their twenty-fifth, thirtieth and thirty-fifth an-
niversaries, Valery's high school and college graduations.
He had missed all those occasions.

He had missed so much.

At the end of the corridor, he paused in front of the last
door, balancing on his crutches as he wrapped his fingers
around the cool crystal knob. With no more than curiosity
and the expectation of seeing something new, he pushed the
door open, then stepped inside...and came to an abrupt
halt.

A wave of nostalgia, bittersweet and intense enough to
hurt, swept over him as he stood there in the dreary afternoon chill. Nothing had changed—not a single thing. His
books, including college textbooks that he'd thought worth
keeping, still filled the shelves. His stereo and a collection
of record albums and tapes were still on one corner of the
desk. Photographs and posters hung on the walls, and the
letter he'd been awarded for his one and only season on the
Belclaire High baseball team was still attached by a tack to
the bulletin board.

Slowly he sank onto the bed, its dark green coverlet faded
now where the afternoon sun came through the big windows, and he let his crutches slide to the floor. His parents

hadn't changed a thing. They had kept Valery's room for her, and they'd kept his room for him.

Finally, for the first time in fifteen years, he truly was home.

Chapter 6

It wasn't difficult for Susannah, when she awoke, to locate Remy: she simply followed the trail of lights he'd left burning. She took her time, though, studying each of the portraits and photographs in the hall, lingering over those few including him, before finally approaching the open door at the end of the hall where yellow-tinged light fell onto the worn rug.

Now she stood there, waiting to be noticed, to be invited in—or out. As moment after moment ticked by without him becoming aware of her presence, at last, she cleared her throat. "I take one little nap, and you go off climbing the stairs you're supposed to stay away from."

He looked up from the book he was paging through—a yearbook, she saw, slender and filled with yellowing pages of black-and-white photos. He didn't offer a welcoming smile. For a moment he didn't do anything at all, but finally he spoke. "Sorry. I didn't hear you."

"Am I intruding?"

"No. Come on in." He turned another page, then closed the annual and set it on the desk. "I just wanted to see what Mom and Dad had done with my room."

"Looks like they left it alone. They must have been hoping for you to come back someday."

"You think so?"

She ventured past him to stand at the foot of the bed. By nature there was something incompatible about fine old furniture sharing space with a very young man's keepsakes, but in this room it worked. Maybe it was the plain lines of the four-poster bed, the dresser and armoire, the desk and the chairs, along with the simplicity of the drapes and bedding.

Or maybe it had nothing at all to do with furniture, drapes or bedding. Maybe it was simply Remy himself—the force of his personality—that made it work.

"I was still living at home when I got married," she said in response to his question. "After the ceremony, I was saying goodbye to my father, and I told him that finally he had a room to convert to an office. He shook his head and told me that he planned to leave my room exactly as it was, in case I ever needed a place to go."

"He didn't have real high hopes for your marriage, did he?"

She smiled wryly. "My father met Guy once and had him all figured out. He tried to warn me, but..." She ended with a shrug.

"You married against your father's wishes? That's not what I'd expect from you."

"I was in love. It makes you do foolish things."

"Are you still in love?"

After a still moment, she turned to study the bulletin board on the wall in front of her. There wasn't much on it: a fifteen-year-old calendar turned to the month of May, a hand-printed list of names and phone numbers belonging mostly to girls, a bumper sticker advertising Louisiana State University, a photograph of a pretty redhead wearing a dark green-and-cream-colored cheerleader's uniform and an athletic letter, a swirly *B*, in the same green-and-cream shades. The letter was dusty, faded and marked with a circle of rust where the thumbtack pierced it. "What did you letter in?" she asked absently.

"Baseball."

"Were you any good?"

"Yeah. But I only played one year. My parents kept missing games because they were busy with Valery. Their excuse was always, 'We'll come next time,' or 'There'll be plenty of games next season. We'll make it up to you then.'"

"So, to get back at them, you made sure there wasn't a next season."

He looked sheepish. "It sounds pettier now than it did at the time."

Susannah glanced around again. Besides the chair he was sitting in, there was one other tucked into the corner. It was wooden, oversized, the seat polished to the sort of sheen that only years of use could give. She made herself comfortable in it before responding to his last comment. "It doesn't seem petty now. No matter how much your cousin needed your parents, their first obligation was to their own child."

Leaving his crutches where they were, he cautiously moved the few feet to the bed, propping his leg on a pillow. "You didn't answer me."

"Again?" She tried for a faint smile, but it wouldn't come. She didn't feign ignorance, didn't pretend that she'd forgotten the question. "No. The answer is no. I'm not still in love with Guy. I'm not in love with anyone, and I don't want to be. Like I said, love makes you do foolish things, and I've done enough foolish things to last a lifetime."

"Somehow I have a great deal of trouble imagining you behaving foolishly."

"Keep trying. The image will come."

He shook his head. "You know what image I'll always have of you? That night in the emergency room. Everyone was doing something to me, and they were shouting at each other, and I already hurt like hell, and they were making it worse. No one was looking at me or talking to me or even noticing that I was there...except you. You were so calm. So serene."

"Serene," she echoed, injecting skepticism into the word even though his compliment touched her deeply. "That's a new way to describe it. Guy always preferred words like dull. Uninteresting. Boring."

His voice rang with annoyance. "Then Guy was an idiot."

"Careful," she gently warned. "In some ways you remind me of him."

"What ways?"

"Well, there's the superficial. You're both tall, blond, blue-eyed and handsome."

Immediately Remy grinned a charmingly unrepentant grin. "You think I'm handsome?"

"Don't most women?"

"I don't care what most women think. I want to know what *you* think."

"There's that, too," she said thoughtfully. "The ability to say lines like that and actually make a woman think you're sincere. You're both very brash, very confident. You're very certain that you deserve to have what you want at exactly the time you want it. You're both more than a little forceful."

While she spoke, his expression shifted from charming and amused to stony. "And what about our differences? There have to be some."

"I don't know," she admitted. The similarities were easy. They were right there on the surface for all the world to see. But the differences... Oh, she knew they were there. She knew Remy was a better man than Guy could ever hope to be, knew Remy was a *good* man, but differences ran deep. They took time to uncover. They took knowledge—intimate knowledge—to sort through. While she had lived intimately with Guy for four years, she'd been with Remy only a week, and they certainly weren't intimate. They weren't even exactly living together but simply sharing quarters.

But there was one very obvious difference. "I don't be-lieve you would ever be deliberately cruel."

"And he was."

She shrugged. "It was a way to amuse himself when nothing else was going on." Insults, hurts, comments cal-culated to undermine her confidence—that had been the way of her marriage. He had piled them one on top of an-other, so subtle at first that she'd been convinced she was imagining them, so skillfully that later she had blamed her-self. If she was prettier, she had reasoned, he wouldn't flirt with other women in front of her. If she was more outgo-ing, he wouldn't snub her when his friends were around. If she was more interesting, he wouldn't neglect her so much. If she was taller, shapelier, more exciting, better skilled, more imaginative or any of a hundred other things, he wouldn't have affairs with other women.

It had taken four years to catch on to what he was doing to her. Four years to see how he was manipulating her, making her take the blame for his failures. Four long, un-happy years before she got smart...and by then, the dam-age had been done.

At the end, the very end, she had confronted him regard-ing how badly he had treated her. He had shrugged it off as if the issue were unimportant—as if *she* were unimpor-tant—but, in his own defense, he had replied, "At least I never hit you." As if that counted for something. As if his words hadn't been, in their own way, every bit as painful as a physical blow might have been. As if his restraint was something to be proud of.

"I'm sorry, Susannah," Remy said quietly. "I'm sorry your ex was a bastard. I'm sorry he hurt you and that things didn't work out the way you wanted them to. But, you know, people go through bad relationships, they get over them and they go on with their lives. They fall in love again. They get married again. They find happiness again."

Leaving the chair, she walked around the perimeter of the room, giving a wide berth to the bed where he sat. "You don't have to be in love to be happy. You certainly don't have to be married.''

''Logically I can agree with that. Emotionally I can't. I can't imagine finding happiness in a life that you're living alone.''

''I'm not alone. I have friends. Family.''

''Your family is halfway across the country in Nebraska. So are your friends, except for the ones you've made in the last few months. How can that be enough to satisfy you?''

She came to a stop in front of the bookcase, which held fewer than a dozen books and shelf after shelf of mementos. In a prominent place was a framed photograph. It was different by far from those hanging outside in the hall. There was nothing professional about it, not in the composition, the taking or the framing. It was just a snapshot in a two-dollar frame, but it held the place of honor in the room.

Taking it down, she cradled it in both hands. There were four young men on the steps of a slightly shabby house, the sort that college students, no matter what their background, were always happy to call home. She easily recognized Remy, the fair-haired charmer, and Michael, intense even then. She didn't know enough about either Evan or Smith to decide which of the handsome boys—the tall, serious one beside Remy and the shorter one with the dark mischievous eyes—was which.

In this moment frozen in time, they were all so young, so innocent, each facing a future that was full of possibilities. Now the youth was gone, and so was the innocence, and the future. At least Michael's was full, with his upcoming marriage to Valery. Again, she didn't know enough about Evan or Smith to guess at their futures.

And she knew too much about Remy.

Still holding the frame, she went to the bed and sat down facing him. ''Which one is Smith?''

He pointed toward the serious boy, then touched his fingers lightly to the glass over the dark-eyed youth. ''And this is Evan. I haven't told you about him, have I?''

"You said he was one of your roommates in college and that he's a cop."

"He *was* a cop. He was a good cop."

There was such emotion in his voice that Susannah knew what was coming, and she knew that she didn't want to hear it. Still, she sat quietly, waited and listened.

"He died last spring. He and Michael were trying to help a little girl who had been kidnapped. Michael went in after the girl, and Evan went after the bastard who'd taken her. She came out of it unharmed—physically, at least—but Michael got shot and Evan—" Breaking off, he sighed. "Risk comes with the job, you know? Criminals tend to be people who don't have a lot to lose. This guy knew that if he got caught, prison would be sheer hell—it usually is for child molesters—so he figured that he'd check out rather than give in. And since he was going to kill himself, hell, why not take a cop or two with him?" Sighing again, he withdrew his hand from the photograph, leaving it unsteady in her hands. "He's the only friend I ever lost. We thought we would be together forever, the four of us. And then there were three."

And soon would there be only two?

Susannah forced the morbid thought out of her mind, forced the guilt back into the darkness where she would deal with it later, and returned to the point she had intended to use the photo to make. "How old is this picture?"

"Eighteen years. That was our sophomore year in college. We'd met the year before when we all lived in the same dorm. That picture was taken the day we moved into that house together."

"Michael and Smith are still your friends, aren't they?"

"Best friends."

"And they've been enough to satisfy you for nineteen years—or, at least, the fifteen years since you argued with your parents."

"No." He leaned back against the pillows and faced her. "I see the point you're trying to make, Susannah, but you're wrong. They were a very important part of my life. They have been and always will be. But they weren't enough to

make up for the things I was missing. One person can't satisfy all our needs. A friend can't make up for the lack of
parents or a husband or wife or children. Your father
couldn't take your mother's place when she died. Michael,
Evan and Smith couldn't replace my parents. Michael,
Smith and I couldn't fill the emptiness in each other's lives
when Evan died." He paused, then softened his voice as he
finished. "And you're never going to be happy with just
friends and long-distance family in your life."

She wanted to argue with him, wanted to tell him that he
was wrong, but how could she when he was more right than
he could imagine? She *wasn't* going to be happy, not here
and now and certainly not anytime in the future. Once she'd
done the job she had come here to do, once she had safely
returned Skip to their father's home, she was going to be so
alone. How could she make new friends when she knew how
little she deserved them? How could she face her father
when she knew how her actions would shame and shock
him? Not even her relationship with Skip could survive, not
when, for the rest of their lives, she would blame him for
what she'd had to do.

She was going to be so totally alone.

And so incredibly unhappy.

Striving for cynicism to ward off the pain accompanying
those last thoughts, she asked, "And what do you think I
need in my life, Remy? *You?*"

"Don't sound so thrilled by the idea," he said dryly; then
immediately that small bit of humor faded. "Are you afraid
that this is just a line? That I'm bored and looking for
something to amuse myself with? That when the cast comes
off and my life returns to normal, I'll no longer need either
the amusement or you?" He paused, but not long enough
for her to answer. "I would never hurt you, Susannah."

"Maybe I'm afraid that *I'll* hurt *you.*" Her manner was
careless and hard-edged, but inside all she felt was the ache.
She had thought it bad this afternoon when she had curled
up in bed and silently cried herself to sleep, but that was
nothing compared to the pain now. "That's a hoot, isn't it,

considering who you are and who I am. You could have any woman you want, and I'm supposed to be grateful that for now you've decided you want me. It never occurred to you that maybe I could hurt you."

His smile was fleeting, a little unsteady and a whole lot sad. "Honey, I have no doubt that you could break my heart."

"So go find someone else."

"What if I think you're worth the risk?"

"You're wrong, Remy. I'm not worth anything." She rose from the bed, intending to escape before he could get to his crutches, but abruptly he reached out and stopped her with his hand on her wrist. It was warm where his skin touched hers, soft and nubby where the black glove did, and his fingers were gentle where they held her.

His voice, though, was anything but gentle. "Damn it, Susannah... Is this what he did to you? Is this how your ex-husband amused himself? Telling you that you should be grateful for his attention? Teaching you that you don't have anything to offer, that you aren't worth anything?"

Too ashamed to answer his questions, having no answers that she could possibly give him, she stared hard at their hands, her vision blurred by the tears that burned her eyes. "Please let me go," she whispered. She pleaded.

His reply was every bit as much a whisper, every bit as much a plea. "I can't." But he did exactly that, releasing her wrist, freeing her to walk away.

It took a moment for his action to sink in, took another moment for her to gather her strength and turn away. But she made it only as far as the door before he spoke again, his tone more determined this time, more of a warning.

"I'm sorry, Susannah, but I can't. You're going to have to deal with that."

Over the next few days, Remy realized that, in a sense, one of Susannah's fears had been true: he *had* been relying on her to keep him occupied, to stave off the boredom that accompanied his limitations. Since their conversation in his room Tuesday afternoon, she had, for the most part, avoided him. She cooked his meals and ate across from him, washed his clothes and ran his errands, but she spent no time in his company that wasn't necessary.

The strain between them didn't seem to be taking much of a toll on her. Of course, she was keeping busy with her job. She was taking long walks around the grounds and, lately, venturing into the woods behind the house where he and Valery had played when they were kids. She spent the better part of Wednesday helping Mrs. Holloway when the housekeeper came for her every-other-week cleaning, chatting and, apparently, enjoying the other woman's company.

She had things to do. All *he* could do was brood.

That was why he'd decided to return to New Orleans this afternoon. Not to stay, he had explained when he'd seen the startled look come into Susannah's eyes as he'd made his announcement over breakfast. He had an appointment with the orthopedic surgeon tomorrow morning; rather than get up early to make the drive down, he'd chosen instead to go back today. He had called Michael and Valery, back from their trip to Arkansas, who had invited him, Susannah and Smith over for dinner. Then they would spend the night at his apartment, see the doctor in the morning and, sometime Monday afternoon, return to Belle Ste. Claire.

Susannah certainly didn't seem enthusiastic. It had taken a moment for that unnerved look to fade, only to be replaced by the distant, troubled expression he'd seen so much of lately and was coming to hate with a passion. That was a good idea, she had agreed in a distant voice, and she had gone off to pack their bags. Now they were in the city, and she'd barely spoken since then.

He would wager half this month's salary that she was planning to ditch him tonight. She would wait until the last minute, he figured, probably until they were standing outside Michael's door, and then come up with some excuse for why she couldn't join his friends for dinner. There would be friends of her own to visit or errands of her own to run and, after all, it wouldn't be an inconvenience to him because his cousin and friends would be more than happy to give him whatever assistance he might need.

But she wasn't going to get away with it.

"Take the next exit," he directed, and she turned her head for a moment to look at him. Dark glasses hid her eyes, but he could feel the cool steadiness of her gaze.

"I remember the way to your apartment."

He would like to think that there was something significant about that. After all, much of the city was still unfamiliar to her, and she *had* been to his apartment only once. But he knew better than to flatter himself. She was a capable, efficient woman who was probably good with directions. "We'll drop off our bags and then go someplace for a drink before we head over to Michael's."

He waited a moment to see if she would put her getaway plan in motion now, if she would display any reluctance to spend the evening with his friends, but she said nothing.

She did, indeed, remember the way to his place. She pulled into the single parking space he was allotted in addition to the private garage where his own car was stored, then got their bags while he made his way over the curb and up a short flight of steps to the square stoop at the apartment's entrance.

The apartments had been built in the twenties, and they had everything more modern places lacked: large rooms, high ceilings, quality work and personality. The floors were cypress or tile; there were large expanses of high-gloss terracotta running through his. The walls were thick, the windows deep-set, and there were steps everywhere. He had lived there so long—and had been fortunate to be in such good health—that he'd practically forgotten the three steps down into the living room, the two steps up to the dining room, the four up into the kitchen.

Susannah closed the door behind her, set their luggage down and gave the foyer a cursory glance. He watched her, searching for some sign of approval, of like or dislike, on her face, but her expression didn't change. Just once, he thought, he would like to see a little sheer, unanticipated pleasure on her face. He would like to see something take her by surprise, something that she liked so much, she couldn't begin to hide it.

Even more, he would like to, if not *be* that something, at least be responsible for it.

"What do you think?" he asked.

Her gaze brushed across him, then skittered away. "It's pretty."

Pretty. The word was universally accepted as a compliment, but it seemed to Remy—at least when spoken in that tone of voice—to be just one more of those damnably bland and meaningless words. Nice. Sweet. Pretty.

"Do you want to go by your place while we're in town and pick up anything?"

That brought her gaze back to him, along with a too-abrupt answer. "No."

"Are you sure? It's not too far from here, is it? Three or four miles?"

She shoved her hands into the pockets of the jacket she wore, then leaned back against the banister. "Three or four miles can be a long, long way."

He supposed that was true anywhere, but especially in New Orleans. Traveling a few miles could take you from gracious, old-money elegance through government-supported projects and back into affluence. Cross one street—the wrong street—down in the Quarter, and you traded historic ambience for a no-man's-land where your life wasn't worth the slug it would take to end it.

"Are you embarrassed by where you live, Susannah?"

Ready with a denial, she opened her mouth, then her face grew red and she slowly closed it again. She turned away from him and stood at the top of the steps descending into the living room, where her sigh seemed to echo from the tile floor to the sparsely decorated walls to the high ceiling. "I'm not embarrassed by it," she said at last, "although I understand why you might think so. It's nothing like this. Calling this place and my place both apartments is sort of like calling a two-foot-deep ditch and the Grand Canyon both holes in the ground. It's a plain, average apartment in a plain, average complex. Nothing fancy, nothing expensive. Fifteen, maybe twenty, years old, a little the worse for wear. It's what I can afford on my salary with my expenses, and it suits my needs just fine."

She faced him then and, for the first time in days, her smile wasn't forced. It wasn't filled with pleasure, either—in fact, it was slightly self-mocking—but it was real. "The apartment and I have a lot in common."

Plain, average, nothing fancy, a little the worse for wear.

Remy covered the distance between them with a few easy paces, then balanced on his crutches in front of her. He lifted one hand to her hair, which was pulled back today and fastened with a plastic clip so that it cascaded down in soft waves, and stroked it gently. "You're not plain, there's nothing average about you, and, honey, we're all a little the worse for wear."

The smile came again, a little different this time, touched with a hint of longing and the mocking now directed at them both. "Lines, Remy," she murmured. "Those are just lines."

"Truths, Susannah. Someday you're going to recognize the difference between the two." Bracing against the crutches, he placed both hands on her shoulders, then waited for her to step back, to effortlessly glide away from his touch, to do something, anything, to break the contact between them. When she didn't, he slowly drew her closer. At first she was hesitant, and under the circumstances, she had to be the one to move; because of the cast, the crutches and their position, he was physically incapable of it.

One step, he silently pleaded. Just one small step at a time.

Finally, when he was about to give up hope, she took that last step that brought her into his arms. For a moment she remained still and stiff; then, with a soft, weary sigh, she relaxed against him, resting her head on his shoulder, pressing her cheek to his sweater, settling her hands at his waist.

It was a simple embrace—not passionate, not joyful, not sexual in the least. He had experienced more intimate encounters with total strangers in crowded elevators or in a Saturday night throng on Bourbon Street.

More intimate... but not sweeter. Never sweeter.

For a moment he was content to simply hold her and to stroke her hair, the exposed curve of her neck, down her spine. But it wasn't long at all before contentment turned to greed. Holding and touching should lead naturally to caressing, to kissing and more. He wanted more. Always more.

But was she ready to give it?

Was she ever going to be ready?

"I wish I'd met you before he did," he said regretfully. He didn't have to clarify that by "he," he meant her ex-husband. He could feel the tension of acknowledgment ripple through her. Raising both hands to her face, he gently forced her back, gently forced her to look up at him. "Want me to make life miserable for him?" he asked with his best grin.

She almost smiled. "He's in Nebraska. What could you do from down here?"

"Plenty. I could call the nearest field office up there and give them his name and address. They would call the local sheriff's department and pass it on. It would be strictly unofficial and off-the-record, one cop doing a favor for another—it happens all the time. Good ol' Guy wouldn't be able to leave his house without getting followed, stopped, warned or ticketed. They would make his life hell."

This time she did smile. "That's harassment."

"That's satisfaction, sweetheart. You deserve that much." He couldn't resist tracing his thumb across the curves of her smile. "Say the word, and I'll make it happen."

Wide-eyed and innocent, she shook her head. "Guy likes to drive fast and reckless. The insurance company had told him just before we separated that if he got one more ticket, they would cancel him. I couldn't be responsible for that."

Remy pretended disappointment—although he'd known, if he had made the offer seriously, what her answer would be. "You're a better person than I am. I'd let the sheriff have him."

His words faded and stillness grew between them as their gazes locked and held. She was a beautiful woman—not merely pretty, as he'd first thought, but quietly, dazzlingly beautiful. When had she changed? he wondered. The answer, of course, was that she hadn't. *His* perception of her had. The more time he spent with her, the better he came to know her, the more deeply he cared for her, the more beautiful she became to him.

On impulse he leaned forward to kiss her. Instinctively—as he'd half expected—she drew back and turned her head so that his kiss, if completed, would graze her cheek rather than her mouth. "Oh, Susannah." His voice was soft, his breath warm and ticklish, sending a shiver through her. "What will it take to convince you to trust me?"

She had no answer—he didn't expect one—but slowly she tilted her head back until her gaze met his again. The position moved her body into closer contact with his, into damned intimate contact, he thought, suppressing a groan even though he couldn't suppress his body's response.

"You've got to help me out here, sweetheart. I feel as if I'm playing a game that I can't afford to lose, but I don't know the rules. Tell me what you want, tell me what you need that I haven't offered, and I'll give it to you."

"Tell me what *you* want," she said quietly, her voice curiously cool when their bodies were undeniably hot.

"I want *you.*"

"What exactly does that mean?" Acknowledging his arousal, she gave a tiny little shrug that sent shocks through him everywhere they touched. "Besides the obvious."

He considered all the ways he could answer, weighing the merits of one reply against another. When he finally spoke, his words came haltingly. "From the first time I saw you, I felt . . . connected to you."

"You were afraid and in pain. Sometimes, in a time of great stress, a person develops an emotional attachment to someone who can help him—a patient to a doctor, a victim to a police officer. It's not an unusual response. But it's not enough to build a relationship on."

"It's not the same, Susannah, and you know it." While stroking her hair, he worked the clip open and pulled it free so that her hair swung loose over his hands. "It's ironic. I *was* afraid that night . . . but you've been afraid ever since. Look at me, Susannah, and tell me that you don't feel something for me. Tell me you're not curious about what could develop between us. Tell me you don't care."

Stiffening, she pulled away. He couldn't force her to stay in his arms, but he did catch her wrist, holding her close, close enough so he could see the shadows in her hazel eyes. "Tell me, Susannah."

"You want an affair, Remy—"

"Yes," he interrupted. "I do. I don't deny that. Hell, right now I *can't* deny it. I want to make love to you, Susannah. I think about it at night when you're asleep across the hall. I think about it when I watch you work and when you sit in the parlor in the evenings and read, and I damn sure think about it when you take those long baths every morning. I'm a normal, reasonably healthy man and you're a lovely woman, and I would like to spend the next fifty or sixty years indulging my desire for you. Is there something wrong with that?"

"Don't say things like that," she insisted. "You don't know me!"

Giving in to the demands of his leg, he moved back to the half wall that separated the entry from the living room, pulling her with him, and leaned against it. "I know that your ex-husband hurt you tremendously. I know that you're a generous, nurturing woman. I know that you're not as afraid of believing in me as you are of believing in yourself. And I know that there are things troubling you." He smiled faintly. "I also know the important things, Susannah. I know that you have the gentlest eyes I've ever seen. I know that you brighten a room just by walking into it. I know that you have a healing touch. And from the first time I saw you, I've known that you were the woman I wanted—not just for a nurse, not for a friend, not for an affair, but for always."

She shook her head, almost frantic in her denial. "I could be a terrible person. I could have awful things planned for you."

"I've known terrible people, sweetheart, and I've seen awful things. You're not capable of hurting anyone."

"You don't know that," she whispered, "because you don't know me."

"I do know, Susannah."

She tried to pull her arm free, but still he held her. "This is ridiculous. Let me go, please. I need to unpack bef—"

Breaking in, he repeated his earlier request. "Look at me, tell me you don't feel something for me, and I'll let you go."

Her gaze settled somewhere around the waistband of his jeans. "I . . . don't . . ."

"Susannah. Look at me."

At last she forced her gaze up until it locked with his.

"Say, 'I don't want you, Remy,' " he demanded, even as he silently prayed for her to deny it.

She didn't say it . . . but neither did she deny it. She simply said nothing.

"Say, 'I don't feel anything for you.' " *Please, damn you, tell me you do.*

Still nothing.

His voice grew harsh and tight, and his breathing sounded strained in his own ears. "Say, 'I don't give a damn about you, Remy.' "

The gentlest eyes he'd ever seen were also now the saddest. He'd never felt such sorrow...such longing...or such regret. "I'm sorry, Remy," she whispered.

He stared at her a long, long time, until the emptiness growing inside him was complete, until the pain lost its raw edge and the shock began turning everything numb. Finally he released her, and he took a clumsy step away, followed by another. "No, Susannah," he said at last, his voice hollow and unsteady. "*I'm* sorry. I thought... I assumed that anything I felt so strongly couldn't possibly be one-sided, but obviously I was wrong. I am sorry."

He turned away then, feeling aches that he hadn't felt in days as he made his way down the steps and across the living room to the overstuffed sofa. As he gingerly eased down onto the cushions, she came to the second step. "Remy..."

Whatever she was about to say, he didn't want to hear it. Not now. Not yet. "My room is the first one at the top of the stairs. You can have either of the two guest rooms. Go ahead and unpack our bags now." He drew a deep breath that stung. "Michael and Valery are expecting us about six, so I'd like to leave here around five-thirty."

"Maybe... maybe I shouldn't go."

He smiled mockingly. There was no maybe about it; she *definitely* shouldn't go. He didn't need to spend an entire evening watching her with his friends. He certainly didn't need to see how naturally she fit in, how easily she belonged. But more than that, he didn't need the questions that showing up without her would generate. "They're expecting both of us," he said pointedly. "Be ready at five-thirty."

Then, using a coolly polite tone that he'd learned years ago from his grandmother, he dismissed her as effectively as any servant had ever been dismissed. "That's all for now, Susannah. You can go."

Shortly after arriving at the third-floor apartment overlooking Jackson Square that Valery and Michael shared, Susannah accepted Valery's invitation to step outside to take in the view of St. Louis Cathedral. While the other woman went to get jackets to protect them from the damp evening chill, Susannah left Remy, seated at the dining table, and Michael, cooking their dinner in the small kitchen, and went on out alone. It *was* cool outside, but she swore she would have been just as chilled inside, alone with the two men.

Remy was treating her exactly as she had expected to be treated on her first day at Belclaire—as a servant, someone paid to see to his needs, to follow his orders and to remain more or less a nonperson the rest of the time. She had been sure in the beginning that an all-business relationship was exactly what she wanted, but now that she had it, it hurt. It hurt to see that cool impersonal look in his eyes. It hurt to watch him distance himself from her.

Most of all, it hurt to know that he was doing this because *she* had hurt *him*.

And she hadn't even meant to.

He had misunderstood her in the foyer this afternoon. She hadn't been apologizing because she couldn't deny the things he was saying. She had apologized because she couldn't confirm them, because she couldn't tell him that she didn't care. She *did* care, God help her, entirely too much. She cared more than he would ever know.

And she had no right.

A shiver rustling through her, she turned to face the cathedral, lit against the encroaching night, at the far end of the square below. Although she had been a regular churchgoer from the time she was born, it had been shamefully easy not to find a new church once she'd moved here. There had been other priorities in her life—getting a job and dealing with Skip—and a new church home wasn't one of them.

She hadn't even looked. She had known she would never find a church like the one she'd left behind—the one where she'd been baptized, where she had taken part in every Christmas play and Easter pageant in twenty-five years, where she had for a number of years taught Sunday school, where she and Guy had been married. They'd had the same minister her entire life and, it seemed, more or less the same congregation. Oh, there had been marriages and births and deaths, but the heart of the church had stayed the same. More than half the members were related to her in one way or another. Uncle Richard was a deacon, and his youngest boy was the youth leader. Aunt Salley, who lived just down the road from the farm, played the organ, and a cousin on Susannah's mother's side was the pride and joy of the informal choir.

Since she couldn't replace what she'd had at home, she hadn't even tried. It had felt funny at first—awakening on Sunday mornings and not putting on a pretty dress or doing her hair or makeup. A lifetime of Sunday morning services had been a hard habit to break, but she had managed. Oh, she had still tried to follow the teachings and the preachings, had tried to live a good Christian life, and for a time there, as she uncovered the extent of Skip's problems, her prayers had grown more fervent, more impassioned, more regular.

Until the day that lawyer had called.

Although she knew she needed divine guidance and help more now than ever before, she didn't feel she even had the right to pray. She was committing a crime, was conspiring with an evil man to commit an even greater one. Why should God hear her prayers? Why should He care?

"The cathedral is a beautiful place, isn't it?" Closing the French doors behind her, Valery joined Susannah on the balcony, offering her a heavy woolen shawl for protection from the damp evening chill. "Sometimes I go inside and just sit there. It's so peaceful." She pulled on her own jacket, then leaned on the wrought-iron railing. "You look as if you could use a little peace."

Susannah offered her a sad smile. "I could use a new life."

"One away from Remy?" Valery didn't wait for an answer. "You know, Susannah, we've all been kind of enjoying the way Remy's pursued you. Granted, I haven't been around him much in recent years, but Michael and Smith both say this is pretty much out of character for him. He's never been so single-minded about a woman before. They also say it's a sign of how important this is—how important you are—to him. But if you really aren't interested in him, if you don't feel what he feels, maybe it would be kinder for both of you if you made it clear to him now."

On a not too distant street corner, a single horn—a saxophone, Susannah thought—was playing a sweet, rather mournful tune. She didn't know the name, but she'd heard it before. She remembered one line. *Do you know what it means to miss New Orleans?* Oh, yes. She was standing right there in the heart of the French Quarter, in the heart of the city itself, and she already missed it. She already felt the ache that she knew was going to follow her forever.

As the last notes died away in the night, she turned to Valery. "It's not a question of being interested. There's much more to it than that."

"Do you want to talk about it?"

She missed that, she thought regretfully—talking. Confiding. When she was a girl, she had told all her dearest secrets to her mother and later, after Janet Crouse's death, to her girlfriends. She had cried over the gradual breakup of her marriage with Traci Lynn Williams, the best of her best friends, and she'd made more than a few long-distance calls back to Nebraska to discuss her concerns about Skip with Traci Lynn.

But she couldn't confide in anyone anymore. This time her secrets truly were secrets. Telling them would do more than cost her the respect and possibly even the love of people who had always loved her. Telling, at best, would put those friends in the difficult position of having to choose between protecting a friend and obeying the law.

At worst, it could put their lives in danger.

"I wish I could. But I can't." She held the other woman's clear blue gaze for a long moment, then looked away to the square. "You and Michael have a lovely place here. If you're going to live in New Orleans, I can't imagine a more perfect location."

After another long moment, Valery let the change of subject stand. "I know. We'll both miss it when we move."

"Then why do it?"

"We both want babies—lots of them—as soon as we're married, but the apartment is just one bedroom. Besides, an apartment is no place to raise kids if you can avoid it."

"When is the wedding?" Susannah asked, telling herself that it was all right to discuss marriage, weddings and babies. That twinge around her heart had nothing to do with wanting any of that. It was simply a little sorrow left over from hearing that song. In the right hands, the clear tones of a sax on a cool, foggy evening could turn the cheeriest song in the world into the blues.

"A few more weeks. As soon as Aunt Marie and Uncle George get back from their trip."

A few more weeks. Everything would be settled in a few more weeks. She would be gone. She would never see New Orleans or Valery or any of her friends here again.

She would never see Remy again.

Unless . . .

Unless she found some way out.

Unless she somehow managed to rescue her brother and to save Remy at the same time.

Unless she betrayed Jimmy Falcone.

She pulled the shawl closer, burrowing her fingers into the soft woven fabric. It was an impossible suggestion. Jimmy Falcone had a nasty little way of dealing with people who betrayed him. He made sure they couldn't do it to him or anyone else ever again. He didn't give them a chance to live to regret their deeds.

He simply had them killed.

Life meant so little to him that he'd had Nate Simmons murdered merely as a means of framing Remy. Now, for whatever reasons—because Remy had escaped his trap, because he was still an irritant, because for too long Remy had headed the case against him—now Falcone intended to have *him* killed.

And to accomplish that, he was threatening to do the same to Skip.

And if she tried to stop him, he would simply add her to his list.

God help her, she didn't want to die.

But did she want to live at the expense of someone else's life?

The three soaring spires of the cathedral drew her gaze. Only moments ago she had wondered why God should listen to her prayers; a person committing the terrible sin that *she* was committing wasn't deserving of His attention.

But she had been taught better than that. Saints weren't quite so needy of God's direction.

Sinners were.

And she was sinning in the worst possible way. That meant she probably ranked pretty high right now on the Lord's list of priorities.

Her hands clasped tightly together, she stared hard at the church as she offered a silent prayer, a silent plea for help. There had to be a way to escape this nightmare, hopefully with their lives intact, but she didn't know what it was. She couldn't see any way out, but then, all she could see was her own fear, her own worries. There *had* to be some solution, some way to save both Remy and Skip, some way to stop Jimmy Falcone before he destroyed any more lives.

Failing that, there had to be some way to save Remy. He was the only innocent one involved. Whatever else happened, he had to survive.

Dear God, she whispered silently, he *had* to.

Beside her, Valery stirred, disturbing, then breaking, the tense silence that surrounded Susannah. "Ah, there's the answer to my prayers," she said with a smile. "Now we can eat."

The answer to my prayers. Susannah blinked back the moisture that glazed her eyes. There was no justice, she thought, not when she and Valery could share the same small space, could look at the same church and offer such different prayers.

There was certainly no justice when it was Valery's prayers that brought an answer.

After mouthing one final, silent *please,* she turned to face the brightly lit apartment. The curtains across the wide windows and doors were sheer, allowing a filmy, hazy look inside at the new arrival. He was as tall as Remy and as lean as Michael. Although he was as casually dressed as they were and was sprawled as comfortably as they were around the table, something about him screamed—no, wrong word—something about him *whispered* refinement. Breeding. Pure class. It was indefinable, unmistakable.

Intimidating.

But, curiously, she didn't feel intimidated. "Is that Smith?"

Valery nodded.

"Tell me about him."

"Ah, Remy hasn't filled you in?" Valery considered her request a moment. "Well, his name is Smith Kendricks. You've probably heard of him. No, I forgot, you're a newcomer. Stay around long, and you'll see a lot of him—if not in the headlines, then in the society pages. He's *the* most eligible bachelor in the city for obvious reasons. He's incredibly handsome, sexy as hell and very, very rich with very old money. He comes from back east, from Connecticut or Rhode Island or someplace. I think his family owns New England."

Susannah smiled weakly at that, and it felt surprisingly good. She had smiled so little in recent months and she missed it.

"For reasons that escape me, he turned his back on all those venerable old institutions where people like him usually go to college and came here instead. That's how he met Michael and Remy. He went back to Harvard or another of those venerable old places for law school, then got a job here with the U.S. Attorney's office. He's very bright and very talented. He's already inherited a number of fortunes and has more just waiting for him, and the best part of it, Susannah, is he's such a nice guy."

"Right," she said. "Those are qualities *I* always think of together. Incredibly handsome, sexy as hell, bright, rich and nice." But Remy was all those things, too. He was incredibly handsome and sexy, and he came from money, but he was sweet, nice, charming and thoughtful.

"I know. Isn't it a hoot?"

"Sounds as if he'd be the answer to a lot of prayers. With all that going for him, why isn't he married?"

"I imagine it's difficult to find someone whose bloodlines and bank balances measure up. That seems to be his only flaw. He chooses his women based on their suitability for a relationship with the heir to the Kendricks empire rather than something as unimportant as physical attraction or compatibility." Valery shivered as a breeze rustled across the square. "In all fairness, I'll also say that he *is* dedicated to his job. Michael says he's the best damn prosecutor around. He believes very strongly in what he's doing."

"And what exactly is that?"

"He prosecutes federal cases, primarily organized crime. When they finally get Jimmy Falcone for the murder that I witnessed and for trying to kill Remy, Smith will take the case to court." The easiness disappeared from Valery's voice and was replaced by a tougher, colder tone. "He'll send the bastard away forever."

Susannah studied him for a long, still moment. A federal prosecutor, scheduled to prosecute Jimmy Falcone if the government ever got him to court. One of Remy's two best friends, one who hopefully wouldn't take an immediate dislike to her as Michael had, and such a nice guy.

Maybe Valery had been wrong earlier. Maybe Smith Kendricks wasn't the answer to *her* prayers.

Maybe he was the answer to Susannah's.

Chapter 7

A blast of cold air swept into the room when Susannah and Valery returned from the balcony. Sitting near the door as he was, it should have sent a chill through Remy, but he already felt pretty damned cold inside. The air temperature outside couldn't begin to compete.

Valery came in first, wearing a welcoming smile and offering a friendly greeting to Smith. Behind her, Susannah took her time, making certain that the billowy curtain didn't get caught in the door as she closed it, before she finally joined them at the table. He wondered if anyone else could recognize her reluctance to be there at all. It wasn't obvious, wasn't anything that couldn't be mistaken for shyness at spending an evening with a bunch of people who were mostly strangers, but he could see it. She didn't meet anyone's gaze, didn't speak unless spoken to, and even though she did join them around the table, she somehow managed to also stay apart. She sat straight, kept her feet together and her hands clasped in her lap.

Valery performed the introductions with little fanfare as she went about setting the table. "Susannah Duncan, Smith

Kendricks. Susannah's taking care of Remy until his folks get back from Europe.''

"Susannah." Smith leaned across the table and offered his hand, forcing her to also lean forward. When she did, Remy caught a whiff of fresh, cold air, of the sweet, flowery fragrance that clung to the shawl still wrapped around her shoulders and, barely noticeable beneath the rest, her own fragrance—subtle and simple. The mix of scents was appealing. So was her wind-ruffled hair, the pinkness slowly fading from her cheeks and the faint glitter the cold had put into her eyes. The whole damn image was appealing.

There was just one problem.

She didn't want to appeal to *him*.

Damn her.

And damn his own judgment for being so far off. He'd never missed before. He had always known when a woman was attracted to him, when she would welcome his attention. He had never approached anyone who wasn't happy to be approached, who didn't share his interest.

So how had he managed to be so wrong about Susannah?

Maybe she'd been right. Maybe it had been some sort of gratitude complex. Maybe he had fixated on her because she had helped ease his fear and his pain, because she had offered him assurances at a time when he badly needed them. Maybe he was simply grateful to her, and he had let it get out of control.

No way. If he was grateful to anyone in the emergency room, it was the doctors. They were the ones who had spent hours putting his leg back together. They were the ones primarily responsible for his recovery.

Besides, he was a smart man. He could tell gratitude from attraction. He could damn sure recognize desire.

But he had failed to recognize her lack of desire. He had failed to notice that she didn't reciprocate his feelings. Maybe he wasn't so smart, after all. If he was, he never would have forced that scene back at his apartment. He never would have asked her to admit that she didn't care about him if he hadn't believed with all his heart that she did.

A smart man? he thought bitterly. No. Except for her ex-husband, he was the sorriest fool that ever lived.

"Remy."

Susannah's voice, soft and all too sweet, broke into his thoughts. For a moment, he ignored her. In forcing an answer from her this afternoon, he had done more than destroy the future—the fantasies—he had built around her. He had put himself in an impossible situation. He couldn't continue living with her, knowing how she felt. He couldn't pretend that it didn't matter. He couldn't see her every day and know that there was no hope for them.

But how could he let her go and never see her again?

"Quit daydreaming, Remy, and take the food," Valery commanded from across the table. "There are hungry people here."

Finally he focused his gaze on the dish Susannah was offering. Red beans and rice. Michael could cook anything, but he preferred Cajun. Tonight he had fixed a sampling—beans and rice, crabmeat gumbo and crawfish etouffée—with something equally rich for dessert. Ordinarily the mere smell of his cooking was enough to make Remy's mouth water, but tonight he had little appetite.

Taking the bowl from Susannah, he ladled a portion onto his plate before passing the dish on to Smith. He passed the other bowls around as they came to him, ate and even took part in the conversation, but he didn't notice what he was eating. He couldn't remember what was said.

God, he wished he could go home.

Alone.

Before he realized it, the meal was over and Susannah, Valery and Smith were clearing the table. Michael offered him the crutches that had been put in the corner out of the way and suggested that they move to the sofa where he could stretch his leg out.

"What's the problem?" Michael asked once they were settled in the living portion of the large room.

"What problem?" Remy arranged a pillow underneath his foot to protect the coffee table, then leaned back.

"Between you and Susannah."

Somehow he kept his expression even and blank. "Who says—"

"I do. You two haven't looked at each other since you got here. What gives?"

"There's nothing wrong between Susannah and me." And that was the truth. How could something be wrong when there was nothing between them?

"Right. That's why you've been off in another world most of the evening, and she's been afraid to even look up from the table, much less open her mouth."

Remy stubbornly refused to back down from his first response. He had always been honest with Michael, had confided practically everything in him, but he'd be damned if he'd sit here with Susannah across the room and repeat this afternoon's conversation to him now.

After a moment, Michael apparently decided to let it slide. "So you have a checkup tomorrow. What good news are you hoping for?"

"That my leg's healed, the cast can come off and I can go back to work." Then he shrugged and offered a more realistic response. "That my leg has healed enough to bear weight, I can trade the crutches for a cane and can finally take a shower again."

"When is the cast supposed to come off?"

"A couple more weeks."

"And then what?"

And then he had no excuse for having Susannah around any longer.

But that was already true. He had no excuse now. He had never been interested in her nursing, her housekeeping or cooking or driving. He'd never had any interest at all in a paid servant/companion, and that was all she was willing to be. The smart thing to do would be cut her loose now. Pay her the rest of the month's salary and send her back to the city, back to her apartment, her friends and a new job. Hell,

she might not even have to look for a new job; after only
two weeks, she might be able to get the old one back.

But he wasn't feeling particularly smart right now.

In fact, he felt pretty damned masochistic.

With a sigh, he turned his attention to Michael's last
question. "Then I begin physical therapy to rebuild the
muscles in my right leg, I rely on a cane until I can manage
on my own, and I go back to work on a limited basis. I have
checkups every month for six months, then every three
months. The doctor says I'll even be able to start jogging
again…oh, after a year or so. And after only one and a half
to two years, if everything's okay, they'll put me back in the
hospital, open my leg and remove the titanium plate. It's
something to look forward to, isn't it?"

Michael ignored the sarcasm that tinged his voice.
"You're alive, Remy. That's a hell of a lot to be grateful
for."

Immediately Remy felt ashamed of his attitude. He knew
how easily he could have died that night, and he knew that
if he had, it probably would have destroyed his friend. For
months Michael had blamed himself for Evan's death, because it had been *his* visions of the little girl in trouble that
had drawn Evan into the case. He hadn't wanted to survive
his own injuries, and when he had lived in spite of himself,
he'd done his best to drink himself to death.

It had been a tough time for all of them, but Remy and
Smith had finally reached Michael, had finally gotten him
out of the bottle and brought him—unwilling but coming
along anyway—back into the world. Then the visions of
Valery had started and, in the end, Remy had gotten shot.
If he had died, Michael would have once again blamed
himself, and there was no way he could have survived it a
second time.

"I know," he said quietly. "And I am damned grateful.
I just wish…" Letting the words trail off, he looked away.
He'd been given a precious gift—his life—but it wasn't
enough. He wanted someone to share it with. He wanted to

share it with Susannah, who didn't think that what he had to offer was worth taking.

After a brief silence, Michael spoke again. "I ran into Shawna Warren Friday."

Mention of the agent who had replaced him on the Falcone case lessened Remy's moodiness slightly. Shawna was a good agent, tougher than most of the men in the office and with an IQ that was practically off the charts. He liked her—had liked her enough, in fact, when she was first assigned to the office to spend a few evenings and one particularly memorable night with her before they had both decided that a personal relationship wasn't worth jeopardizing their professional relationship. He couldn't have asked for a better agent to take over his case.

Even if it had—pardon the bad joke—almost killed him to give it up.

"What's going on with her?" he asked.

"She was in her usual bad mood. She asked about you. Said she's not getting anywhere with Jimmy and that, as far as she's concerned, when the doctors let you return to work, you can have him back."

Remy scowled. "So she says. Let me try to take him, though, and she'll bite my hand off at the wrist. I was hoping they'd made some progress against Falcone."

"No, you weren't. You were hoping that things would just sort of idle along until you were back at work so you could bring the bastard down yourself. But you know that's not going to happen."

"I know. I can't be the case agent when I've become part of the case itself." He shook his head wistfully. "But it would have been nice to be the one to get him and all the sons of bitches who work for him. I'd like to see them all locked up for the rest of their worthless lives and know that I put them there."

"At least you'll know you helped. Probably ninety percent of the evidence you guys have against Falcone is stuff you dug up."

"Yeah, but I'd sure like to supply that last ten percent."

In the silence that followed, Remy's gaze shifted unwillingly to the small kitchen. Valery and Smith seemed to be doing most of the talking, while Susannah quietly washed the dishes that wouldn't fit into the dishwasher. Occasionally bits of their conversation drifted out and across the room, but not enough to make eavesdropping worthwhile.

Occasionally the sound of Susannah's laughter drifted out, too. Had he heard her laugh before tonight? he wondered bleakly. No. All he had managed to coax from her was a rare smile, and even those were usually tinged with emotions other than pleasure.

He had thought her ex-husband or some other problem, maybe whatever had put that sorrow in her eyes, was to blame for the rarity of her smiles. Now he knew it was because she didn't find any pleasure in his company. Because, while he'd wanted an affair, a commitment, a future, all she had wanted was to do her job. Because he hadn't given her the space and the peace of mind to do it.

Setting his brooding aside—after all, he had plenty of time for that back at Belle Ste. Claire—he turned his attention back to Michael. "How did it go with your family and Valery? Did they make any unfavorable comparisons to Beth?"

"Are you kidding? You know my folks weren't too fond of Beth. They weren't happy when we divorced, but it was more because there had never been a divorce in the family before, not because they were sorry to see her go." Michael looked at Valery with a tenderness that Remy envied—rather, what he envied was the fact that Valery always looked back with the same tenderness. "My grandmother adored her," Michael continued, "and she pretty much ruled the rest of the family."

"So you've got her blessing, and theirs. Is your father going to conduct the ceremony in his church?" At his nod, Remy chuckled. "Not many people can be married by their fathers even once, and here you'll be doing it for the second time."

"For the last time," Michael corrected, and Remy had no doubt his friend was right. He and Valery would be spending the rest of their lives together.

How long would it take, he wondered, for *him* to find someone to spend the rest of his life with?

How much longer would he have to live alone?

In the kitchen, Susannah dried her hands, then laid the dish towel on the counter. It had been a long time since she had shared a family meal—and even if there were no blood ties here, these people were, undoubtedly, family. Back home such meals had been as regular a part of her life as work on Monday morning and weekends off. Every Sunday after morning services, every holiday, every time a wandering relative passed through town and on any other occasion a person could think of, the families had gathered at one house or another. Being a very traditional bunch, the women had shared the cooking, the child care and the cleanup, while the men had eaten their fill and discussed crop prices, weather and politics. At the time such events hadn't carried any special significance for her; they were just a part of belonging to the Crouse family.

Now she knew how special they were. Now she missed them.

"You like chocolate, Susannah?" Michael asked, joining them in the small kitchen and wrapping his arms around Valery's waist.

"Doesn't everyone?"

"I don't know. Remy only eats it in cookies. Valery, on the other hand, inhales it as if it were vital to sustain life as we know it." He ignored Valery's teasing scowl as he released her, then eased past to the refrigerator. "Go on in and make yourself comfortable, and Val and I will serve dessert."

Susannah saw that Smith had already left and was seated in the chair directly across from Remy on the sofa, where they were deep in conversation. "First, do you mind if I use your phone? It's a local call."

"It's right there." He gestured toward a nearby table, where a cordless phone rested. Although she saw that he was clearly aware of her hesitation, for a moment, he didn't say anything else. Finally, though, he added, "It's the only phone I've got. You can take it into the bedroom."

"Thank you." Picking up the unit from the base, she made her way across the living room and into the bedroom, where she closed the door quietly behind her. There was only one chair in the room, placed between the windows, and she headed straight for it. It was big and comfortable, the sort of chair made for curling up and dreaming in.

But she had no time for dreams. Not this evening.

Quickly she dialed the number that had become too offensively familiar to her and asked for the man she had never met face-to-face but had come to hate with a passion. She didn't know if this number reached his home or office, or if possibly his office was in his home. All she knew was that she could use it to contact him anytime, night or day.

Nicholas Carlucci's voice was smooth, charming and underlaid with steel—with threat—as always. If he was annoyed to have his Sunday evening disturbed with business, he gave no hint of it. "I was beginning to wonder when I would hear from you."

"I've kept to our schedule," she said defensively.

"Yes, you have. But you were also told to call when schedules changed."

So he knew they were in the city. She was as sure of it as if he'd come right out and said so. And if he knew, then that meant he was still having them watched. It meant that he already didn't trust her. If she started lying to him now . . .

"I didn't know about Remy's plan to spend the night in town until he told me this morning. This is the first opportunity I've had to contact you."

There was silence on the other end for a long, unnerving moment. Then, at last, he spoke. "Are you staying at his apartment?"

"Yes."

"Is that where you're calling from?"

"No. We're at his friend's place."

"Which friend? Bennett or Kendricks?"

"Michael Bennett." She hesitated. "But Kendricks is here, too. And Valery Navarre."

"What are Remy's other plans for this trip?"

"Just the doctor's appointment in the morning."

"And after seeing the doctor, you'll be returning to Belclaire."

"As far as I know."

"Does it seem to you, Susannah, that he's keeping you in the dark? That perhaps he doesn't trust you with his plans too far in advance?"

Her voice turned haughty and cold. "I'm his employee, Mr. Carlucci. He tells me what he wants me to know when he wants me to know it. If you don't like the way things are going, release my brother and find someone else to help you."

The cynicism that had shaded his voice disappeared, leaving it smooth—oily smooth—again. "Things are going just fine, Susannah. I believe we'll hold on to young Skip a while longer. Mr. Falcone does enjoy his company." There was an interruption in the background, then his manner became all business. "Very well, Susannah. I'll expect to hear from you...shall we say Friday? Unless, of course, something changes before then."

Before he could hang up, she spoke abruptly. "I want to talk to Skip."

"I'm sorry. He can't come to the phone now. Goodbye, Susannah." There was a click, followed by a dial tone.

Muttering a curse, Susannah returned the phone switch to Off, then stared for a moment into the distance. After a time she realized that she was staring at a portrait of Valery, beautiful and as ethereal as any angel. It was the work of an artist passionately involved with his subject—Michael's work. How wonderful it must be, she thought wistfully, to know passion like that.

Remy had offered *her* such passion. If she found some solution to her predicament, and if she could convince him

to give her a second chance, maybe she could accept . . .
temporarily, at least. Maybe she could know just once in her
life what it was like to experience such ardor. Maybe she
could believe in him and, for a time, believe in herself.
Maybe she could gather enough memories to last the rest of
her life.

Until he found out the truth about her.

Until he knew how she had lied. How she had betrayed
him.

Until he started hating her with as much passion as he had
ever wanted her.

From the next room came a burst of masculine laughter.
She needed to rejoin them, but first there was one more call
she wanted to make. This was a familiar number, too—her
home number. On the second ring the answering machine
picked up. She listened to only a few words of Skip's *We
can't take your call* message before pushing the proper buttons to access the messages.

There were only three—one from a friend for Skip, one
for her from an X-ray technician at work and a second for
her from . . . She whispered a little prayer.

"Hey, Suzanne, I don't know if you'll be checking for
messages, but this is the only way I know to get hold of
you," came Skip's voice. "I've got to be quick—I don't
know when they'll be back. I'm sorry about all this, Suz. I
know that's not good enough . . . I know I really screwed up
this time . . . but it'll never happen again, I swear. I promise, really. When this is over, I'm going home, and I'll never,
ever—" Suddenly his voice dropped to a whisper. "Gotta
go. Love you, Suz."

Her hands trembling, she pressed the button to replay the
last message. When the machine signaled the end the second time, she disconnected and gave a great shuddering
sigh. He was her brother, one of the dearest people in her
life. She had promised their mother on her deathbed that she
would always take care of him, had promised their father
that she would look out for him and keep him safe.

Could she really break those promises now? Could she do anything other than exactly what Nicholas Carlucci was asking of her? Could she take any chances at all when, with the slightest slipup, it was Skip who would have to pay the consequences?

Could she trust someone else—Remy, Smith, Michael or anyone—to care about her brother as deeply, as intensely, as she did, to put his best interests ahead of everything else as she did?

She didn't know.

God help her, she just didn't know.

Rubbing the ache that throbbed between her eyes, she wearily got to her feet. She couldn't think about this anymore, and she'd been in here long enough to surely arouse suspicion, at least in Remy and Michael. It was time to return to the living room. Time to pretend that nothing was wrong.

Time to, once again, start living her lies.

Sunday evening had been chilly and damp with fog— suitably dreary for February—but Monday was as sunny and clear as any midsummer morning. Susannah stood at one of the three wide windows in Remy's guest room, gazing out across the grounds. A broad expanse of ground separated his building from the next, and it was heavily planted with trees—weeping willows, crape myrtles, dogwoods and oaks. Shrubs provided natural barriers between neighbors, and bulbs bloomed along the winding sidewalks.

It was a lovely place, she thought with a smile. Three and a half miles and a world away from the apartment she shared with Skip, where the few trees that hadn't been uprooted were scraggly, where not a single flower bloomed and—thanks to the neighbors' kids—where the grass grew best in the cracks of the sidewalks.

She hadn't lied yesterday—for once—when she'd told Remy that she wasn't ashamed of where she lived. Granted, it *was* a world away from his life, but she knew better than to judge people by such things. After all, she'd grown up on a farm, where extra money went to improving the operation, buying new stock, replacing worn-out equipment, hiring extra help or saving for the inevitable bad season. A fancy place to live came pretty low in a farmer's priorities. A house in good repair was enough to satisfy most people she knew—and her apartment, while not luxurious like this place, was in good repair.

It would be different when this was all over. Skip would be back home in Nebraska, their father's responsibility once more, and she would be supporting only herself. For the first time in her life she would be truly on her own. Before her marriage she had lived at home—apartments or rental homes were scarce to nonexistent in Homestead. After the wedding, she had moved in with Guy with the assumption that it would be a partnership, that they would each contribute to the household expenses, only Guy had had other ideas. *She* had paid all the living expenses, including his car payment, and he had spent his money on...

She smiled faintly. To this day, she didn't know where his money had gone. No doubt he had blown much of it partying and playing poker with his buddies, and another substantial chunk had likely been spent on his other women. He liked to impress the women he dated, the way he had impressed her.

After the divorce, she had moved back home, back to the room her father had kept waiting for her, and then she had come to New Orleans. Skip had been more than happy to have her live with him; his roommate had moved out a few months before, and the rent was killing him. She had naively believed his promise that they would split expenses right down the middle. Of course, that was before she had discovered that he didn't have a regular job, that when he was working, he spent his money on things more important—meaning more fun—than necessities.

The day she moved in, he had hit her up for a loan. The rent was past due, as were the electric bill, his car payment and his car insurance. The telephone company was threatening to disconnect the phone, and his long-distance bill—for all those calls to his old buddies back home—was astronomical. "It's no problem for you, Suz," he had said with his most charming grin. "You're so reliable about saving. I'll pay you back, I swear."

I swear. Two of her brother's favorite words. *I'll pay you back, I swear. It'll never happen again, I swear.* And why shouldn't he use them so casually? That was all it took to win forgiveness from anyone in the family—Uncle Richard, Aunt Salley, their father and Susannah herself. They were all suckers for Skip's grin accompanied by an "I swear...."

Look how he had paid her back this time.

With a sigh, she turned away from the window, pulled her robe on and took a large freezer bag from the dresser. Inside were her shampoo and conditioner, toothbrush and toothpaste and a smaller zippered bag containing the bare essentials from her makeup case. She crossed the plush rug and a chilly section of wood floor to the door, then stepped out into the hall just as Remy came out of his room, directly across from hers.

They both stopped abruptly, and she uncomfortably pulled her robe tighter. He was already dressed in sweatpants and a T-shirt. His jaw was clean-shaven, and his hair was slicked back, a dark, wet gold. He looked well rested and handsome. So handsome.

For a moment, she thought he was going to smile, the way he did every morning, but he caught himself and instead simply looked at her. He had, in the past eighteen hours or so, developed a way of looking right at her and straight on through her, as if she were nothing of substance but simply a vague visual disturbance. It made her feel small and insignificant.

It hurt.

Clutching the plastic bag in both hands, she offered him a taut smile. "Good morning."

He didn't speak.

Wetting her lips, she tried again. "I noticed last night that you don't have any food in the house. Would you like me to go out and get something before your appointment, or would you rather stop on the way?"

He looked away then, directing his gaze toward the stairs—no doubt wishing he had escaped down them a moment or two sooner and damning his cast and crutches for slowing him down. "I'm not hungry."

Such simple words to send such a shiver down her spine. She had never heard a colder, emptier voice. "All right. What time do we need to leave for your appointment?"

"Eight-thirty."

"I'll be ready. Do you want me to pack first, or will we come back here before returning to Belle Ste. Claire?"

His gaze flickered across her face, then away again. "Get everything taken care of now. I want to get home as soon as possible." With that, he walked away, easing past her, then carefully making his way down the stairs.

He wanted to get away from her as soon as possible, she knew. This morning he had to spend time with her—here in the apartment, in the car, at the doctor's office—but back at Belle Ste. Claire, avoiding her would be relatively simple. There were very distinct territories in the old house—family quarters as opposed to servants'. He could go wherever he wanted, while she could, quite fairly, be restricted to the back of the house—the kitchen, the laundry room and her own room. Except for the little tasks of daily straightening and cleaning she had taken on in the parlor, there was no reason for her to set foot in any of the family living areas.

She didn't know if he would put such restrictions on her, although it was only fair if he did. After all, *she* was the one who had wanted a strictly business arrangement. *She* was the one who had insisted there was nothing personal between them. *She* was the reason he felt this need to stay away.

But if he did, if he limited her to her working areas, if he began taking his meals in the parlor or the dining room

while she ate in the kitchen, if he spent his long, free hours
ignoring her...

It was going to be a very lonely way to live.

At the bottom of the stairs, Remy listened for the soft
shuffle that meant she had finally moved from where he'd
left her. When he heard it at last, he swung away on his
crutches, crossing the foyer to the study. The room was
large, high ceilinged, done in dark woods and rich colors.

He realized for the first time that it was very much like his
father's study at Belle Ste. Claire. When he had chosen these
colors, this furniture, had he subconsciously been trying to
duplicate a little bit of home here in his apartment? Possibly. Probably.

He settled in the chair and leaned back. Like his father,
he kept photographs on his desk. There was one of himself
with his three friends, taken only a few months before
Evan's death. A picture of Valery, which was taken a year
or two ago, obtained by the FBI from his parents when she
had disappeared after witnessing Nate Simmons's death.
Copies had been distributed to everyone involved in the
case, and his had ended up here in a small brass frame.
There was a snapshot of Evan and his wife Karen. He saw
her around town from time to time, but the basis for their
friendship had been lost when her husband died. She had to
get on with her life and, he suspected, having little contact
with him, Michael or Smith made that easier.

The last frame held a picture of his parents. He wasn't
sure how old it was—more than fifteen years. In it his
mother's hair was still blond, while his father's was just
starting to show a little gray. They had been an attractive
couple, and they still were. They had aged well, partly because they had aged together.

He thought of Susannah, who didn't want to grow old
with anyone, least of all him, and he felt as if he were already old. But he would get over it, he told himself. He just
wasn't used to misjudging a woman. He wasn't used to being rejected by a woman. But he had no doubt he could deal

with it, because he was very used to not being able to have what he wanted.

It would just take time.

And distance.

He was still sitting there, doing nothing, when she came looking for him a short while later. He had never known a woman who could shower, dress, fix her hair and do her makeup as quickly as Susannah. He had never known a woman who looked so good.

She wore suede moccasins that were run-down to the point where they were truly comfortable, faded jeans and an ivory sweater with the sleeves pushed to her elbows. Her hair was down, pulled back on each side with a tortoiseshell comb, and her expression was sad. He wished he could pull her into his arms, wished he could hold her there in his favorite chair in his favorite room and simply stroke her cares away.

He wished he didn't have to remember to keep his distance, physically and especially emotionally.

She was carrying both of their bags, small and lightly packed. She set them on the tile before venturing into the room. "Everything's ready."

By that he had no doubt that she meant she had made the beds, straightened the bathroom, repacked every single item she had unpacked yesterday and probably even plumped the pillows on the sofa where he had lain yesterday. Except for the faint scents they would leave behind them—her perfume, his after-shave—the apartment would bear no sign that they'd even been there.

When she didn't say anything else, he gestured for her to have a seat. "How long will this appointment take?" he asked, careful to keep his tone perfectly neutral.

She sat stiffly on the edge of the chair. "If the doctor's on schedule, it should be fairly quick. He'll ask if you've had any problems and get an X ray. If everything looks good, they'll fit you with a boot—a sort of sandal made of canvas with Velcro closures and a rubber sole—and a cane. That'll be it."

"A cane," he repeated softly. "My grandfather walked with a cane. I don't think he needed it, though. It was just awfully convenient for getting someone's attention."

She started to smile, but didn't get past the faintest beginnings. A part of him was tempted to go ahead and coax it out of her. The stronger part, the part in charge of self-preservation, knew it was wiser not to try.

"What if everything doesn't look good?"

Gradually she settled back in the chair. "The biggest problems would be with nonunion, meaning the bone isn't healing properly, or infection. I don't think either one would be much of a concern at this point. When they changed the cast before you were discharged from the hospital, the gunshot wound was nicely healed and the X rays looked good. You've followed their instructions, stayed off your leg and used the crutches. You're probably in good shape."

Swiveling his chair just a bit, he shifted his gaze from her to the wall where three framed certificates hung together. One was his college degree. The second was his law degree, and the third was the certificate he had received upon finishing training at the FBI Academy. "What are the chances—" He broke off. The question on his mind had occurred to him not immediately after getting shot—then he had been concerned about whether he would live—but soon after arriving at the hospital. But he had never found the courage to ask it. He preferred to ignore the possibilities, preferred to be optimistic and to believe that everything was going to be just fine.

The closer it came to the time for removing the cast, though, the more often the question popped up, and this morning he was feeling just morose enough to ask it.

Except that he didn't have to. "That there could be a problem?" she asked softly. "It's a possibility. Because of its weight-bearing job, the femur is a nasty bone to break, and your break was particularly bad, with the added complication of the gunshot wound. There's always the possibility of a not-so-good result. But it's remote."

"How remote?"

"I'm not a doctor. I can't give you a definite answer. But your recovery has been normal so far. There's no reason to believe your prognosis is anything less than good." She paused, then added, "There's no reason to think you might not be able to continue working as an FBI agent."

He started to deny it but, of course, that had been exactly what he was wondering about. "You know," he began, his gaze fixed on his degrees, his tone soft and distant as if he were speaking to himself, "when I joined the bureau, I was just looking for a job. I went through the academy with these people who had wanted to be FBI agents all their lives, people who had grown up knowing that was what they were going to do, but I didn't have that certainty, that dedication or zeal. I just wanted a job that would make use of my education, pay a decent wage and maybe someday make my parents proud of me. It's funny. Some of those dedicated people didn't make it through the academy. Some of them did and have since quit. But I'm still here. I know now that this is what I want to do. *Always.*"

He glanced at her, then immediately looked away again. "I don't know what I would do if I couldn't be an agent."

"You would make use of that education," she replied. "You've been one of the good guys. Now, if necessary, you can be a lawyer." He heard the soft creak of the chair as she got to her feet. "Don't go looking for trouble. All you need to worry about today is whether you get off the crutches. In a few weeks you can worry about getting the cast removed, and after that happens, you can worry about how long it takes for things to start feeling normal again. The time to worry about any long-term problems is when you find out that you have them. Not until then."

"That's an easy enough attitude for you to take," he said, glancing at his watch, then also standing up, though without her grace. "*You're* not the one who would have to be a lawyer."

She left the apartment first, carrying their bags and her purse. Behind her, he pulled the door shut and locked it, then for a moment simply stood there and watched her. The

sunlight glinting on her hair brought out the reddish high-
lights and deepened the faint golden hue of her skin. There
was something about her, something missing in the other
women he knew. Something innocent. Something whole-
some.

If this was what growing up on a farm did for you, he
thought with a reluctant smile, then hurray for America's
farmers and every one of their daughters.

By the time he reached the car, she was waiting at his door
to take his crutches. She stowed them in the back seat, then
circled to the driver's side. After he gave her directions to the
medical complex where the orthopedic surgeon's office was
located, the rest of the trip passed in silence. There had been
many silences between them, but none, he thought, as uncomfortable as this one. It was because he wanted to talk to
her, wanted to share one thing or another with her. Several
times he caught himself about to speak, and then he remembered the new order: strictly business.

He'd said more than he should have this morning, but at
least it had been medically related. In the future he had to
restrict their conversation even more. There could be no
more confidences, no more reminiscing. He had to remember that she was his employee. Not his friend. Not his companion. Certainly not anything more intimate.

As soon as she pulled into a parking space in front of the
doctor's office building, he unfastened his seat belt. "If
you're right and the doctor's on schedule, this shouldn't
take long," he said as he opened the door, then carefully
swung his leg out. "You can wait here."

Although his back was to her, he could tell that she'd become very still. Then he heard the slithering sound as the
seat belt she had already unfastened rewound in its case.
"All right," she agreed quietly. She got out of the car anyway, retrieving his crutches from the back and brought them
around to him. She avoided looking at him and, after one
glance to see that, he avoided her, too.

She hadn't parked far from the door, but it seemed to take
him forever to reach it. This was the first time in a month

that he'd been allowed to go anywhere without someone at his side. It felt odd.

It felt freeing.

And just a little bit lonely.

Surprisingly the doctor was on schedule. Not surprisingly, the appointment went exactly as Susannah had predicted. He asked Remy a few questions, sent him off for X rays, told him the films looked fine and had one of his assistants—girls, he called them—fit him with a boot. Lastly they gave him a cane—simple, wooden, with a rounded handle. When he got home, he thought grimly, he would look for his grandfather's cane; knowing his mother, it was stored somewhere in the house. If he had to rely on an old man's cane to get around, it would at least be a cane with character.

Susannah was out of the car when he hobbled outside, seated on the curb in the empty space beside the car. Abruptly she got to her feet, brushing her jeans off as she rose, and came to meet him. She took his crutches, then matched her pace to his. "Does that feel better?"

"It's definitely easier." He hesitated. "Is my leg supposed to be a little sore?"

"That'll go away in a day or two. Remember, you haven't had any weight on that leg in more than a month. You'll get used to it." She didn't speak again until they were in the car. "Back to Belle Ste. Claire now?"

Two weeks ago, he had been absolutely thrilled by the prospect of returning to Belle Ste. Claire. He had gone with such hopes, such anticipation. If he could go back to Belle Ste. Claire, could once again call it home, then anything was possible.

Even building a relationship with Susannah.

Especially building a relationship with her.

But he'd been wrong.

With a weary sigh, he reclined the seat and fixed his gaze out the side window. "Yeah," he agreed listlessly. "Back to Belle Ste. Claire."

* * *

Susannah rarely had trouble sleeping, but after more than four hours of tossing and turning, she was no closer to drifting off than when she'd first crawled between the covers. Finally pushing them back, she pulled her robe on, felt around on the floor for her fuzzy booties and pulled them on, too. Then she quietly slipped out of her room and down the hall. She didn't bother with lights; by now, she knew her way to and around the kitchen with her eyes closed.

At the table she pulled out the chair closest to the window, propped her feet on the sill and gazed out across the lawn. Moonlight shone on the old barn and the tumbling fence but got lost in the trees behind them. Once the Sinclairs had kept horses and a few cattle, but not in Remy's lifetime. The barn, she knew from her explorations, held a few pieces of ancient farm equipment, some musty old hay and some junk. It really ought to be torn down, the realist in her admitted; it was generations past its prime and no longer served a purpose.

But her romantic side thought that it, like the fence, added a certain charm to the landscape. Someday the honeysuckle and jessamine vines that climbed the sides and wound in through the doors and between the slats would completely cover the building. They would help support it at the same time they overtook it, until one day it would collapse, a heap of rubbish beneath wiry vines and fragrant flowers.

She felt rather like the barn herself—fragile, none too stable, with a tough web of delicate vines pulling her apart even as they held her together. Her promises to her mother and father, her promises to Skip, her deceit and betrayal, Nicholas Carlucci's demands, Remy's offers, Jimmy Falcone's evil and her own honor... Everything was wound together to pull her in a dozen different directions—and all of them down. She knew what she should do, what she wanted to do, what she had to do, and she knew of no way to do it all.

Rescue Skip.

Protect Remy.

Save herself.

But rescuing Skip required sacrificing Remy, and saving herself required protecting Remy, which meant sacrificing Skip. There was no way out.

Was there?

How much easier it would be if she could simply turn her back on her brother. He was, after all, twenty-three, an adult by any legal standards. But he was a very young twenty-three—immature, spoiled, irresponsible—and she was, in part, responsible for his irresponsibility. The family had never set any standards for him. They had never taught him to take care of himself. They had failed him in so many ways.

She knew there was a time to stand back, to wash her hands of him, to leave him to sink or swim on his own.

But that time wasn't when he'd gotten himself caught in a life-and-death situation.

He would get one last assist from his big sister, she silently promised, and then no more help. No more advice. No more money. No more support. Nothing but love.

As for Remy, how could she protect him without help? She could watch out for strangers, could keep him close to home, could be alert for anything suspicious, but she doubted that would be enough. She didn't know how Falcone planned to have him killed. It seemed that those people had preferred methods of killing, but maybe that was only on TV. Nate Simmons had been shot at close range walking down a public street in the middle of the day. Remy had also been shot at close range, only at a private meeting on a wharf under cover of darkness. This time they could be planning a drive-by shooting, a bomb, a hit-and-run accident, a break-in, a fire. The possibilities were endless.

The responsibility was enormous—more than she could bear.

Everything was more than she could bear.

Too weary to worry any longer, she drew her knees up and rested her chin on them. She would relinquish half the years allotted her if only she could start this job anew. If Skip wasn't in trouble. If she wasn't deceiving Remy. If she could accept what he had offered.

If things were different, she would have long since left Guy and all his hurts and cruelties in the past.

She would have discovered what it was like to know true passion.

All her old wounds would have healed. All her broken dreams would be mended.

If things were different, she would be facing a future filled with hope, with family, with marriage and children.

She would be well on her way to in love with Remy.

If things were different...

She smiled tearfully in the quiet, moonlit kitchen. She'd never been one to fool herself. Things *weren't* different and weren't likely to change. The only passion she was likely to find with Remy would be temporary, only until he discovered the truth about her. Her old wounds *would* heal, but the wounds in the making would last forever. There was no hope in her future—and no family, no marriage, no children.

And as for love with Remy...

Only in her dreams.

Chapter 8

He just wasn't cut out for the role he was playing.

By Wednesday morning, Remy knew things couldn't go on the way they were. He couldn't ignore Susannah, couldn't avoid her, couldn't take his meals separate from her. He couldn't live in the same house with her, couldn't sleep across the hall from her, and not acknowledge her presence. He couldn't continue treating her as if he didn't give a damn about her because, whether she wanted him to or not, he did.

He cared too damn much.

When he went looking for her, he found her in the laundry room, seated in an old slatted rocker, placed to take advantage of the morning light coming through the tall windows. Between the sun and the heat from the dryer, the small utility porch was warm, and Susannah, only occasionally rocking back and forth, looked drowsy. Maybe that was because she wasn't sleeping well at night. No matter how quiet she was, he heard her when she slipped from her bed in the middle of the night. He listened to her pad down the hall in those silly furry slippers of hers, heard the scrape of the chair as she sat down at the table and heard her when, after an hour or two, she padded back to the privacy of her room.

Last night he thought that, while she was up, he had heard her crying. He had wanted to go to her, to find out what was wrong, to somehow make it right, but self-preservation had kept him in his room. Middle-of-the-night rejections were hard on a man, especially one whose ego was as fragile as his was right now.

And so he had lain there in the dark, listening and waiting, and after a time, she had wandered back to her bed.

He navigated the few steps down onto the porch with care, then leaned against the washer. Her eyes closed, her hands loosely clasped across her middle, she rocked on, unaware of him until he spoke her name. "Susannah."

Abruptly she looked at him; then, just as quickly, she dropped her gaze in a manner that could be described only as subservient. He hated it. "I'm sorry," she said in that unnaturally quiet voice that was all he'd heard lately. "I didn't hear you."

"I guess this is a comfortable place to be on a cool morning."

She murmured her agreement as she uncrossed her legs and settled both feet on the floor. "Did you need something?"

He walked over to the door, pretending to gaze out across the lawn. In truth, his peripheral vision was focused on her. She was sitting upright now, all the lazy drowsiness gone. He liked her when she was soft and relaxed; she seemed more approachable that way. Now he could fairly feel the tension humming through her, could see it, he thought, in the way she held her head and clenched her jaw . . . and all because he had walked into the room.

His regret was almost enough to make him walk out again, to leave her to her sunshine and the rocker and the low, hypnotic tumble of the dryer. But he couldn't keep walking away.

After a moment, he turned his gaze outward. "We need to talk, Susannah."

There was a blur of movement—auburn hair, white shirt, blue jeans—as she rose from the chair and opened the dryer door, bringing it to a stop. She removed a selected armload of towels, closed the door and started it tumbling again, then began folding the towels. "You want me to leave."

He turned around, watching her openly now, admiring each efficient move. She gave each towel a shake, then smoothed it out across the top of the washer, folding it in half, then again and again. The scent of fabric softener and tiny particles of lint drifted into the warm air. "No, Susannah, I don't want you to leave," he admitted. "I want..." He thought better of finishing, sighed heavily and went on. "I want to be friends with you."

That caught her attention. Slowly she became still, and even more slowly she turned to face him. She still held a brightly patterned bath towel, and as she brought her gaze to his, she wrapped her hands tightly over and over in the terry cloth. "Friends?" she repeated. "Just friends?"

Damn his ears for playing tricks on him. He could swear that she sounded almost disappointed that that was all he was asking for. "Just friends."

"Why?"

"Because I don't like the way things have been the last few days. I thought it would be easier under the circumstances if we had little contact with each other, but it's not easier. It's just lonely."

She twisted the towel tighter. "It would be easier if you fired me," she suggested, her voice brittle.

"Is that what you want? To be fired? So you can go back to New Orleans and say, 'I did my best, but working for him was impossible'?" He meant his words as gentle mockery, but there was guilt in her hazel eyes. Such guilt. "Who do you need an excuse for, Susannah? Who are you answerable to?"

"No one," she murmured.

He wasn't sure he believed her. It was possible, he supposed, that she merely needed the excuse for herself. She *was* the sort of person who took failure personally, regardless of whose fault it was. Her marriage was proof of that. But he wasn't entirely sure he believed that there was no one waiting for her back in the city. After all, there were those secretive phone calls, and the fact that she paid to have her mail delivered in town when she could have almost as great a guarantee of privacy if it came here.

"Is it the money?" Maybe she thought that, if he fired her, instead of giving her notice, he would pay the remainder of the month's salary. It would only be fair—and it was exactly what he would do. "You'll get the full month's pay whether you're here, you quit, or I fire you."

"Why would you do that?" She sounded not exactly interested, as if she might take him up on it, but rather curious. As if it didn't matter but she would like to know anyway.

"Because the only reason I would fire you is if we can't find some way to get along. And the only reason you would quit is if I make it impossible for you to stay. Either way, I would be at least partially responsible. Paying your full salary would be the least of my obligations."

At last she began unwinding the towel from around her hands. She turned back to the washer and to the folding that awaited her. "I don't want to quit," she admitted in a soft, husky voice.

"And I have no intention of firing you. So that leaves getting along." He joined her near the machines, where a wooden shelf painted white had been nailed to what had once been the house's outer wall. The paint was peeling now, and the wood showed gray underneath, but it was still sturdy enough to support his weight when he leaned on it. "I'll admit, Susannah, that I'd still like to have a whole lot more than friendship with you, but... I'm willing to settle for whatever you want to offer. I don't like the way we've been living. I miss you. I miss talking to you. I miss being in the kitchen with you while you cook. I miss spending evenings in the parlor with you."

She gave him a sidelong glance, accompanied by what might have been a shy smile if it had managed to form. "I've missed you, too."

He couldn't resist his answering grin even as he gently warned, "Careful there, or I might start thinking you like me a little bit, after all—and after you've spent two weeks convincing me that you don't."

After folding one last towel, she turned to face him. For once her gaze was incredibly direct. "I never said that I don't like you, Remy."

His grin disappeared as he straightened and leaned on the cane instead of the shelf. The particular conversation they were discussing had been too painful to take lightly. "I asked you to tell me that you didn't give a damn about me, and you said—"

"That I was sorry."

"Right. Sorry because you couldn't deny it. Sorry because you *didn't* care. Sorry—"

"I said that I was sorry because . . . I do care and because I don't have the right to. I was sorry because I was lying and I knew it would hurt you and there was nothing I could do about it. I was . . . I am very sorry."

Slowly he went to stand at the door again. There he stared out a long time, watching birds on the newly budded trees. If he opened the door, he could hear their song, a sure sign that spring with all its lush growth and beauty was on its way.

But he didn't open the door. He concentrated instead on Susannah's answer. He had never heard words both so hopeful and so lacking in hope in the same sentence. In one breath, she admitted that she did care for him, and in the next she made it sound as if that caring was inconsequential. She cared enough to not want to hurt him, but not enough to stop herself from doing it anyway. And that last sentence seemed to indicate that nothing had changed.

"Why don't you have the right to care?" he asked at last. "Are you married?"

"No."

"Are you in love with another man?"

"No."

So far, so good. Of course, he had already known those answers. Now for the tough one. "Are you involved with another man?"

She sighed audibly over the dryer. "Remy..."

He turned to face her. The sunlight, warm on his back, unmercifully lit her face. She couldn't hide even the slightest nuance of emotion. "Are you involved with another man? Are you seeing someone, dating someone, living with someone? Are you having an affair with someone? Are you some guy's mistress?"

Sighing again, she shook her head. "No."

He believed her. Those eyes couldn't lie. They were too clear, her gaze too direct, too open and honest. "So what's to stop you from getting involved with me?"

Leaving the dryer, she took the few steps necessary to close the distance between them. "Common sense. A sense of honor. You keep insisting that you know me, Remy, but you really don't. Maybe you like what you've discovered so far, but that's not who I am, not entirely. I've done things that I'm not proud of. I've made mistakes. I've created problems. I know myself better than you ever will, and I don't see a whole lot of possibilities here for us."

"That's because your vision is so narrow. You judge yourself more harshly than anyone else ever will. You're not open to a whole lot of possibilities because you're afraid of getting hurt again. I'm not. I would never hurt you, Susannah."

"But I might hurt you," she whispered.

She had warned him of that before. He responded in much the same way as he had then. "Maybe you will, but I'm willing to take that chance. Anything worth having is worth taking a risk. And who knows, Susannah? Maybe we'll surprise you. Maybe we'll fall in love and live happily the rest of our lives.''

A fleeting wistfulness crossed her face, convincing him far more than her words that she did care about him, more than she wanted him to know. More, perhaps, than she was even aware of herself. She wanted that, wanted to fall in love and live long and happily.

But she was afraid. ''And maybe you'll die, regretting the day we met,'' she whispered.

''That won't happen.''

''It could. You don't know—''

He laid his fingers across her mouth, silencing her. ''I'm not a naive man, Susannah. I've seen more bad things, more problems and mistakes and hurts than you could ever imagine. I've seen all the evil one person can do to another. Believe me when I say there is nothing you or anyone else could do that would ever make me regret meeting you.''

She pushed his hand away. ''You're too trusting, Remy.''

His laughter was spontaneous. ''I don't believe anyone has ever accused an FBI agent of being too trusting.''

''You trusted your partner, and it almost got you killed.''

''True. But I won't be fooled again.''

Oh, but he would be. He was being fooled right now, Susannah thought with an ache around her heart. But at least he would live to regret it. She would see to that.

She had spent hours last night mapping out her strategy. She knew nothing about making deals and even less about negotiating with an Ivy League prosecutor who was, according to Michael Bennett, the best damn prosecutor around. No doubt Smith Kendricks played hardball and played to win.

But she had a few things in her favor. Smith and Remy were like brothers—closer, even, than most brothers—and just as she would do anything to protect her brother, so would he to protect Remy. There was also the fact that she, God help her, had become a more important part of Jimmy Falcone's organization than her brother had ever been. If she offered herself in his place, surely Smith would agree to let him go. After all, as Skip had told her—and Nicholas Carlucci had verified—her brother had never been involved in any major undertakings for Falcone. Yes, he had committed some minor crimes, and yes, he deserved punishment, but not the long-term prison sentence Falcone had threatened to set him up for.

He certainly didn't deserve to die for his foolishness.

So she would make a deal with Smith. She would make it clear to him that keeping Skip alive and safe had to be as important to the government as keeping Remy safe. She would make him understand that she was offering information against only Falcone, Carlucci and herself—not the three of them, plus Skip.

She would make certain he understood that Remy's life depended on their working together.

She had no doubt that Smith would deal with her. Why shouldn't he? He would be protecting his best friend *and* getting evidence to use against the man he was trying to lock away.

And what would she get?

Skip's safety.

Remy's life.

And a few more days with him.

Carlucci had scheduled her next check-in for Friday. Surely that meant he had nothing planned before then, didn't it? She didn't trust the lawyer to tell her when it was going to happen—she sure as hell didn't trust him to give her any warning so that she could stop them—but surely he wouldn't have planned another phone call if he intended to conclude their business before then.

So she would call him Friday.

After she called Smith.

After she'd shared just these next few days with Remy.

Abruptly she realized that he was watching her, waiting patiently for her. In some ways, he was the most patient man she'd ever known. In other ways, he was as impatient as hell.

He was smiling whimsically when she finally focused her attention on him. "Where do you go when you disappear into your thoughts like that?"

"Just away," she murmured. After a moment, she sighed. "You're a persuasive man, Remy."

"What does that mean?"

"It means I still don't have anything to offer. That I can't promise you won't regret this. That it might wind up costing both of us more than we can afford to pay. But . . . I do want you. I do care about you." She smiled very, very faintly. "I'm willing to take a few risks."

He remained still and unresponsive for a long, long time. Then, as he took her hands, a slow smile came to him. "Such a romantic proposal, Susannah," he teased as gently as he touched her.

"You said you preferred the honest approach. That's as honest as I can be. If we both go into this with our eyes open . . . maybe we can both come out of it okay."

"Maybe we can come out of it better than okay," he said, pulling her into his arms. "I'll be the optimist."

And she would be the realist, she whispered silently as she pressed her cheek to his shirt. Of course, it was easier to be realistic when she knew everything she was keeping from him.

He held her only a moment before filling his hands with her hair and tilting her head back. "I haven't even gotten to kiss you yet."

"You kissed me outside that day," she reminded him.

"Doesn't count. That was a pale imitation of the real thing."

A pale imitation? It had left her barely capable of breathing and utterly incapable of moving. It had touched her more sweetly, more deeply, than a thousand of Guy's most passionate kisses. "How about letting me be the judge of . . ."

Her remark died away unfinished as he covered her mouth with his. A pale imitation? Oh, yes. Who needed breath or the ability to move? Who needed anything more than this—his mouth on hers, his tongue stroking hers, his body supporting hers?

He kissed her sweetly, gently, then hungrily, his tongue alternately teasing, then satisfying. He stirred her arousal to life with no more than his kiss, without caresses, without tender touches. He heated her blood, made her weak and stole all thought from her mind. All she could do was feel, and all she could feel was need—sweet, fiery, demanding, throbbing need.

There was a time, Remy thought hazily, for finesse, for subtlety, for seduction, but this wasn't it. He was too aroused, and she was too willing. He had waited so long, had wanted so long, and now he craved, could damn near taste, the satisfaction his dreams and his fantasies and her body had promised him. Holding her tight, still kissing her hard, he moved blindly to the side, seeking and finding the old rocker. He sank into it, pulling her with him, settling her across his lap where his erection pressed intimately against her, and he pulled her shirt free of her jeans. He opened the buttons easily and pushed the garment off her shoulders, then dispatched her bra with as little care.

He cupped her breasts in his hands, blindly stroking them, teasing her nipples and making her groan. Ending the kiss at last, he was bending his head to her breast when, with surprising strength, she stopped him.

"Remy, no."

For a moment he simply stared at her, certain he had misunderstood. His heart was pounding, his blood was rushing, his entire body was throbbing. Surely he hadn't heard properly.

But that long look said he had. She sat there astride him, her hair mussed, naked to the waist, her breasts soft and her nipples achingly hard, and with such an exquisite look of regret on her face.

"Remy, we can't..."

Leaning back against the chair, he deliberately stroked his fingertips across her breast, bringing them together on her nipple in a gentle squeeze. The action made her gasp, made her eyes close, made her go all soft and weak right before his eyes. "Don't tell me you aren't interested," he said quietly.

When she looked at him again, she looked drowsy and too perfectly aroused to put up a fuss over anything but stopping. But with a few unsteady breaths, she gathered her strength. "I couldn't lie about it if I wanted to."

"So what's the problem?"

She touched his face, stroking his cheek and along his jaw. "It's me." With an awkward little smile, she started to push away, to climb clumsily off his lap. "I can't talk sitting like this."

He caught her, though, one hand on each of her thighs, and held her, pressed hard against him, for a moment, savoring the pain and the pleasure of being so close…and yet so far. At last, though, he released her, and, taking her shirt, she retreated to sit on the top step leading into the house.

She smoothed the shirt, then slipped her arms into the sleeves and pulled it on. She didn't button it, though. With each breath she took, he could see the full curves of her breasts. When she was still, he could make out the swell of her nipples underneath the fabric. Sitting there like that, her hair needing brushing, her cheeks pink and her mouth obviously well kissed, she presented, he decided, quite possibly the most erotic image he'd ever seen.

After searching for a way to begin, she offered him a faint smile and said, "You've never asked much about my marriage."

"I know the important stuff."

"What's that?"

"I know that your ex-husband lied to you. That he was cruel to you. I know that you're not still in love with him. That you wouldn't go back to him if he asked." He hesitated. "I know that he was unfaithful to you."

"Did I tell you that?"

"The first day. You said that you were married, but your husband wasn't." He scowled as he realized where she was going with this. "He was involved with his new wife before he left you, wasn't he?"

She nodded. "But she wasn't the first. I don't know how many there were. I don't know who they were. I don't know what precautions he took with them, if any at all, but he didn't take any with me. Do you understand what I'm saying?"

With a grin, he used his good foot to set the rocker in motion. "You're saying that if I can't produce a condom within the next few minutes, the fun stops here."

Her responding smile was far less confident and far more regretful as she nodded.

"Hell, sweetheart, the days when I was always prepared ended about ten years ago. If you had asked me at my apartment, I probably could have come up with at least one, but I'm fresh out here." He softened his words with another grin. "I wasn't counting on getting lucky."

"Me, either," she admitted. With a deep sigh, she sat straighter and began buttoning her blouse.

Rising from the chair, he joined her at the door and brushed her hands away. "Let me do that." But instead of fastening the buttons, he slid his hands inside the shirt, filling them once again with her breasts.

"Remy...please...don't..."

"Don't worry," he murmured in her ear, making her shiver. "We're both responsible adults. We won't go too far..." Oh, but it was a temptation. It was tempting just this once to be irresponsible, to forget caution and make love anyway, right here in the warm morning sunshine. But when he had told Susannah that he was willing to take a chance, he had meant with his heart, not his life. Certainly not with her life.

At last he got her shirt done up properly, and he sat down on the step next to her. "How about if I help you fold this last load of laundry and then we drive into town?"

"To Belclaire?"

"Actually I was thinking Baton Rouge."

He looked uncomfortable, Susannah thought, but she completely understood why. She had come from a small town, too—not as small as Belclaire, but small enough that

she'd known the salesclerks and owners of every store in
town. Small enough that she, too, would have driven to an
other town to make such a purchase. "All right," she
agreed.

"We can have lunch while we're in town."

"Hmm."

"Do a little shopping, maybe even take in a movie."

"Hmm."

"Or..." He gave her a wicked grin. "We could find a
drugstore, get what we need, come straight back here and
spend the rest of the afternoon and on into the night..."

"Indulging our desire?" she prompted him with a smile.
As his expression grew more serious, hers grew more un
easy. "Having sex?"

He cupped his hands to her cheeks and kissed her. It
wasn't passionate or heated or teasing. It was a solemn kiss
the sort used to seal a bargain. The sort that often followed
promises like "I do." "Making love, Susannah," he re
plied quietly, intensely. "It will always be making love."

Always. Their *always* was going to last about forty-eight
hours. Once she talked to Smith, he would undoubtedly tell
Remy everything, and that would be the end for them. It
would be the shortest *always* on record.

And she intended to make the most of it.

"Leave the laundry, and we'll go as soon as I clean up."

"You look fine."

She gave him a chiding look. "My bra's on the floor, my
shirt's wrinkled and untucked, and my hair needs to be
combed."

"So you look as if you've been engaged in a little illicit
passion. We're going to buy condoms. We'll look like we
need them." Still, he got to his feet and let her get up. "You
go on. I'll fold the clothes."

She made it as far as the hall before he called her. "Oh,
Susannah? Wear your hair up."

"I thought you liked it down."

"You noticed that." His smile was sweet, charming and, at the same time, sexy as hell. "I think this time I'd like to take it down myself."

With a smile of her own, she went to her room, where she changed into another shirt, this one the color of crimson. After tucking it into her jeans and putting on shoes, she spent the next fifteen minutes fashioning her hair into the most intricate braid she could manage.

When she was finally ready, she found Remy waiting at the kitchen table. He locked up while she got his mother's car from the garage, and then they set off for Baton Rouge, taking the river road instead of the interstate.

"Anything else you want to tell me about your marriage?" he asked once they'd gone a few miles.

"Like what? You know the important stuff, remember?"

"Like why you stayed married for four years."

She flexed both hands around the steering wheel. "I loved him."

"But he treated you badly."

"It was the way he did it. He could be so subtle that, in the beginning, I thought I was just overly sensitive. By the time I realized what was going on, my self-esteem had been worn down to just about nothing." She could smile at the memories now, but three years ago, two years, even one year ago, that had been impossible. "From the time I was a little girl, all I wanted when I grew up was to get married and have a family and be like my mom and dad. Guy convinced me that he was my only chance of having that. That I had to put up with him because no one else would put up with me."

Reaching across the seat, Remy claimed her right hand. "You were a fool to believe him."

"If you're told something often enough, no matter how outrageous or wrong it is, you start to believe it, at least a little. When he left me, I was so afraid of admitting failure, of being alone, of finding out that he was right and no one else would ever want me, that I actually considered pleading with him to stay. He made my life miserable...but I was

familiar with misery. I knew what to expect. I didn't know
what being divorced and alone would be like.''

"What was it like?"

"It wasn't easy. Everyone in town knew about his affairs. They all knew when he didn't come home at night or
when he took women to our house while I was at work during the day. I had a lot of support—so much of the town's
related to me—but there was a lot of gossip. A lot of whispers and catty remarks. Pitying looks.'' She had hated those
most—the looks. She couldn't endure pity.

"You know, my offer from Sunday still stands. One
phone call, and you can spread some of that misery where
it belongs.''

She thought of Guy on the receiving end of someone else's
harassment. It sounded tremendously satisfying, but it
wasn't something she needed. "You wouldn't really do
that.''

"Why do you say that?"

"Because it would be an improper use of your authority.''

"What's the good of having authority if you can't use it
improperly once in a while?'' he replied, then he relented.
"You're right. I wouldn't do it...except for you.''

Coming into the edge of the city, she pulled into the
parking lot of the first shopping center they passed. It was
a strip mall, about a block long, very new and generic
looking. It could have been picked up and set down any-
place in the country and fit right in.

But it had a pharmacy. That was all that counted.

"Would you be more comfortable waiting in the car?''
Remy asked.

She wanted to say, "No, of course not. I'm not embarrassed.'' But the truth was she *was* a little embarrassed. It
was one thing to talk about making such a purchase. It was
another entirely to actually do it. "Yes,'' she said deci-
sively. "I would.''

"Then why don't you pull up to the curb in front? Save
me a few steps.''

She did as he directed, letting him out, then drumming her fingers on the steering wheel while she waited for him to return. Her stomach seemed to be tying itself into intricate little knots. Nerves. She was thirty-one years old and having a bad case of nerves. Of course, it was one thing to talk about spending—how had he put it?—the rest of the afternoon and on into the night making love.

It was another entirely to actually do it.

But after an all-too-short drive back to Belle Ste. Claire, that was exactly what Remy expected of her, and in her heart, it was exactly what she wanted.

But what if that was one thing Guy hadn't lied about?

What if she disappointed Remy?

She couldn't let herself consider the possibility. She had to believe that what she lacked in skill and experience, she would make up for in sincerity. In genuine affection. In the intensity of her desire.

In love?

She shied away from the thought. It was too dangerous. Considering that, after her phone call to Smith in two days, Remy would surely hate her, that line of thinking was entirely too hopeless. Too hurtful.

She had the rest of her life to be hopeless and hurt.

But only forty-eight hours with Remy.

Remy made his selection from the display near the cash registers, paid a young clerk who popped her gum through the entire transaction, then left the store. He was a little more agile with the cane, but his mobility was still limited tremendously by the hip-to-toe cast. He hoped Susannah wasn't averse to taking the lead, because, quite frankly, he didn't see how he and the cast were going to cope otherwise.

But they would manage. They had to. Otherwise, he just might die of need.

As he approached the car at his usual hobbling pace, he could see her tapping her fingers nervously. Given the circumstances, it was remarkable that they'd gotten themselves to this point. After that conversation Sunday afternoon, he'd been convinced that his chances with her were somewhere between slim and none. After what her bastard of an ex-husband had put her through, it was no surprise that she'd been unwilling to try again, to trust again.

Guy Duncan should be strung up for what he'd done to her. She had been right, on the drive up here, when she'd said that Remy wouldn't misuse his authority to harass Duncan. But it would be only natural, after they were married, for them to take a trip to Nebraska so he could see where she'd grown up and could meet her family and friends. And if he happened to run into her ex while they were there, it would be only appropriate that they exchange a few words. And if most of the words were his, and most of his words were threats... Who could expect less from a loving husband?

"Great, Sinclair," he murmured as he gingerly stepped off the curb. "She agrees to go to bed with you, and you've already got yourself married. One step, partner, remember?" *One small step at a time.*

As she started the engine, he maneuvered into the car; then they pulled away from the curb. Susannah was quiet, and he let her remain that way for the major portion of the drive back. At last, when they were only a few miles from home, he looked at her. "I wish I'd met you when you were twenty."

She gave him a curious glance. "Why then?"

"Because you were young, sweet and innocent. I was twenty-six. I had completed the academy and moved to New Orleans. I wasn't sure I was ever going to make a good FBI agent, I bitterly missed my family and I was much too friendly with far too many women. I could have used someone young, sweet and innocent in my life then."

"You wouldn't have given me a second look."

"Always," he disagreed. "Even if you'd been young enough to land me in jail."

"I was very young at twenty."

He chuckled. "Honey, you're very young at thirty-one."

"I was very naive."

"Some things don't change."

"I was also very idealistic."

He waited until she turned off the highway into the driveway at Belle Ste. Claire before he reached across and drew his fingers lightly along her arm. "I wouldn't have disappointed you."

She brought the car to a stop near the parlor door and turned to face him. "I was a virgin at twenty."

Growing serious, he let his fingers come to rest on her hand. "I would have been honored."

He swore, before she blinked and looked away, that he saw a tear form at the corner of her eye. But it was gone when she looked back. "Guy found it more a chore than an honor."

So much information in such a brief statement. She had remained a virgin until her mid-twenties, when she'd met the man she had eventually married. And after all that waiting, her first time had been less than special. And *he* was going to be only her second lover.

And her last.

He really did feel honored.

"Guy was an idiot." Lifting her hand, he pressed a kiss to her palm, then leaned closer to her. "Why don't we try really hard to see if we can't exorcise him from your memory?" he murmured, brushing his mouth across hers.

She warmed to his kiss immediately, opening to his tongue, raising her hands to his shoulders and drawing him closer. He felt the heat rush through him, from every place they touched and every place they didn't. He felt the blood rush through, collecting, hot and heavy, in the lower part of his body. With one kiss, he was hard, damn, and desperate for relief.

Drawing back, he stroked her hair from her face. "Put the car away later and come inside with me now."

"It'll only take a minute."

A minute. Sixty seconds. He could endure anything for sixty seconds, couldn't he?

Releasing her, he collected the small plastic bag and his cane and climbed out of the car. A walkway of brick laid unevenly in a herringbone pattern extended from the edge of the shell driveway to the steps. By the time he had crossed that distance and climbed the seven steps, Susannah was approaching behind him. She waited quietly while he unlocked the door. For once, he could hold the door open for her—as a gentleman should, his mother would say—instead of struggling through with crutches and cast while *she* opened doors for *him*.

Inside, he turned to lock the door once again. For a moment, the house seemed inordinately quiet; then he heard the ticking of the grandfather clock in the front hallway, the faint hum of the refrigerator in the kitchen and the settling creak of ancient wood somewhere up above.

He could also hear the uneven tenor of Susannah's breathing and the less-than-steady beating of his own heart.

Returning his keys to his jeans pocket, he faced her. Her gaze was directed demurely downward, and her hands were loosely clasped in front of her. She looked impossibly shy, but he had no words that would reassure her. Besides, didn't actions speak louder than words?

Taking both of her hands in his free hand, he gently pulled her along with him as he made his way down the hall, through the kitchen and into the servants' wing. For a moment, he hesitated; then he chose his room. Susannah's room was her only private place in the entire house. Until she invited him in, he couldn't take that from her. Besides, he wanted her in *his* room. He wanted to see her in his bed, wrapped in his quilt, her hair spread out across his pillow.

The curtains were drawn across the windows, but the fabric was sheer enough and the sunlight bright enough that the room needed no additional lighting. It was warm inside and smelled of potpourri, aged wood and after-shave—a good place to be lazy and cozy and intimate on an early spring day.

He came to a stop beside the bed and turned to face her. He had seduced a number of women in his life—and had been seduced, in turn, by a few more. After the first time or two, he had never been unsure of what to say or do, of what approach to take with each particular lady.

Until today.

But then, it had never been so incredibly important until today.

Offering her a sheepish smile, he admitted, "I don't know what to do."

She smiled the dazzling sort of smile that he'd been waiting all his life for, the smile of sheer pleasure that he'd thought he would never see her wear. "Let me give you a few pointers," she suggested, her voice husky, her hands unsteady as they clasped his and lifted it to her cheek. "You touch me here..." Pressing his palm gently against her skin, she guided his hand down across her jaw and her throat to her breast. "And here..." Her fingers trembling, she drew his hand slowly across her nipple, so slowly that he could feel it bud and harden beneath her shirt; then, pressing harder, she led him over her stomach, from soft cotton to coarser denim, directing him until his hand was spread flat and low across her belly. "And eventually here..."

Letting his cane fall, he raised his right hand to her breast, covering it, gently caressing it. "Here, like this?" he asked hoarsely. Her only answer was a faint murmur. "And like this?" His left hand inched lower, feeling the heat that radiated through her. "And what do you do?"

"I—" She caught her breath as he lightly pinched her nipple. "I go weak and collapse on the bed and sigh, 'Oh, Remy.'"

He chuckled and wrapped his arms around her, pulling her close. "I like the way you say that."

"Kiss me, and I'll say it again."

He did kiss her then, and Susannah did go weak, reaching for him for support. She supposed there must have been a time when Guy's kisses had affected her so, but she couldn't recall it. She couldn't recall their grandest, most passionate moment even coming close to what little bit she and Remy had so far shared.

When he raised his head and she could at last speak again, she smiled drowsily and sighed, "Oh, Remy."

"Do you ever touch me?" he asked, still playing along with the game she'd started.

"I get to undress you." Summoning her strength, she curled her fingers where they rested at his waist and gathered handfuls of his T-shirt.

"Because I'm clumsy and slow and need the help?" The teasing was still there in tone but not in feeling. She realized it bothered him that he wasn't at his physical best, that his natural grace was overshadowed by the awkwardness of the bulky cast and its restrictions.

"Because it gives me an excuse to see you everywhere. To touch you everywhere. Because, when I'm done and your clothes are out of the way, then you can help undress me."

She pushed his shirt up, drawing her fingers over warm skin. His muscles rippled where she stroked, and his nipples, even though she skirted them, puckered. Pulling the garment over his head, she dropped it behind him, then once again drew her hands over his skin. There was only the faintest discoloration left from the contusion where his bulletproof vest had saved his life. If she hadn't known exactly where it was, she wouldn't even notice the shadow that remained. As for the other injury, there was a reddish-tinged entry wound on the front of his arm, about three-quarters of an inch in diameter, slightly sunken in and healing nicely, and a matching exit wound on the back.

"You're a very lucky man," she murmured, pressing a kiss to the base of his throat.

"I know. No other man in the world has ever done what I'm about to do with you."

She tickled along his ribs and made him squirm. "I'm talking about your wounds. Not many people get shot three times at close range and live to tell the tale."

"A bulletproof vest is a wondrous thing."

Sliding her hands flat across his ribs, she came to a stop when she encountered his jeans. "Besides, are you forgetting that you're not the first?"

It took him a moment to realize that she was referring to his earlier statement; then he grinned boastfully. "Maybe I can't be the first, but I can be the last, and I promise you, sweetheart, I'll be the one who loves you the best." As she had done before, he claimed her hand and, molding it, controlling it, he guided it lower, over his jeans—the waistband, the zipper—and down to his arousal. "Oh, Susannah," he murmured. "See what you do to me?"

She touched him gently, tentatively. He was hard and hot, and she... She felt like that young, naive virgin they had teased about in the car. Her hands felt clumsy, not quite her own, not really sure of what to do or how to do it. Undressing him—that was what she was supposed to be doing. But the metal button on his jeans didn't want to come free. The zipper didn't want to slide down.

"Honey..." His voice was hoarse, thick, as unsteady as her fingers. "Are you doing that on purpose? Because— oh, hell—you're going to finish me off right here if you don't..."

His last words faded away on a groan as she worked open the zipper, then began peeling his jeans away. Underneath he wore only briefs—and brief was certainly an appropriate description. Aside from the fact that they were cotton and white, they shared nothing in common with the underwear the men in her life had favored.

She knelt in front of him, working his jeans down over his good leg and the cast, following them with his briefs, tugging his shoe off and loosening the straps on the boot. Finally he was naked, and she was still fully dressed, and sometime in the last few minutes she had lost her shyness. He pulled her to her feet again, back into his arms again, and kissed her while she stroked him gently, curiously, greedily, everywhere.

Everywhere.

Desire, barely controlled, strong enough to make him weak, rippled through Remy in ever-widening spirals. He had always enjoyed intimacy before, but he had never really bought into the theory that an emotional connection with his partner could make a good experience better. He'd had great sex with women he'd known he wouldn't see again and lukewarm sex with women he had genuinely cared about.

But he had never experienced anything like this before.

He had never wanted so desperately.

He had never ached so intensely.

He had never craved such torment, had never anticipated such satisfaction.

He had never known such sweet need.

For the second time that day he pulled Susannah's blouse from her jeans and opened the buttons with ease. When she had returned to her bedroom earlier to change for their trip into town, she hadn't bothered with replacing her bra, so when he slipped his hands inside the cool fabric, he touched bare skin. Soft skin. Warm, tantalizing, utterly feminine skin. Her breasts were heavy in his hands, her nipples hard against his palms. When he rubbed them, she shivered. When he lowered his head and sucked one nipple into his mouth, she cried aloud.

"Remy..."

"I know. Help me...your jeans..."

Disentangling herself from his embrace, she removed the rest of her clothing while he settled on the bed. He ripped open the plastic bag from the pharmacy, opened the box and shook out the square packages inside. By the time he taken care of that, Susannah was standing beside the bed, naked and nervous and...

He gave her a long, hard look, then exhaled heavily. "You're a beautiful woman."

She smiled hesitantly. When he extended his hand, she took it and placed one knee on the mattress. It barely dipped beneath her weight. When he pulled, she came to him, her gaze locked with his, her mouth steady in that uneasy little half smile.

"I wish I could give you moonlight and romance... seduction... sweet words..." He grinned as he stroked a light, feathery caress from her cheek all the way down to her breast and beyond. "And an able body. I wish I could make love to you the way I want, the way you deserve... but right now I can't. You'll have to... I can only lie on my back..."

Her smile blossomed, sweet and slow, starting in her eyes and lighting her face, dazzling him with its sensuality. "I don't care about moonlight," she replied as she moved into place above him. "Or romance... or seduction. I don't care who does what to whom... as long as we do it together. I care about this, Remy." She lowered her body to his, taking him slowly, painfully slowly, inside her. She was hot and slick and held him tight, so tightly that he swore, right there in the middle of the day in his sun-filled room, he saw stars.

"And I care about this." Leaning forward, bracing her hands flat against his chest, she bent her head to his for a kiss, sweet and breath-stealing.

"I care about this, too." She began moving against him, withdrawing, then pushing forward, taking him again, all of him, sometimes fast, sometimes slow, but each time creating sensations of pure, raw pleasure.

"But most of all..." She was whispering now, her breathing as ragged as his, her skin growing damp with a flush, her breasts swelling and her nipples drawing up even tighter.

"Most of all, Remy... I care about *you*."

Chapter 9

Shadows drifted across the walls as, outside, clouds drifted by overhead, occasionally blocking out the afternoon sun completely but more often just filtering it through their cottony edges. Susannah knew it was well past lunch—her stomach told her that—and that they had made an impressive dent in the contents of that small box that had been well worth this morning's drive into the city, but beyond that she had no clue as to what time it was. There was a clock on Remy's side of the bed and the watch on his wrist was only inches from her nose, but she didn't bother to look.

She didn't want to know how many of her forty-eight hours were gone.

She didn't want to face how little time was left to them.

She was lying on her side, her back to Remy. As he'd pointed out, he had to lie on his back, but he still managed to mold her body to his. He still managed to hold her close, his arm curved around her, his hand resting on the swell of her breast. He still managed, every few minutes, to kiss her or stroke her or find some other way to send a shiver down her spine.

Behind her, he yawned, then drowsily murmured, "Oh, Susannah." After a moment, he asked, "When you were little, did the kids ever tease you about that?"

She thought of the old-time folk song whose name she shared, the song she'd heard a thousand times more than was funny. *Oh, Susannah, oh, don't you cry for me...* She faced the prospect of plenty of tears in her future. She would cry for Remy and for herself, for everything they might have had and everything she had cost them.

"Oh, yeah," she replied, focusing on the past and not the future. "I used to plead with my mother to let me go by Susan or Susie, but she refused. She had named me Susannah, and no smart-mouthed little kids were going to change her mind."

"That's because she wanted a beautiful name for her beautiful daughter."

Beautiful. She smiled bittersweetly. "When you say that...I can almost believe it."

"That you're beautiful?" He tugged until she rolled over to face him. "I'll tell you often enough in the next fifty years that you'll have to believe it. You'll see it for yourself."

Her desire for that, fifty years with him, was so strong that it made her heart hurt and her eyes tear up. Smiling to disguise it, she asked, "Has anyone ever told you that you're awfully sure of yourself?"

"Maybe a time or two."

"You'll be getting that cast off in a few more weeks, and your parents will be home around then. You'll go back to work and back to your regular life, and you won't need me anymore."

Taking her chin in hand, he forced her to look at him. "My need for you has nothing to do with this cast or my parents being gone," he said fiercely. "I'll always need you, Susannah. *Always.*"

"Remy, you don't—"

"Remember what you told me the other day?" he interrupted. "Don't go looking for trouble. The time to worry about problems, sweetheart, is when you find out we've got them. The only thing you've got to worry about right now is whether or not I intend to let you out of this bed anytime today.''

She let him silence her protest because it was easier than arguing with him. Because it was too wonderful a time to spoil. Because the idea of a future with him was too sweet. Because she had never been a dreamer and for two days she wanted to be.

And because reality—with its disillusionment, betrayal, anger and hatred—would intrude soon enough.

Shivering a little, she snagged the quilt folded across the bed with her foot and managed to pull it up to cover them without leaving his side. ''Do you know why Valery gave you this quilt?''

He shrugged. ''She thought I would like it.''

''But do you know why she chose this particular one?''

Another shrug. ''The colors are nice. So's the pattern. It's a family heirloom. I don't know.''

Leaning on one elbow, she spread the coverlet over his chest, smoothing out wrinkles. ''I understand she manages an antique clothing store. Do they sell quilts there?''

''I don't know. I've only been there once, and that was when she disappeared after Nate Simmons was murdered.''

''I come from a family of quilters,'' she remarked with a smile. ''My mother quilted, and my aunts and my grand-mothers. Life slows down on a farm in winter. It kept them busy, and it kept the family warm on those cold prairie nights. Mama kept her quilt frame in the dining room—we usually ate in the kitchen because it was cozier. She balanced the frame on the back of the dining chairs, and she worked in there for hours at a time. Sometimes one of my aunts or my grandmothers came over and helped, although special quilts—those she was planning to give away—she made all by herself. I used to play in there on the floor underneath the frame, or sometimes I sat in one of the chairs and watched her.''

''Did you learn to quilt, too?''

"I always intended to, but I never did. There were chores to do, games to play, friends to visit. Then Mama died, and there was dinner to cook, laundry to wash, a household to run." And a baby brother to help raise. To help spoil.

"You can learn now." He stroked her bare shoulder as she stroked the swirling stitching on the quilt. "You can make a quilt for us."

She knew it was reckless to ask, knew it was a risk she was ill prepared for, but she asked anyway. "And what kind of quilt would you have me make?"

"I don't know. Something with a big heart that says, 'Susannah loves Remy.'"

She had to swallow hard over the lump in her throat to get even the simplest of responses out. "Uh-huh. Sort of..." Forcing a deep breath, she strengthened her voice. "Sort of the fabric-art equivalent of carving initials into a tree, huh?"

His grin was charming. "I could do that for you. My old pocketknife is upstairs, and we have some live oaks out front big enough around to spell out your entire name."

He was too sweet. Too dear. And too right. Susannah did love Remy...even if she never could tell him so.

"Hush," she admonished, shifting slightly so he couldn't see her tears. "I'm getting to the point here."

"I thought you were reminiscing," he teased. "I didn't know there was a point."

"I was, but there is. The point is I never learned to quilt, but I learned a lot about them. I learned how to piece the tops and how to secure the layers before they went into the frame. I learned how to choose fabrics and patterns and colors, and I became very familiar with most traditional quilting patterns. Apparently Valery is familiar with at least one pattern, because she chose this quilt to give to you. I have one in the same pattern at home, one my mother made all by herself."

He was serious now. "A special one," he said, and she nodded confirmation. "These traditional patterns...they have names?"

She nodded again.

"What's the name of this one?"

Turning at last to face him, she whistled a few bars of an old-time folk tune and watched his smile as it grew.

"Oh, Susannah? My quilt is named Oh, Susannah?"

For the third time, she nodded.

He looked as smug as a man could. "You see, sweetheart? It's fate."

"What do you mean?"

"Long before you and I were even born, some Sinclair relative knew that one day one of her descendants was going to have reason to treasure a quilt named Oh, Susannah. We were meant to be together."

Fate. The idea made her want to laugh and cry at the same time. Fate had brought them together, all right, but its form was nowhere near as harmless and sweet as the image of some long-ago Sinclair woman piecing together a fine quilt by lamplight. It was a stupid, twenty-three-year-old kid who didn't have the brains to stay out of trouble. It was a slimy, repulsive lawyer who twisted the law for his own purposes, justice be damned. It was an evil man who thought nothing of destroying human life for his own greed, maybe even for his own pleasure.

"Remy, please don't—"

He cut off her words with a kiss, hard and hot, demanding a response, and she gave it in spite of herself. She twined her arms around his neck, welcomed his tongue into her mouth, rubbed her body sinuously against his, arousing him, arousing herself.

Just as abruptly as he had taken her, he pushed her back. For a moment he subjected her to a long, hard look, a look that left her feeling naked in a way that had nothing to do with her lack of clothing. A look that, God help her, could open her soul and see every one of her lies.

And then the chill was gone, and the sweet, teasing, sexy man was back. "What are the chances," he asked with his most endearing smile, "that we could get some lunch, then pick up where we just left off?"

Her breasts were aching, and in that one brief moment, heat and moisture had begun gathering between her thighs. She was surprised that she could want him again so quickly, surprised that her body could take him again...but then, she needed to store up memories—a lifetime's worth. "I'd say they're pretty damned good," she said evenly.

"Good. Would you mind getting me a pair of sweats out of the armoire?"

She wriggled out from beneath the quilt and located her shirt where he had dropped it. It offered some degree of modesty while she opened the cabinet door and fished out a pair of black sweatpants. After handing them to him, she picked up her underwear and jeans and started toward the bathroom to finish dressing there.

Remy waited until she reached the door to speak. He knew what he was about to say wasn't going to thrill her— but, damn it, someday it would, so he was going to say it anyway. He wanted her to know. "Susannah?"

She paused, looking back at him.

"Did I remember to mention that I intend to marry you soon?"

Her face went blank. Absolutely blank. "No. You didn't."

"Then consider yourself warned."

Thursday afternoon found them sitting—reclining, more accurately—on the gallery on the sunny side of the house, being lazy and quiet and, oddly enough, intimate, although they weren't even touching. This was exactly the sort of idyllic time Remy had been looking for when he'd first made his plans to come home to Belle Ste. Claire to recuperate and exactly the sort of romantic time he had hoped for when he had chosen Susannah to come with him. They had spent Wednesday afternoon in and out of bed and most of the evening stretched out on the sofa in the parlor, a fire burning in the fireplace and the television tuned to some show or another. They had touched a lot, talked a little and said nothing, and it had been the most satisfying evening he could recall.

There was one thing he wished she would mention, though—since she hadn't last night, then sometime today: yesterday's warning. He wished she would say, "Gee, Remy, I'd love to marry you," or "I'm just waiting for you to ask," or even, "I'm not sure that's what I want."

Instead she had said nothing. Right after he'd said it, she had given him a long look, then walked out of the bedroom and down the hall to the bathroom, where she had very quietly closed the door and stayed for a long, long time. When she had finally come out again, he'd been in the kitchen, gathering the makings for sandwiches at the table. She had brushed and rebraided her hair—he'd forgotten his request to take it down himself—and finished dressing, and for the first time in weeks she had looked almost but not quite serene again.

But she had pretended his promise of marriage had never been made.

With a sigh, he thought back to last spring and early summer, after Evan's death, when he'd spent so much time in French Quarter bars—literally hours looking for or sitting with Michael while he drank, convincing him to go home, half carrying, half dragging him out the door. He had put his friend to bed when he could afford the time to sleep it off, had given him coffee and food when he couldn't. Remy had sat with him when he was sick and when he was hung over and had tried reasoning with him when he was sober. The limits of Remy's patience had never been tested before that time, and he had been surprised by how far they extended.

Susannah just might test them even further before he got her to stand up beside him in front of God and their families and make vows of forever.

But that was all right. He could counter every argument she might make. He could eliminate every excuse she might give him. He wouldn't even have to try very hard. "I love you" pretty much took care of everything she might come up with. Someday she would run out of reasons for holding back and she would have to replace her don'ts and can'ts with "I do."

Someday she would find it easier to quit making excuses and start making that quilt with the big heart that said "Susannah loves Remy."

From the wicker chaise longue set at an angle to his, she unexpectedly spoke. "Want to take a walk?"

"A walk?"

"Around the grounds."

He glanced down at the cane leaning against his chair, the smooth silver handle gleaming in the sun. It was his grandfather's and he had found it not buried away in the attic, with only his mother knowing where, but so prominently placed in the front hall that he couldn't help but wonder if he'd left it there, the ebony and silver all brightly polished, specially for him.

"I can do that now," he said, surprised by the realization. He had become too accepting of his limitations in the past month. While there were still things he couldn't do—run, take a bath, drive a car or make love to Susannah the way he would like—there were a few new things he could do, such as taking a shower and sharing an afternoon walk with her.

"Is that a yes?"

He was already on his feet by the time she finished asking. Together they descended the steps and started across the grass. Susannah, her hands hooked in her hip pockets, stayed close to his side, naturally adjusting her stride to his. "This is a great yard for kids," she remarked. "I can't get used to these trees. They're perfect for climbing."

They ducked underneath a massive branch of the live oak he was gesturing to. "You can go all the way to the top of that one, and I swear, you can see all the way to Texas," Remy remarked. "If you're reckless or a little adventurous. You, being the sensible sort, probably wouldn't make it more than twenty feet."

"And you, being the adventurous sort, have been to the top and have seen Texas." Trailing her fingers lightly over the bark, she turned in a complete circle around the trunk, disappearing from sight for a moment or two before reappearing. "They're wonderful trees."

"They are that. This one is Claire."

She gave him a doubtful look. "Claire," she repeated. "You named this tree."

"Not me. It's been Claire—actually, La Belle Claire—for as long as I've been alive. I imagine my grandparents named it." He studied her for a moment, reading the good-natured skepticism in her eyes. "Ah, you don't believe me, do you? You wound me, Susannah. I could tell you something totally outrageous, and you would probably accept it as fact. I tell you something perfectly logical—such as that I'm going to marry you or that this tree has a name—and you don't believe me."

"I can see that your definition of outrageous varies significantly from mine," she retorted. "You know, in my part of Nebraska, trees are a little on the rare side. We admire them. We try not to cut them down. We even plant them, water them and nurture them, hoping to get more. We get awfully attached to them. But we do not name them." She gestured to the next closest tree. "And who is this? Thomas? Henry? No, wait. Your people are French. Beauregard? Philippe?"

With a grin, he approached her, not stopping until she was leaning against the trunk of the second tree and he was holding her there with his hands placed on either side of her head. "Don't be silly. This is a magnolia. Who would name a magnolia?"

She raised her hands to his chest, rubbing him through the thin, worn cotton of his shirt. "You Southerners are a strange lot," she teased softly.

"We have our eccentricities."

"And you're proud of them."

"Hmm. I think it'll make for awfully interesting kids—my southern peculiarities and your midwestern conventionality."

Her smile faltered at the mention of children. That was all right. He could give her time—a little, at least—to get used to the idea.

"So tell me," she said, her voice soft and as warm as sunshine. "Why does your oak tree have a name but not your magnolia?"

"Actually—" he pressed a kiss to her forehead "—Claire is a live oak, not an oak. There's a difference." His next kiss landed beside her eye. "Claire is a member of the Live Oak Society, which is a collection of live oaks around the state that are at least a hundred years old. It can't very well be listed on the society's rolls as 'the big tree at Belle Ste. Claire,' so someone—"

As he placed his next kiss on her cheek, she took over for him. "Likely your grandparents."

"—in keeping with the name of the house, the family and the town, named it La Belle Claire." He was about to kiss her mouth when she ducked away, sliding underneath his arm. She circled the magnolia, then resumed her leisurely stroll. After retrieving his cane where it had fallen, he went after her, catching up when she slowed to wait for him.

"Will you live here someday?" she asked, looking out across the field where the family had once kept horses. "Like your parents and grandparents and generations of Sinclairs before you?"

"Probably. When we're retired and the kids are grown and on their own." He grinned at her refusal to react to his assumption that they would still be together when retirement came. "Every morning we'll sit on the gallery and drink lemonade and watch the traffic and the birds and the grandkids, and every afternoon we'll sneak off to the servants' quarters and make mad, passionate love."

Lowering her gaze to the ground, she kicked a pine cone, sending it skittering away. "Remy, please don't..."

"Susannah." He stopped right where he was and waited for her to turn, to come back and face him. She did stop, but she didn't turn right away. "Tell me that the idea of spending the rest of your life with me holds no appeal for you. Tell me that the prospect of being my wife doesn't interest you. Tell me that the possibility of carrying my baby inside you doesn't fill your heart, just the littlest bit, with pleasure."

Finally she did turn, but her expression was so sad that he almost wished she hadn't. "All those things sound wonderful, Remy, but... we can't always have what we want. Sometimes we just have to take what we can get."

"Not in my world."

"Then your world is privileged. But in *my* world—in the *real* world—sometimes you have to settle."

He shook his head. "The night I got shot, when I thought I was dying, I looked back at my life and about all I had were regrets. When I knew I was going to live, I swore I would change that. I know now what I want. I want you—*you*, Susannah. Do you understand that? I want to marry you, to have children with you. I want to spend the rest of my life loving you." He looked away, then back at her, finishing fiercely, "And I'll be damned if I'm going to settle for anything less."

"You are the most stubborn man!"

"Damned right I am."

"You *aren't* God. You can't just decide what you want and make it happen."

"Why not?"

She sighed wearily. "Because life doesn't work that way, Remy."

"We'll make it work."

"Some things *can't* work."

In an effort to lighten the mood, he wryly remarked, "You're certainly no optimist, are you?"

"No," she agreed. "I'm a realist."

"That's all right, Susannah." Taking her hand, he gently pulled her along with him. "I've got dreams enough for both of us."

* * *

The night was quiet and still. Susannah sat in the barrel chair in the parlor, her feet tucked beneath her, her head resting on one hand, and let her gaze move slowly around the room. What would it be like to live here, to call this place home? To have pictures of her husband, her children and herself on those tables? To make this homey room *her* family room? To gather here on holidays with children and grandchildren? To become part of the centuries-old Sinclair family traditions?

It would be closer to heaven than she was ever going to get.

She sighed a little, and her head sank a little lower. From that position it was easy for her gaze to settle on the sewing basket, its lid decorated with intricate cross-stitch, underneath the chair-side table. Marie Sinclair did needlework, she remembered. Some of her work decorated pillows in here; other signed pieces were framed in the kitchen and the upstairs bedrooms. That basket likely contained her equipment—floss, needles, scissors, probably even a few pieces of fabric.

From the sofa Remy switched the television from the movie that had just ended to a program she found interesting, then got to his feet. "I'm going to take a shower."

"All right," she murmured, still looking at the basket.

"When I get out, maybe you'll be ready for bed."

"I'm sure I will."

He brought the remote control to her, then bent and kissed her cheek. It was such a natural gesture, so husbandly. It frightened her how easily she accepted it . . . and how soon she would face a life without such gestures. Without Remy.

When he reached the door, she abruptly spoke his name. "I noticed that your mother does needlework. Do you think she would mind if I borrowed some of her supplies? Just a small piece of fabric and a little floss?"

"Of course not. If you don't find what you need in that basket, she keeps a bigger one on the window seat in their bedroom."

For a time after he left, she remained where she was. Finally, though, she knelt on the floor and pulled the basket out. Inside she found exactly what she needed, including an eight-by-ten-inch piece of linen in a fine ivory shade. Feeling impossibly romantic for an avowed realist, she chose her colors—one the golden hue of Remy's hair when the sunlight touched it, the other to match his eyes, bluer than the snatch of song she'd heard on Michael and Valery's balcony the other night.

She also took out a needle, a threader, a pair of small pointed scissors and—the miracle of modern sewing—a disappearing marker. She had never possessed much artistic talent, but what she was doing didn't require much. It would be a simple, unfinished piece, an apology of sorts that would probably never be accepted.

But she had to offer it anyway.

She worked through Remy's shower, not stopping even when she heard the distant sound of the blow dryer. He wasn't drying his hair, she knew—he preferred to leave it be, even though it meant waking up with some interesting styles in the morning—but rather his cast. The doctor's suggestion of covering it with a plastic bag worked only partially. Remy always completed his showers with damp places on the foot and leaks inside at the top opening of the cast.

When the hair dryer shut off, she smoothed the linen across her lap. She was working without a hoop, so she would have to press the piece when she was done. But even wrinkled and unfinished, it had charm. It wasn't the best embroidery she'd ever done—not surprising, since she hadn't done any at all in more than fifteen years and had never been particularly skilled—but it wasn't the skill that mattered.

It was the sentiment.

Gathering the supplies in the center of the piece, she folded everything together and stored it in Mrs. Sinclair's basket. Then, after shutting off the television and the lamps, she went toward the back of the house, where she met Remy coming out of the bathroom. "Why don't you make sure everything's locked up?'' she suggested as she slipped past him. ''I'll meet you in your room in fifteen minutes.''

Without giving him a chance to reply, she closed the door and began hastily undressing. The bathroom was steamy and smelled of him. Having deliberately left her own bath supplies in her room, she used his—shampoo, shaving cream and even, when she was done, his cologne—so she smelled of him, too, without even getting close to him.

Wearing nothing but a towel, she turned off the bathroom light and stepped into the hall. The only light on was in his room, spilling out through the open door to light her way. She didn't go there, though. Instead she went to her own room, leaving her door open, turning on the bedside lamp. A quick glance across the hall showed that he was sitting in bed, pillows propped behind his back, the quilt pulled to his waist, and watching her.

Good.

She sat down on her bed and began smoothing lotion over her left leg, starting low at her toes and working all the way up to her hip, rubbing it in with slow, lazy, long strokes. After repeating the procedure on her right leg, she applied a small amount of the cool cream to her face, then her hands.

Another furtive glance showed that Remy was still watching her... and that he was very definitely interested.

Leaving the bed and his line of sight, she dropped the towel across her laundry basket and took a nightgown from the dresser. It was soft, thin and white, one she'd bought on a whim but rarely wore. She wasn't sure why she had even brought it with her, unless maybe the poet's ruffles along the neckline, the billowy sleeves and the yards of flowing fabric had seemed dreamily appropriate for a sojourn in a wonderfully romantic antebellum southern mansion. In reality, the gown, falling to her knees, was so full, ruffled and flowing that, whenever she tried to wear it, it wrapped itself in a choking tangle around her when she slept.

But tonight it would be on the floor long before she fell asleep.

Taking her hairbrush with her, she moved to stand in the doorway. This time she didn't pretend that she was unaware of Remy watching her. She didn't pretend that being watched, and enticing him in the process, wasn't exactly what she wanted.

She had towel-dried her hair in the bathroom. Now she drew the brush through it, slowly working out each tangle. When that was done, for a time she simply brushed her hair, each stroke drawing back from her face, long and sensuous, each movement causing her gown to shift and swirl, pulling the soft fabric across her breasts and her impossibly sensitive nipples.

At last, when she knew from her brief, but intense, experience that he couldn't get any harder, that she couldn't get any hotter, she laid the brush on the night table, turned off the lamp and slowly crossed the hall that separated them. She placed one knee on the bed, then swung her leg over him and settled across his lap. Her quilt—that was how she'd begun to think of it—was between them, trapping, exchanging their heat, rubbing sensuously over his hard flesh, abrading her tender flesh.

Wrapping her fingers around the iron bars of the headboard, she leaned forward to kiss him—gentle little nips along his ear, his jaw, finally reaching his mouth. He opened to her immediately, inviting her in, and she tentatively accepted. It was a new experience, being the aggressor, one that, with practice, she could come to like. She mimicked the way *he* kissed *her*, exploring his mouth with her tongue, teasing, tasting, before slowly withdrawing.

He started to speak, but she silenced him with a light, fluttery kiss before she leaned aside to reach the nightstand and the small pile of plastic packets there. She tore one open and removed its small coil of latex, then pushed the quilt back and...

And her confidence faltered. Her seduction scene fell apart.

Recognizing the reason for her falter, he brought his hands to hers, guiding her. "Hold it here," he instructed in a voice that was hoarse and sharp with desire, "and put it here . . . now unroll it . . ." He groaned. "There."

A soft giggle escaped her. "So much for seduction. I'd never . . ."

"I know . . . and, sweetheart, I find that incredibly seductive."

"You do?"

"That I'm the only man you've done this for? Done this to? Hell, yes."

In thanks she gave him a quick kiss, then softly admonished, "Be serious again. I can manage from here on out."

Without further play, she lifted her gown and took him inside her, controlling her movement, sinking a millimeter at a time until their bodies were as closely, as perfectly, joined as was physically possible. For a time she simply sat there, eyes closed, breathing uneven, and felt the changes— the fullness, the heat, the stretching. Then he moved just the slightest bit, and satisfaction quickly gave way to hunger.

For one instant she cursed his cast, cursed that she would never know what it was like to make love with him any other way, cursed that she would never experience the full expression of his passion. Then the instant passed, and she began making love to him. She began loving him.

She took him slow and deep, withdrawing, then returning, feeding her arousal with every stroke. With his hands underneath her gown, he stroked her breasts and her belly and occasionally slipped his fingers between her thighs, helping her, pushing her, guiding her, faster, harder. He was close, she knew from the rhythm of his breathing and the tightening of his body, and she— Sweet mercy, she had gone beyond close. Her lungs were tight, her heart pounded mercilessly and her body had gone hard and quivery with a pure, relentless ache that threatened to consume her.

When it happened, it was sudden, violent in its intensity, painful in its pleasure. The ache exploded from the inside out, stealing her breath, robbing her of her voice, her strength, her soul. It made her tremble and plead, words with no sound, sounds with no meaning.

But it left her with enough awareness to hear Remy's throaty groan. To feel the clenching of his muscles. To feel—sense?—the protected emptying of his body inside hers.

It left her with enough awareness, when he gathered her into his arms, when he stroked and held and soothed her, to hear the low, quiet promise he whispered.

"I love you, Susannah. I always will."

And it left her with enough awareness to literally feel her heart break.

Remy awakened Friday morning to empty arms and an empty bed and a future that couldn't have been more full. He knew Susannah loved him, knew it with a certainty that he couldn't explain. Call it instinct. Intuition. Whatever it was, he *knew* it.

And he knew *she* knew it.

It was just a matter of getting her to admit it.

Then they would get married. Get pregnant. Have the first of at least three or four babies. Begin living the rest of what was guaranteed to be a long and happy life together.

He wondered what she would think of his parents and all the Sinclair-Navarre relatives. They would probably intimidate the hell out of her. But his father—being a typical male—would surely adore her, and his mother, he had no doubt, would, too. Susannah and Marie shared much in common: they were both gentle, quiet, sensible women. They understood family ties and obligations. They gave freely of their time to those who needed it and of themselves to those they loved.

And what would her family up in Nebraska think of *him*? On the whole, he wasn't a bad catch. He came from a good family. He was well educated and had a reputation as a damned tough FBI agent. Even though he'd come into his share of the family money when he was twenty-five, he worked hard and had no intention of slacking off.

Still, there *were* those resemblances she'd said he bore to her ex-husband. And he was a stranger who would be keeping her in a distant city far from the farm where she'd grown up. And after her first marriage, her family would have to be leery about seeing her try again. And the simple truth was he didn't deserve her.

But he could make them promises that Guy Duncan never could have: that he would always love Susannah. That he would always treat her with respect. That he would never be unfaithful to her. That he would never hurt her. That her love and her happiness would always be the most important things in his life.

He was persuasive. Susannah had said so herself. If he could win her over, then he could win anyone over.

But, he reminded himself, he hadn't *quite* finished winning her yet.

Pushing back the covers, he swung his feet to the floor and slowly, with his usual morning stiffness, stood up. He was tired of sleeping on his back all night, and he was damned tired of lying there passively while Susannah made love to him. He wanted to trade positions with her, wanted to cover her body with his, wanted to lean over her while her hips cradled his. He wanted to feel her legs wrapped around his hips, wanted to share the work of their lovemaking as well as the pleasure.

A few more weeks. The words had become a promise. A prayer.

After dressing and a trip to the bathroom, he went in search of Susannah. Her room was empty, the door open, her bed unslept in these past few nights. The kitchen was empty, too, with no sign of breakfast having been started, and the parlor was still and untouched from last night.

But the locks on the door leading to the gallery were undone.

He circled the house, at last locating his mother's sewing basket on a bench on the south side. He stopped at the top of the steps and was staring out across the lawn when a voice called out from above him. "Good morning."

It was the swinging of her feet in midair that gave away her location. With a grin, he moved down the steps and approached the giant live oak, where she sat, her back against the trunk, on a branch some fifteen feet from the ground. She looked so smugly self-satisfied and so damned beautiful that he would give almost anything for a camera to capture the moment. "What are you doing up there?"

"Isn't it a beautiful morning?"

"Louisiana's full of beautiful mornings." After a curious pause, he repeated his question. "What are you doing?"

"I was sitting on the porch—"

"The gallery," he corrected with a grin.

"—doing a little embroidery, and I remembered what you said yesterday."

"I said a lot of things yesterday, ranging from 'I'm going to marry you, Susannah,' to 'I love you.'"

"I'm referring to the conversation where you said I was sensible and dull while you're reckless and adventurous."

"I never called you dull," he argued good-naturedly. "Hell, I never said that *I* was reckless and adventurous."

She gave him a look that was so haughtily superior. "Oh, please . . . what do you think sensible means?"

"Rational. Reasonable. Logical."

"Predictable. *Dull.*"

"Take my word for it, sweetheart. *Nothing* about you is dull."

She moved from her perch to the next branch below, then to the immense limb, bigger around the middle than she was by at least three times, that sagged all the way to the ground before rising up again. She was right in front of him now and only six feet or so off the ground. "Anyway, I was sitting on the porch—sorry, on the gallery—enjoying the morning and doing some embroidery and admiring La Belle Claire, and I realized that I had never climbed a tree before. I had never been reckless or adventurous. I had never seen Texas before."

"Honey, if that's how you're defining reckless and adventurous," he teased, "then you 'saw Texas' two days ago, when you took a chance with me."

She held out her arms, and he reached above to grasp her around the waist. He pulled, and she leaped—well, sort of slid—and he helped her to the ground. When her feet were safely on firm earth again, though, he didn't release her.

"No, Remy," she seriously disagreed. "That was heaven."

His laughter was quick and easy. "Damn, Susannah, I've never met a woman who amuses and arouses me at the same time."

Giving him an innocent look, she stepped closer and rubbed tantalizingly against him. "Are you aroused?"

"Sweetheart, I'm horny as hell."

"Hmm. *I'm* hungry. I was thinking about having a big breakfast and then maybe settling into that chaise longue on the gallery and not moving the rest of the morning."

That held a certain appeal, too, Remy admitted. And, after all, they did have all day.

In fact, they had the rest of their lives to indulge their desire.

Keeping his arm around her shoulder, he steered her back toward the gallery. "Come on, and I'll help you with breakfast."

"I thought you couldn't cook."

"Anyone can fry bacon or scramble eggs." They paused at the bench so she could scoop up the sewing basket, then continued their leisurely walk around the house. "What about your embroidery?"

"Oh, I finished it. It wasn't anything much."

"Do I get to see it?"

She considered it for what seemed an extraordinarily long time before finally looking up at him. "I suppose so. Sooner…" She walked inside the house and straight into the parlor, looking at him over her shoulder as she returned the basket to its place. "Or later."

It was approaching three o'clock when Susannah finally stirred from the chaise longue where she was watching Remy alternately doze and watch *her.* It had been the laziest of days, one that she couldn't bear to bring to an end.

But she had to.

She had to bring everything to an end.

Sitting up, she stretched, then brushed her hair back where it had come loose from its braid. "Hey, Remy?"

"Hmm."

She opened her mouth, but no sound came out. Her throat had closed in a knot and required a moment's swallow to clear. "I've got to go into town to pick up some things. Do you mind?"

Tilting his head to one side, he opened only one eye to study her. "I take it you're not inviting me to go along."

"No. I thought..." She cleared her throat again. "I'd kind of like to go alone."

She waited for him to protest, but instead he grinned. "You don't have to sound so hesitant, sweetheart. We're not permanently joined at the hip, although I wouldn't object if we were."

Relief washed over her. "Is there anything special you want while I'm out?"

"Nah. Just bring yourself back."

Rising from the chair, she bent and kissed his mouth. It wasn't the sort of kiss she wanted to give him, full of passion and fire and love. It was just a simple goodbye kiss. *Goodbye.* It damn near broke her heart.

"Be careful," he called as she disappeared inside.

She combed her hair and got her purse, with the number she had looked up in Mr. Sinclair's study early this morning, then went out to the other side of the house. Her little car was parked near the back, unused since the day she had moved in here. It seemed appropriate, under the circumstances, that she should drive it today.

The engine turned right over, an amusing little putt compared to the powerful purr of the car she'd been driving. She rolled the windows down, turned the stereo on and drove onto the highway. At the first junction, she turned east toward Belclaire, but when she reached the small town, she kept right on driving. At the interstate, she debated between New Orleans and Baton Rouge, finally settling on the capital city.

She would call Smith Kendricks first, she decided. She would explain her situation, would tell him that she wanted to help, would offer the terms under which her cooperation was available. Then she would call Carlucci, take care of a little shopping, then return home . . . Not home. Because of what she'd done, it would never be home. Then she would return to Belle Ste. Claire.

By the time she got back, she had no doubt that Smith would have already called Remy. What action would the U.S. Attorney's office and the FBI decide to take? Would they put Remy someplace safe and unreachable? Would they leave him at the house, under protection, and try to catch Falcone's men in the act? If that was the case, would they allow her to remain also, so Carlucci—and, therefore, Falcone—didn't suspect that they'd been double-crossed? Or would Remy hate her too much to let her stay in his precious family home?

And what would they do about Skip? How could they protect him when he was being held at Falcone's house? How could they get him out safely when he was surrounded by people who wouldn't hesitate to kill him if their boss so ordered?

She didn't have any answers, didn't even have any guesses. All she could do was trust that Smith would take care of things. She had to trust that he loved Remy enough to make everything work out right.

Pulling into a shopping center on the outskirts of Baton Rouge, she found a parking space, then hurried to the nearest pay phone. It was the same place, she realized, where she had come to buy Remy's gloves. The same phone where she had called Nicholas Carlucci the first time.

Dialing the number she had written for the U.S. Attorney's office in the back of her checkbook, she charged the call to her credit card. A receptionist answered and switched her to Smith's office, where another woman picked up.

Her voice trembling, Susannah asked for Smith.

"May I ask who's calling?" The woman sounded terribly efficient and tough. Getting around her could be a problem.

"Tell him that it's regarding Remy Sinclair and—and Jimmy Falcone."

"Yes, ma'am. And your name?"

She clenched the phone tighter. No names, she had promised herself that. Not until she had Smith's promise that Skip would be protected. "Please." Her voice was little more than a whisper, nothing more than a plea. "Tell him that it's very important."

The secretary put her on hold, and she sighed with relief. There was no way Smith would ignore a message like that, even if it did come anonymously. And as soon as she got his promise, she would identify herself.

She would destroy everything between herself and Remy.

She would destroy her future.

After a moment of silence, a voice came on the line, a man's voice, strong and authoritative. "This is Alexander Marshall. How can I help you?"

Panic made her hand tremble. "There's been a mistake. I'm holding for Smith Kendricks."

"Yes, I understand, Miss . . ." He waited a moment, but when she didn't speak, he went on. "Mr. Kendricks is in court this afternoon. I'm his boss, though, and I'd be happy to help you. Now I understand you're calling regarding Remy Sinclair. You have some information for us?"

"I have to talk to Smith. I don't—I don't know you. I have to—" She gulped a deep breath. "When will Smith be back?"

"I really don't know. But anything you tell me will be in confidence, and I'll pass it on to Smith as soon as he returns."

"No, I'm sorry. I can't—" Abruptly, she hung up. Stupid, stupid, *stupid,* she berated herself. Why hadn't she considered the possibility that Smith—a prosecutor, for heaven's sake!—might be in court today? And why hadn't she come earlier in the day, so that if he *was* gone, she would have the rest of the day to call back? This late in the afternoon, he very well might not even return to the office until Monday morning.

And Monday morning could be too late.

She was a fool to think she could handle this. She deserved whatever punishment the government chose to give her, even prison.

She *deserved* to lose Remy.

Bleakly, pulling her credit card out again, she dialed Carlucci's number. Until the end, the call was virtually the same as the others. She told him that Remy had had no visitors, no phone calls, that except for a brief trip into the city Wednesday, he had gone nowhere and done nothing, and he told her that Skip was still fine. She hated the way he said it—*still fine*—as if that condition was liable to change at any moment.

At the end, though, she gathered her courage. "It's been nearly three weeks, Mr. Carlucci. How much longer?"

"Don't be impatient, Susannah. By the time the Sinclairs return from their vacation, you and Skip will be safely home in Nebraska."

"When will we be leaving? Tomorrow? Monday? Wednesday?"

He was silent for a long, cold moment, then he replied, "Call me Tuesday morning, Susannah." He hung up.

Frustrated, she slammed the receiver down with more force than necessary, and returned to her car. She had to buy some groceries, and there surely would be a pay phone at the store. She would try Smith one last time, and if she didn't get him then . . .

Then she would go back.

And she would tell Remy everything.

Remy was standing in front of the refrigerator, wishing he had asked Susannah to pick up some beer, when the phone began ringing. There was an answering machine in his father's office that would get it on the fourth or fifth ring, but he headed that way anyway. She'd been gone a long time for a shopping trip to Belclaire; maybe she'd had car trouble or had gotten lost or something else had gone wrong. Whatever the problem, he didn't want to leave her to talk to an impersonal machine.

The machine picked up before he reached the office; he could tell by the low tones that it was a man, not Susannah. Before he got close enough to recognize the voice or understand the words, the caller hung up, but only seconds later, the phone rang again.

This time he got it before the machine. He didn't even get out a complete hello before Smith interrupted him. "Where is Susannah?"

Puzzled, Remy eased himself into his father's chair. "What?"

"Where the hell is Susannah?"

"Uh...she went to pick up some things at the store. Why?"

"Do you have your gun up there?"

"Yeah, it's—"

"On you?"

"Of course not. It's in my room."

"Go get it."

"Smith, what's going—"

"*Now*, Remy. I'll wait. And if Susannah comes back while you're gone...don't turn your back on her."

Curious as hell—and wishing his father had a cordless phone like everyone else in the world—he laid the phone on the desk, took up his cane again and went to his room. Once the pistol in its holster was secured to the waistband of his sweats, he returned to the study as quickly as he could. "Okay, I'm back. Now what the hell's going on?"

Chapter 10

It was after five o'clock and growing dark when Susannah let herself into the house and carried two bags of groceries into the kitchen. She stopped at the doorway to flip the light switch with her elbow, then gave a start when she saw Remy sitting there at the table. Was she simply surprised to see him sitting there in the dark? he wondered grimly.

Or was she surprised to see him at all?

She gave him a long, uneasy look—a guilty look. God help him, how many times had he seen that guilt in her eyes and disregarded it? People didn't look guilty for no reason, but he had ignored it, had brushed it off as if it were unimportant.

He was a fool.

After a moment, her gaze dropped to the table and the items spread out there in front of him. There was a small bag—a shopping bag, about the right size for a greeting card, made of a plastic so dark that the first time he'd searched the armoire in her room, he had missed it there in the back. There were the contents of the bag: a sticky note, the kind meant for refrigerators and computers, with a New

Orleans phone number and a five-by-seven-inch photograph.

And there was his gun, within easy reach and, right now, lying there pointed at her.

The shopping bags began sliding from her arms. She caught them about halfway to the floor and eased them down, then straightened again.

"Put your purse down, too, and move away from it."

She obeyed him, taking a few steps closer to the table. After a moment he gestured for her to sit in the chair across from him.

"Remy—"

"Why, Susannah?" he interrupted. "Was it for love? Money?"

She laid her hands on the tabletop, her fingers knotted together but trembling a bit anyway. Nice touch, he thought cynically. "There's no money involved."

"So it's love then." He would have preferred money, he realized with an ache. He would have preferred believing that his life—or, rather, his death—was worth money to her to knowing that it meant nothing more than a favor for someone she loved. "He's a little young for you, don't you think?" Of course, with the appetite she'd shown in the past few days, she probably had to take them young. More energy, better stamina—those were probably important qualities to her.

"So you and young Lewis here... Sort of an old-fashioned name, isn't it? Do you call him that or Lew?"

She reached out, and his hand moved closer to the pistol, freezing her in motion. Drawing her hand back, she quietly asked, "Can I see the picture?"

He looked at it a moment, at Susannah, smiling and beautiful and happy, and at the dark-haired young man whose arms were around her, also smiling, handsome and equally happy. It was relatively recent, taken soon after her arrival in New Orleans, assuming that part of her story was true.

Disgusted, he tossed the photograph across the table and watched her catch it just as it slid to the edge.

"How do you know his name?"

"We have a file on Lewis Crouse. He works for Jimmy Falcone...but, of course, you know that." He shook his head grimly. "I have to be honest. I don't know how we missed you, living with Crouse and on Falcone's payroll yourself. We got sloppy. So...you call him Lewis or Lew or what?"

"Actually I call him Skip." She gave the couple in the photo a sad smile, then laid it on the table and looked at him. "Lew is our father."

Remy stared at her. "Lewis Crouse is your brother," he said skeptically. "How does an only child three weeks ago suddenly come up with a twenty-three-year-old brother?"

"I lied to you." Ignoring his muttered curse, she went on. "I thought that, with the trouble Skip was in—with the trouble that *we're* in—it would be best to deny having a brother."

He wasn't sure he believed her, but that could be sorted out later. "So what's the deal, Susannah? You help them kill me—that's easy enough to figure out—but what do you get in return?"

"I get my brother back safe."

"Get him back? From where?"

She drew a deep breath. "For the last month or so, they've been keeping him at Jimmy Falcone's house."

"Keeping," he repeated. "You mean as a prisoner."

"Yes."

He considered the plausibility of that for a moment. It was certainly a prettier tale than he'd expected. It had a much nicer, much more innocent, ring to it than admitting, "I'm conspiring with a known organized crime figure to murder a federal agent because it's how I get my kicks or because my kid brother asked me to or because it's been a slow month in the emergency room with not enough people dying to satisfy me." *He* would certainly rather believe that she'd done all this—come here, betrayed him, put his life in danger—because her brother's life was in danger.

But then, he was crazy in love with her. He would rather believe any story, no matter how outlandish, in which she was acting against her will.

Without waiting to be asked, she began her explanation. Her excuse. "Skip came down here about two years ago to go to school. He had always been pampered at home— smothered, he called it—and he wanted to get away, wanted to get out on his own. I don't know how he got tied up with Jimmy Falcone. I guess he's just that kind of kid...if there's trouble around to be found, he'll find it. I had no idea what was going on when I moved down here. I was eager to get out of Nebraska myself, and when Skip invited me to come down and live with him ... It seemed like the answer to my prayers. I could start all over in a new place, but I wouldn't be totally on my own. I'd have family. I'd have Skip."

She closed her eyes for a moment, then blinked them rapidly to control the dampness that had collected. "As soon as I got to New Orleans, I discovered that Skip was in debt, that he wasn't going to school and couldn't—or wouldn't—hold a regular job. His friends were rougher, tougher, than back home, and he was more reckless, more irresponsible, than ever. He was getting into trouble and staying out late. And then he got the job with Jimmy Falcone. It seems that, after that, all we ever did was argue. I wanted him to grow up, and he was having too much fun playing the tough guy. Then..."

Remy stared at her as she spoke, his expression stony and hard, but inside he felt a strange, almost giddy sense of relief. She was telling the truth. It was in her eyes, her voice, her expression and her gestures. She had lied to him, true. She had betrayed him, when he had sworn that he would never let anyone betray him again.

But she hadn't done it willingly. This was what she had meant all those times she had insisted that he didn't know her at all. When she had said that she didn't have the right to care about him. When she had sworn repeatedly that she had nothing to give, that she was worth nothing. When she had warned that she might hurt him.

I could be a terrible person. I could have awful things planned for you.

And maybe you'll die, regretting the day we met.

She'd been warning him from the beginning, only he had been too intent upon seducing her to recognize it.

Realizing that she had fallen silent, he prompted her. "And then?"

"One day I got a phone call. Skip wasn't home—I hadn't seen him in a day or so, but that wasn't so unusual. When we argued about the way he was wasting his life, he often stayed over at a friend's place a night or two. Anyway, the phone call was from a lawyer named Nicholas Carlucci. He told me that he was Falcone's lawyer, that he knew Skip. He said that he knew the details of every job Skip had ever done for Falcone, that he had documented everything. It was all minor stuff, nothing really bad, but it would be such an easy thing, he said, to make it look worse, to make the police believe worse."

If anyone could build a tight, credible case against a reckless, irresponsible Nebraska farm boy, Nick Carlucci could, Remy acknowledged. If Falcone had used Nick to construct the frame for Nate Simmons's murder around *him,* he would likely be sitting in a cell somewhere right now. "So in exchange for your help, he wouldn't set your brother up for a crime he didn't commit."

He sounded so cold, Susannah thought. It was useless continuing with her explanation. Even if he believed her, which she doubted, he would never, ever forgive her. Still, she did continue, her voice slight and empty of hope. "He told me that you were looking for a nurse to help you out until the cast came off. He advised me to apply for the job and to do whatever was necessary to get it. In the meantime, he said, Mr. Falcone had invited Skip to come and stay with him for a while, and that was where he would stay until . . ." She paused to recall Carlucci's exact words. "Until the issue of Remy Sinclair had been resolved."

"Why didn't you go to the police?"

"Because he assured me that if I did, my brother would pay, most likely with his life."

"So what were you supposed to do? How far were you supposed to go to protect your brother from his own actions?"

"Carlucci wanted regular reports. He wanted to know your schedule, who you talked to, who you saw, where you went. That's all."

"That's all," Remy repeated scathingly. He pushed away from the table and paced across the room. He didn't forget to take the pistol with him. "That's enough to get me killed."

"I know." The tears that had burned her eyes earlier spilled over now. "I'm sorry, Remy. I'm so sorry."

"So that's who you've been calling—Carlucci. That's why you didn't want your mail delivered here." At the counter, he turned back to face her. "Did he tell you anything? How they plan to do it or where or when?"

She shook her head. "Just . . . sometime before your parents get back from Europe."

He started to speak, thought better of it and turned away.

"I know it's not enough," she whispered, "but I *am* sorry. I thought—I thought I could take care of everything. I thought I could protect you and Skip and that no one would have to get hurt."

He gave her a derisive look. "And how the hell were you going to do that? Make a deal with Smith? Tell him he could do whatever he wanted to you as long as he let your precious little brother go free?"

She wished she dared reach into her purse for a tissue, but he was still holding that gun and he still looked so angry. Instead she wiped her cheeks with her hand. "Is that how you found out? Does Smith's office record his phone calls?"

"Technology's a wonderful thing, isn't it?" he replied sarcastically. "Do you know how much trouble you've caused? You called Carlucci from Michael's apartment, for God's sake. The man is part of a major investigation. Do you think the government isn't keeping track of the phone calls he receives? How do you think it looks when the bureau's doing a routine check of all the phone numbers that have made calls to Carlucci or Falcone or any of the others, and they find a number belonging to a New Orleans cop listed there?"

She huddled a little tighter in her chair. Now Michael had a reason other than simply instinct to dislike her.

"They began a background check on Michael—on my *friend*. Do you have any idea how that looks, for a cop to be investigated by the FBI? It's not exactly a career-enhancing move. They began examining *his* phone records, and today they went to court to get a wiretap order so they could monitor *his* calls. Fortunately for him, they had to go through Smith for the court order, and he remembered that *you* were the only one to use Michael's phone that night. Michael verified that, and so did Valery."

"I'm sorry," she whispered helplessly. *So sorry.*

Gripping his cane in his right hand and the pistol in his left, he came back to the table, this time sitting in the chair closest to her. "When Smith got back to his office this afternoon," he continued, his voice empty of emotion, "his boss had a little tape for him to listen to. Marshall had already notified the FBI, and they had already traced the call to a pay phone in Baton Rouge. Interestingly, a few weeks ago a call was made to Carlucci from that same phone on the same day and at the same time that I saw you using it. Everyone already suspected it was you on the tape, but Smith was the only one who could prove it. He recognized your voice, and he called me. Damn it, Susannah—"

At that instant, the room fell into darkness, and Remy muttered a curse. Susannah prayed that it was just a fuse that had blown or that the power had gone out everywhere along the highway, but that awful sick feeling in her stomach warned her that wasn't the case.

His chair scraped just a little when he stood up. "Come on," he demanded in the hoarsest of whispers, taking her arm and pulling her with him out of the kitchen and down the hall toward the study. She followed blindly, not familiar enough with this part of the house to find her way in total darkness. He went straight to his father's desk and picked up the phone there, then swore again. "It's dead . . . and, sweet God in heaven, so are we."

"Maybe it's just—"

He silenced her with his hand on her mouth as the distant, almost delicate sound of breaking glass echoed through the house. She couldn't tell where the sound had come from—the darkness confused her, disoriented her—but Remy seemed to know. He began moving quietly, around the desk, the chair, the credenza, to one of two French doors that opened from the study to the south gallery. There were multiple locks on every exterior door in the house, and he was in the process of unlatching the second one when footsteps sounded in the hall.

Susannah recognized at least two distinct steps, one heavy like a boot and the other lighter, stealthier. A man and a woman? It had been a man and a woman in that gray car that Sunday afternoon, taking pictures of them when they were outside. Could these be the same two?

After an excruciatingly long moment of stillness, Remy opened the third lock, then began easing the door open. When it creaked, he stopped immediately; when no one came running, he opened it farther. As soon as the space was wide enough, he slipped outside, pulled her after him, then began the slow process of closing the door again.

It was quiet outside; just another peaceful country evening. Susannah shivered, wishing for one of the sweaters in her room. She wished for socks, too—her ankles were cold—and for the car keys she had dropped on the kitchen floor when she had dropped her purse.

Most of all, she wished for the power to stop what she had started.

She wished for some way to protect Remy.

She wished she didn't have to die knowing that he hated her.

Her sudden understanding—that she *was* going to die, that Falcone and Carlucci had probably intended from the start to kill her along with Remy—brought with it a sudden calm. Using her free hand, she tried to pry his fingers from her arm. "Let me go, Remy."

He looked at her in the moonlight. "We've got to get away from the house," he whispered. "They'll search some of the rooms, but maybe not all of them. We've got to get to the woods."

"Let me go back inside. Let me talk to them."

"Are you crazy? You can't reason with people like them! They came here to kill us, Susannah—*us,* not just me!"

"I know. But maybe..." Maybe she could slow them down. Maybe she could throw them off track. Maybe she could do something, *anything,* to give him an advantage.

"No. *Hell,* no. You're staying with me." To ensure that, he held her tighter, tight enough to hurt. "We have to work our away around to the back of the house, then use the trees and their shadows to get to the woods. Stay beside me and stay close. Understand?"

She nodded, and he set off, drawing her with him. They practically hugged the outer wall, following it all the way back to the steps that led down to the yard where La Belle Claire grew. They had to step into the moonlight then, and Remy cringed at the thought of how it shone on Susannah's pale shirt and his own fair hair. Quickly, though, they worked their way back into shadows, squeezing between the house and the shrubs that grew around the foundation.

At last they reached the back wall of the servants' wing. It was the easternmost part of the house and came closest to the woods that offered their only hope. It seemed to have taken forever, but he estimated it had been only a few minutes, maybe five or six at the most, since the power had been cut.

Now came the tough part. Now they had to move, quickly and quietly, through moonlight and shadow. Now they had to expose themselves to a high risk of discovery. All Falcone's people had to do was look out the window at the right moment—and they were in a house filled with windows.

He drew a deep breath, then blew it out again. Before leaving the cover the house provided, he looked at Susannah, expecting to see fear, tears, terror. Instead there on that lovely face was the serenity he'd fallen in love with that long-ago night in the hospital. Serenity, damn it. The woman was facing death, and she was doing it with far more calmness than *he,* an experienced federal agent, could dredge up. He would laugh if he weren't so damned afraid.

She looked at him then, and he mouthed, "Ready?"

At her slight nod, they left the safety of the house, hurrying across moonlit grass to the cover of a live oak. This one wasn't as big as Claire, but it was big enough to hide them both on the other side.

They cut a zigzagging trail from one tree to another. If only he could run, they could take a straight shot for the old barn, then veer off into the woods and use these precious moments to put as much distance between them and the house as possible. But he couldn't run. He could only hobble at a moderate pace, and even that was quickly becoming painful. He wasn't kidding himself: if they made it to the woods, he wouldn't be able to go far. But at least he could get Susannah headed in the right direction. At least he could give her a chance to escape. He might even be able to set up an ambush of some sort and, if he was really lucky, save himself.

At last they reached the last tree. A wide clearing stretched ahead of them, lit by the moon and with nothing, not even the faintest shadow, for cover. Remy leaned against the trunk of the live oak, taking his weight off his favored leg for a moment. "Once you get into the woods, there's a trail," he whispered. "It's probably pretty grown over, but you can find it, and when you do, you run like hell. It winds back for a mile or two and comes out on the next road over. When you reach the road, turn left. There are a half-dozen houses just a few hundred feet away. Go to one of them, call

the sheriff and tell him to call Michael or Smith. Understand?''

When she didn't respond, he gave her a little shake. ''Do
you understand, damn it?''

''Yes,'' she replied with a mutinous scowl.

''Don't worry, Susannah,'' he said with a grin meant to
reassure. ''I'll be right behind you.'' *If I'm not dead.*
''Ready?''

Together they pushed away from the tree, trading its
safety for the lighted clearing. At about the halfway point,
he started to think that just maybe they might make it when,
from somewhere up above, a shout—and, God help them,
a shot—rang out. ''Hey!'' a woman called from the sec-
ond-floor veranda. ''They're out back!''

''Go on, Susannah!'' he commanded, shoving her in the
direction of the woods, but apparently she had other ideas.
She knew he couldn't keep up with her in the trees, knew he
couldn't outdistance their killers and, damn her, she wasn't
going without him. In fact, *she* was the one leading now, the
one pulling him straight into the barn.

It was the worst place they could have gone, the first place
their killers would look. It was old and musty, big and filled
with shapes he couldn't recognize. But Susannah could. She
had explored inside during one of her walks, he realized, for
she led him straight to the best cover—the only cover—the
old place seemed to provide: bales of hay stacked precari-
ously, one atop another, some only four feet high, others
towering over their heads. Releasing his arm, she wriggled
into a crevice between stacks, then disappeared from sight.

Remy hesitated only an instant, then, hearing a screen
door slam, he pushed through behind Susannah. The bales
were stacked unevenly, some pushed up tight against the
rows behind them, others leaving gaps. It was like a maze—
narrow, winding, the dust overpowering. Dropping to his
knees where there was room, he rounded a corner and found
a small breathing space. Susannah sat there in a huddle,
knees drawn to her chest, head bowed. He settled a few feet

away from her, listened and tried hard not to notice the fine
dust that was clogging his throat and his lungs.

"Check the woods," the woman directed from the clearing.

"They wouldn't go into the woods," disagreed a deeper,
male voice. "The guy's a cripple. How far is he gonna make
it in the woods? My money's on the barn."

"There's nothing in the barn except hay and old rusted-
out equipment, and there's only one way out. He'd have to
be a fool to hide in there, and Sinclair's no fool."

"No, but he's got a bum leg, he can't run and he's dragging the deadweight of a woman around behind him. It's his
best bet."

Remy glanced at the woman he was supposed to be dragging around with him—the woman who had dragged *him* in
here. She was no more than a pale shadow in the darkness,
curled up tight as if she were trying to crawl inside herself.
He wished he could reassure her, wished he could somehow
comfort her, but he didn't dare speak or even move. Not
now, not when the powerful beam of a flashlight was playing across the interior of the barn.

"Sinclair!" The man's voice echoed off the rafters, then
dissipated in the still night. For a time it seemed there was
no sound at all, then Remy could make out the man's
breathing and, more distant, a car passing by on the highway.

"We know you're in here, Sinclair. There's no way you
can get away with that bad leg. Give it up now, and we'll let
the woman go."

Although a part of him desperately wanted to believe that
was possible, Remy knew the bastard was lying. Falcone had
never intended to let Susannah or her brother walk away
from this. Their deaths had been part of the plan from the
very beginning. Like Nate Simmons, they were expend-
able, a sacrifice to their boss's ambition.

And this time, Falcone was determined to succeed. He
wasn't using his own people. Remy knew them all by sight,
and there wasn't a woman in the bunch, which meant he'd

brought someone in from out of town. He was paying big bucks for the big guns.

"Come on, Sinclair, don't be stubborn. There's no way you can save yourself... but you *can* save her. Come on out."

What was the worst they could do? Remy considered. Open fire on the bales of hay? Thick as they were, they wouldn't stop the sort of high-powered ammunition these people were sure to be using. There was a slim chance, he supposed, that he and Susannah could survive, but very slim.

If he were in their position, he would save his ammo and take the easy way out: toss a match into the hay, stand back and watch the place go up in flames. As aged as the timbers were, as dry as the hay was, the barn would become an inferno in literally seconds. The best he and Susannah could hope for then would be to succumb to smoke before the flames got them, and that wouldn't be likely.

"Maybe they're not here," the woman said impatiently.

"Oh, they're here." The man sounded supremely confident. "I can smell 'em. Go pull the car up. We can use the headlights to help find them."

What were his chances, Remy wondered, of moving soundlessly with his cast and finding a crack in the stacks of hay that would allow him a view of their hunters? And if he got that view, what were the chances he could take them both out before either of them got any shots off? He was a damned good shot. He routinely spent hours on the range practicing for just such a purpose.

But the targets on the range didn't shoot back.

And these targets would be shooting at Susannah, too.

From outside came the sound of an engine, then light flooded the barn. Hoping their hiding place was more secure than it felt, he took advantage of the increased light to check on Susannah... just in time to see her disappear deeper into the stacks of hay. Damn her, where was she going?

"So what do we do now?" the woman asked after switching off the engine, then rejoining the man in the barn.

"We start pitching hay and see what little creatures come slithering out."

"Don't bother." The voice came from a few feet above and at least a dozen feet away. It was clear, unmuffled by hay and it was definitely Susannah's.

Remy bowed his head against the bale in front of him and whispered a silent prayer, a silent plea. *Dear God, Susannah, what have you done?*

Susannah's hands were in the air, shoulder high, her fingers spread wide. Blinded by the lights, she could see little—two shadowy forms, one slender and about her height, the other bigger, bulkier. She couldn't tell anything about the car, couldn't see their guns, although, of course, they had them.

And they were prepared to use them.

"Please don't shoot me," she said, ignoring the bits of straw that clung to her hair and clothes, that floated in the air and tickled and itched wherever they touched. "I'm unarmed. Please don't hurt me."

It was the man who responded. "This little creature's a whole lot prettier than the rodent I was expecting," he said with what sounded like a grin. "Where is Sinclair?"

"I don't know. He wouldn't come in with me. He said it was too obvious." She forced a tremble into her voice. "He said . . . he said we would have a better chance in the woods, that there's a road back there, and some houses."

"I told you so," the woman muttered.

"So why didn't you go with him?" the man challenged.

"Because he's slow. He can't run with that cast. Besides, it's him you're after, not me. If I stayed with him, you might shoot me by mistake."

The man found that remark worthy of a chuckle. The woman didn't. Ignoring him, she took a few steps forward, partially blocking the headlights' beams. "Come on out here."

Susannah had crawled into a dead end. Now she maneuvered carefully, slowly, lifting herself up onto the bales in front, wriggling and sliding, wasting as much time as she dared. She wasn't sure exactly what she was hoping for—that while she distracted them, Remy would find some way to escape; that she could convince them that he had, indeed, gone into the woods instead and that they could use her to find him; that she might simply give him a little longer to live.

Finally she could delay no longer. She climbed down makeshift stairs of bales and at last stood on the dirt floor in the center of the barn, cold and shivering.

The woman approached her, coming close enough that Susannah could make out her features in spite of the light in her eyes. She was blond, probably in her mid-thirties, really rather pretty. What kind of career choices had this woman made, she wondered, that she found herself in a job where she killed people for a living?

The woman stopped only a few yards—ten, maybe twelve feet—away and raised her right arm, extending it fully. That put the pistol she was holding dead level with Susannah's heart. From that short distance, there was no way she could miss. "You want to watch her die, Remy?" she called. "Because that's what's going to happen if you don't get out here *now*."

Her voice trembling for real this time, Susannah edged a step back. "You can't kill me. I did everything I was asked to. I kept my end of the bargain. I made a deal with Mr. Falcone, and I kept it."

It was the man, still over by the door, who responded. "No, you made your deal with Nick Carlucci. *We* deal with Mr. Fal—"

"Shut up!" the blonde interrupted. "Sinclair, last warning!"

Hearing a scrape of noise off to the side where she had left Remy, Susannah burst into rapid, tearful speech. "I told you, he's not here! I want to talk to Mr. Falcone! I did what I was supposed to, I gave Carlucci all the information, I kept quiet and I didn't tell anyone anything, and he promised, damn you—"

"Susannah, get down!"

Remy's warning shout was followed immediately by a thunderous shot as she scrambled for the nearest crevice in the stacks of hay. Amid more shots, she fell to the floor, then began burrowing backward, feetfirst, seeking more cover, not stopping until something blocked her way. Twisting in the narrow space, she turned to see what the barrier was and whether she could work her way around it....

And found herself facing the blonde and one very deadly looking gun.

Dimly she heard a grunt of pain from across the room, heard the sound of weight hitting the floor and a muttered curse. It came from over near the door, she told herself, over where the man had been standing. It wasn't Remy who'd been hurt. It wasn't Remy who'd gone down. She assured herself of that.

She prayed for it.

And her prayers were answered.

"You have me at a disadvantage," Remy called out in the heavy silence. "You know me, but I don't know you."

Down at Susannah's feet, the woman remained silent.

"Your partner's down. Why don't you come on out and let's get this over with."

She still said nothing, but she seemed to be considering her options. It didn't take her long at all to settle on her best hope. With her pistol and the jerk of her head, she gestured for Susannah to get to her feet. Turning onto her stomach, Susannah prepared to do just that. "Remy? It's me. Don't shoot."

Over in the corner Remy listened to her tearful plea with genuine regret. The serenity had disappeared again. She was afraid—afraid for her life—and there was nothing he could do to reassure her. Nothing he could do to help her. "Come on out, Susannah," he said softly.

Crawling to the opening, she slowly got to her knees, then stood up. Immediately rising behind her was the blonde—why wasn't he surprised?—with the barrel of her gun pressed hard against Susannah's back. "You're right, Sinclair," the woman said. "Come on out and let's get it over with."

After a moment's hesitation, he stepped out from behind his cover and gave them a rueful look. "Hell, Susannah, how did you manage to hide where she already was?" he asked, the mildness of his voice negating the rebuke.

"I do my job very well," the blonde answered. "And for the record, Remy, my name is Greta, and I'm from Chicago."

"Why don't you let her go? It's me you're after. You don't want to kill her."

"Yes, I do. She's part of the job."

He flexed his fingers around the grip of his pistol. When your target was using a hostage as a shield, your best shot was a head shot, but Greta was careful. She was a little bit shorter than Susannah and a good deal thinner, and she was keeping Susannah squarely in between them. From this angle, he couldn't get off any sort of shot at all without sacrificing Susannah.

And he wasn't *that* desperate to live.

But he was desperate enough to stall. To hope that someone had heard the gunshots and called the sheriff. To hope that help would arrive. To pray that somehow, someway, they could find a way out of this.

"Things must be pretty slow in Chicago if you'd come all the way down here to Louisiana to take care of a nurse from Nebraska."

"I wouldn't cross the street to take care of a nurse from Nebraska or her idiot kid brother. Don't be so modest, Remy. You know it's you I'm here for."

"So you kill us, and you go back to Falcone's place and take care of the brother." He regretted saying those last words, regretted the look of sorrow they brought to Susannah's eyes, but he kept it out of his expression. "Then what?"

"I collect the rest of my money and go home."

"Are you sure about that? Jimmy Falcone's developing a reputation for not upholding his end of his deals. He made a deal with one of his own men a while back to help set me up, and when the guy had done his part, Falcone had him killed. He made a deal with Susannah through Nick Carlucci—and you know dealing with Carlucci is the same as dealing with Falcone—and now he's reneging again. What makes you think he's going to keep his deal with you?"

Greta's laugh was low and husky. "Because I can kill him as easily as I'll kill you."

"Sweetheart, he's got two dozen men around him at any time, any one of whom would be happy to put a bullet in your brain when you least expect it. For all you know, they could be right here, just waiting for you to kill us before they kill you."

She laughed again and shifted just slightly to one side so she could see him better. She was opening her mouth to speak when a single gunshot echoed through the barn. The bullet found its target, entering high in the chest and spinning the woman back and away from Susannah, who shrieked and, for the second time tonight, scrambled away seeking safety.

"Dear God," Remy whispered, stunned, looking abruptly around for whoever had fired the shot.

Then Michael stepped out of the shadows near the door, his expression grim, his pistol in hand.

Remy blew out his breath in a rush. "My God, what are you doing here?"

Holstering his gun, Michael crossed to where the woman's body lay sprawled over a bale of hay. He claimed the pistol she had dropped when she'd fallen, then turned to answer Remy's question. "Smith and I figured this would be a good time for me to spend a few days in the country, while the FBI decided how they were going to handle this new development. I got up here in time to see that you already had some unexpected guests. I called the sheriff from my car. They should be here any minute. I told him to notify Smith. Are you all right?''

"Yeah." He put away his own weapon, found his cane where he'd propped it and limped out into the center of the floor. The man he had shot was coming around now, moaning pitifully as Michael dragged him a few feet closer to the old tractor, then cuffed his wrists to it. The woman... He didn't get close enough to check, but it was a good bet she was dead. Michael was too good a shot, and too good a cop to mess around with trying to wound a suspect when a hostage was involved.

As for the hostage, Susannah was sitting on a bale of hay, her head down, her shoulders rounded, her hands pressed between her knees. She looked utterly lost. Bereft. He sat down beside her, stretching out his leg. "Are you all right?"

For a long time she didn't respond, then finally she raised her head and nodded.

"As far as we know, he's still alive, Susannah. When these two don't come back tonight, Falcone will know they've failed. With you and me both still living, it'll be in his best interests to keep your brother alive, too. He'll be all right."

Her gaze held his a long time, searching, then she nodded again, accepting his assurances, just not terribly reassured by them.

"Are you sure you're okay?"

One more nod.

"Then what the hell were you trying to do, surrendering like that?" he demanded. "Are you crazy?"

The blankness in her soft hazel eyes was replaced by surprise, then shock, then anger. "I was trying to give you a chance to do something!"

"By turning yourself over to them? By letting them take you hostage? For God's sake, Susannah, you could have gotten yourself killed!"

She raised her chin stubbornly and replied in her chilliest voice, "Better than getting you killed." Getting to her feet, she crossed the room, pausing only briefly in front of Michael. "I'm sorry for the trouble I've caused you." With a glance back at Greta, she added, "Thank you."

Then she stalked out of the barn and into the cold night air.

In the silence that followed her leaving, Michael looked at Remy, out the door into the darkness, then back at Remy. "Whatever she did must have worked. You were both still alive when I got here."

"What she did was reckless. Crazy."

"People in love do crazy things." Michael waited. "You going after her?"

Remy sighed. "Yeah, I guess I am." Outside, sirens sounded, and a combination of red and blue lights lit up the night. The sheriff and his deputies had arrived, along with an ambulance. "Can you deal with them for me?" he asked Michael.

There was little for the newcomers to do. The ambulance crew could attend to the gunman and verify that Greta was, indeed, dead, and the sheriff could secure the scene, but the investigation would be handled at the federal level. No doubt a team of FBI agents was on its way up from New Orleans even now.

He didn't have to go far to find Susannah. She had stopped at the nearest tree outside, the same live oak where, such a short time ago, he had instructed her to head into the woods—just moments before she dragged him into the barn. He could admit now that her choice had been better. Handicapped as he was, he surely would have gotten trapped in the woods, with no place to hide and little hope of Michael finding him before it was too late.

She was leaning against the trunk, her arms crossed tightly over her chest. He wished he had a jacket to give her; failing that, he wished he could draw her into his arms and see if they could generate some warmth together. But she looked so fragile, so brittle, as if she couldn't quite bear being touched.

Taking up position beside her, he watched as a growing number of people milled around the old barn. "Thank you."

"For what?"

"Giving me a chance to do something."

She didn't respond. For a long time she just stood there, little shivers rippling through her. Then she spoke, soft, sad and distant. "I'm sorry."

This time it was his turn to ask. "For what?"

"All this. Everything I did. Those people. Tonight."

"You're not responsible for all this, sweetheart. Falcone had it in for me long before either of us knew you existed."

"I'm sorry for my part in it. I'm sorry I didn't tell someone sooner. I'm sorry things went so far." Her voice quavered then. "I'm so sorry."

Remy watched as yet another car pulled into the driveway. It was a sedan, clearly marked by its antennae as a government car, and driving it was Shawna Warren. Other agents would be arriving soon, along with Smith. It was time for him to go to work, but not without one question. "Susannah?" He felt rather than saw her look at him. "Can you tell me one thing? Your brother...is he worth what you did here?"

She looked away again, and tears made her voice thick. She took so long to answer that he had already started to turn away when finally she spoke. "No," she whispered. "He isn't."

Hours passed before quiet fell over Belle Ste. Claire again. Susannah had been questioned by Smith and a female FBI agent, while Remy and Michael silently listened. Then Smith had sent her off to her room with the polite advice that she pack whatever she needed. That had been half an hour ago, and she was still waiting for one of them to come and get her.

She hadn't been exactly sure what to pack. What, after all, did you take to jail? So, by candlelight, she had packed everything. Whatever she didn't need or couldn't keep could be stored or delivered to her apartment or shipped to her father.

One thing was certain: she couldn't leave anything here. She would never be coming back here again.

Now she sat on her bed, knees drawn to her chest, listening to the low murmur of voices down the hall. The woman, Shawna something-or-other, had left a few minutes earlier. As far as Susannah could tell, that left only the three men. She supposed Smith would take Remy to his apartment in New Orleans, at least until the power and phone service could be restored here and until he had an opportunity to hire someone else to help out.

And she supposed Michael would take *her* to jail.

The thought of jail terrified her, although it was no less than she deserved. Still, she'd never had so much as a parking ticket, had never told anything more than a white lie. Now she faced charges of aiding and abetting a known felon, participation in a criminal enterprise and conspiracy to commit murder—those were just a few of the charges the female agent who was in authority had tossed around.

And all she'd been trying to do was protect her brother.

Now she didn't know if Skip was all right or if he was even alive.

But at least Remy was safe.

That was one prayer answered.

Outside a car door slammed, then an engine started. Susannah wondered whether it was Michael or Smith leaving and whether Remy had gone with him. Maybe he wanted to get away from her so much that he wouldn't even tell her he was going. She certainly couldn't blame him.

Even if the thought did make her hurt way down inside.

With a sigh she got to her feet. Whichever of the two men had remained behind to take her into custody would be coming for her any moment now, and there was one more thing she needed to do. Earlier, while everyone was still busy outside, she had reclaimed her embroidery from the sewing basket in the parlor. Now she took it and the note she'd written to accompany it from the desk and, finding her way by moonlight, she went across the hall to Remy's room. She positioned the linen on the dresser and the note on top of it; then, with one last touch of her quilt—of Remy's quilt, which he would probably no longer want—she returned to her own room to wait.

It was another ten minutes before footsteps finally approached. Getting to her feet, she pulled on her jacket and was waiting beside the bed, beside her bags, when Remy stopped in the doorway. "Are you about ready?"

He hadn't left without saying goodbye, she thought with a sudden surge of hope, but it faded as quickly as it had come. Did he want to accompany her to jail? Did he want to actually see her locked up for what she'd done to him? "Yes," she whispered.

He played the flashlight he carried across the room, bringing it to a stop on the bags beside her. "You packed an awful lot for one night."

"I—I didn't know what to take."

"I think just a toothbrush and a change of clothes will be plenty."

"Oh. I didn't know."

"Michael's going to board up the door where they broke in, and I'm going to get my stuff together. Then we'll go."

She listened to him leave, then lifted one bag to the bed and opened it, removing a set of clean clothes. From her tote bag she took out a plastic case containing both her toothbrush and toothpaste, then closed everything up again. She wrapped her clothes around the case and slid the entire bundle into her purse. Then, suddenly, his last words registered in her mind. *I'm going to get my stuff together.*

She bolted from the room, crossed the hall in one step and stopped abruptly beside his bed. His flashlight was sitting on the dresser, its beam pointed across the room, and he was holding her note in one hand, the linen in the other. Just holding them. Looking at them.

Tears stung her eyes. She had left them in plain sight to be sure he found them, but she hadn't wanted him to find them before she was gone. She hadn't wanted to be here to face his pain or anger or rejection. She had hoped she could at least be spared that.

He didn't turn, didn't look around, but he was aware of her. "Susannah, where do you think we're taking you tonight?" he asked, his voice oddly pitched.

"To jail."

"Do you think I would let them arrest you?"

"That woman—Shawna... She said..."

"Shawna's in charge of the investigation, and you're right. If she had her way, you *would* be going to jail. She can arrest you, but Smith is the one who would prosecute you. She'll defer to his recommendations."

"But... I broke the law. What I did was wrong."

"You had a good reason for it. And you tried to make it right before anyone got hurt."

"But I almost got you killed," she whispered sadly.

"My *job* almost got me killed. It happened once before I met you, and it might happen again. Susannah, you played the least significant role in Falcone's plan. They didn't do anything that they couldn't have managed without your information. What happened tonight wasn't your fault."

At last he turned to face her. "So... that takes care of this." He held up her note, a simple and very brief apology—*I'm sorry*—then laid it on the dresser. "Now let's talk about this."

Her gaze dropped to the linen. She couldn't see the stitches from this distance in the dim light, but she could picture them: the fat heart embroidered in gold, decorated with a few simple pink flowers and one flowing ribbon, and the message in script across its center. The words were as blue as his eyes, as blue as her own heart.

"Do you mean this?"

"Remy—"

He silenced her with a gesture. "Do you mean this?"

"Yes," she whispered. "I do."

"'I do.' Now there's an answer I've been looking forward to getting out of you. But somehow I thought we'd have an audience of at least a few hundred when you said it.''

She recognized his tone—that sweet, teasing, charming tone he had used so often with her—and slowly sank onto the bed. ''Why aren't you angry with me?''

''I *was* angry. I got mad, I lost my temper and I yelled at you in the kitchen.'' He shrugged. ''I'm not angry anymore.''

''But I—''

''You made a mistake, Susannah, but you did what you could to correct it. Why would I hold that against you?''

''Remy, a mistake is when you add up the numbers wrong in your checking account and write checks for more money than you have, or you forget to put oil in your car and burn the engine up. My 'mistake' almost got you killed!''

He sat down in front of her, still holding the linen. ''You put your life on the line for me tonight. You could have easily escaped into the woods, but you didn't go because I surely would have gotten caught without you. You could have stayed hidden in the barn, but you didn't. You came out and stalled them so I could have a little more time. For God's sake, Susannah, you knew they intended to kill you, but you put yourself out there anyway, just to give me a chance. That more than makes up for what you did.'' He glanced at the embroidery. ''*This* more than makes up for it.''

She stared at him for a long time, wanting desperately to believe him but afraid. ''Can it be that easy?'' she whispered. ''Can you forgive me just like that?''

With his free hand he claimed both of her hands. ''Remember that Sunday afternoon when we sat out in the yard reading, the first time I kissed you?''

She nodded. It was that day that the woman, Greta, and her partner had shown up.

''I announced to you that I intended to get married.''

''Just as casually as if you had decided to have bacon and eggs for breakfast the next morning.''

"And you said that marriage was too important to be taken so lightly. You said I should get married because I'd fallen in love, because I couldn't imagine living without this woman, because she completed who I was, because there was an emptiness to my life that no one could fill but her." He smiled faintly. "That's how I feel about you, Susannah. You're the one I want to spend the next sixty or seventy years with. I could be angry with you for not confiding in me about your brother. I could send you away and nurse a grudge for the next few weeks or months or even years. I could refuse to forgive what you've done, could refuse to understand why you did it. But none of that would change the fact that I love you."

"But—"

With a chuckle, he drew her close. "Sweetheart, you have more arguments than anyone I've ever known. Answer one question for me: do you love me? And don't forget that I already have it in writing."

"Yes, but—"

"No more *buts*. Just a simple yes or no. Do you love me?"

"Yes."

"Enough to live with me? To marry me? To spend the rest of your life with me?"

She was preparing to offer a more complicated answer when he stopped her with a warning shake of his head. "Yes."

"And I love you, enough to live with you, to marry you, to spend the rest of my life with you." His grin was sweetly confident. "So what more could you possibly want?"

It *could* be that easy, she thought with growing delight. With love you could do anything—could resolve any difference, right any wrong, forgive any hurt. If you loved someone, and he loved you, too, what more *could* you possibly want?

"Susannah?"

She wrapped her arms around his neck and hugged him tightly. "I love you, Remy."

"I know. I love you, too." He kissed her, then solemnly added, "And I always will."

It was a lovely March afternoon, springtime warm and sunny. Susannah sat in the dining room of the apartment she shared with Remy, music playing softly in the background, her attention focused on the quilt frame in front of her. She had bought a few how-to books, had visited a quilt shop in the Quarter and had picked up a few tips from Michael's grandmother last weekend when they'd all gone to Arkansas for his and Valery's wedding. Her first project wasn't turning out badly at all.

Remy had chosen the pattern—Oh, Susannah, of course—and she had chosen the colors: ivory, gold and blue. They both had a romantic streak—and a sentimental one, she thought—that was darn near embarrassing. Take, for example, the ivory squares that formed the corners of each block. Most of them were plain ivory-shaded cotton, but two of them, the upper left and bottom right squares of the very central block, were fine linen. Each was embroidered with a gold heart, and a message was inscribed across each heart. The first was in her handwriting. *Susannah loves Remy.* And the second, in his writing—

"The mail's here." Remy bent to press a kiss to the top of her head as he came in. "You got a letter from your dad *and* one from Skip."

She laid her needle and thimble aside and took the envelopes he offered. The FBI had picked Skip up at Falcone's house and arrested both Jimmy Falcone and Nicholas Carlucci the day after the attempt on their lives. After he had cooperated fully with them and Smith's office, he had been allowed to return home to Nebraska. He would be brought back to testify—if they ever made it to court—but in the meantime, he was living at the farm, working hard and keeping his promise to stay out of trouble.

She hoped he managed to keep it for a long, long time.

She skimmed his letter, then her father's, before returning them to their envelopes. Instead of returning to work on the quilt, though, she settled back in her chair and studied Remy for so long that he began to squirm. "What?" he asked at last.

"You look good." His cast was off, and the physical therapists had worked wonders at rebuilding the muscles in his right leg. Of course, she liked to think that the love they made on a fairly regular basis had something to do with his recovery, too. He still needed the cane on occasion, when he was tired or his days at the office were impossibly long, but for the most part he was as fit and healthy as anyone she'd ever seen.

"I feel good." Remy grinned lecherously. "Want me to show you?"

"I'd like that," she replied with a smile that made him slowly turn serious. It was a soft, gentle smile, he thought, full of the serenity that had first drawn him to her. For much of their time together at Belle Ste. Claire, it had been missing, but he lived with it now. He saw it in her smile every night, saw it in the sleepy, drowsy lines of her face every morning.

She gathered her supplies together, then bent over the quilt top to secure her needle in its layers. He wrapped his arms around her from behind, holding her close while he examined her handiwork over her shoulder. He had never taken much interest in any kind of craft, but this quilt interested him. He could sit and watch her work on it for hours. He could imagine all the nights of warmth it would give them.

He was already anticipating all the intimacies they would share underneath it.

"You do good work," he remarked.

"I come from a family of quilters," she reminded him.

He reached past her to trace across the fine stitches, to stroke over the hearts and their sentiments; then he pulled her around and kissed her. "Come upstairs with me, sweetheart," he invited hoarsely. "There's something I want to show you."

Such as how much he loved her.

Or maybe the two embroidered pieces in the center of the quilt said it best.

Susannah loves Remy.
But Remy loves her more.

* * * * *

Another wonderful year of romance concludes with

Christmas Memories

Share in the magic and memories of romance during the holiday season with this collection of two full-length contemporary Christmas stories, by two bestselling authors

Diana Palmer
Marilyn Pappano

Available in December at your favorite retail outlet.

Only from

Silhouette®

where passion lives.

XMMEM

MILLION DOLLAR SWEEPSTAKES (III)

Harlequin® Historical

Maura Seger's
BELLE HAVEN

Four books. Four generations. Four indomitable females.

You met the Belle Haven women who started it all in Harlequin Historicals. Now meet descendant Nora Delaney in the emotional contemporary conclusion to the Belle Haven saga:

THE SURRENDER OF NORA

When Nora's inheritance brings her home to Belle Haven, she finds more than she bargained for. Deadly accidents prove someone wants her out of town—fast. But the real problem is the prime suspect—handsome Hamilton Fletcher. His quiet smile awakens the passion all Belle Haven women are famous for. But does he want her heart...or her life?

Don't miss THE SURRENDER OF NORA
Silhouette Intimate Moments #617
Available in January!

HUSBAND: SOME ASSEMBLY REQUIRED
Marie Ferrarella
(SE #931, January)

Murphy Pendleton's act of bravery landed him in the hospital—and right back in Shawna Saunders's life. She'd lost her heart to him before—and now this dashing real-life hero was just too tempting to resist. He could be the Mr. Right Shawna was waiting for....

Don't miss
HUSBAND: SOME ASSEMBLY REQUIRED,
by Marie Ferrarella,
available in January!

She's friend, wife, mother—she's you! And beside each Special Woman stands a wonderfully *special* man. It's a celebration of our heroines—and the men who become part of their lives.

EXTRA! EXTRA! READ ALL ABOUT...
MORE ROMANCE
MORE SUSPENSE
MORE INTIMATE MOMENTS

Join us in February 1995 when
Silhouette Intimate Moments introduces
the first title in a whole new program:
INTIMATE MOMENTS EXTRA. These break-
through, innovative novels by your favorite
category writers will come out every few
months, beginning with Karen Leabo's
Into Thin Air, IM #619.

Pregnant teenagers had been
disappearing without a trace, and
Detectives Caroline Triece and Austin Lomax
were called in for heavy-duty damage
control...because now the missing girls
were turning up dead.

In May, Merline Lovelace offers
Night of the Jaguar, and other
INTIMATE MOMENTS EXTRA novels will
follow throughout 1995, only in—

INTIMATE MOMENTS®
™ Silhouette®

IMEXTRA

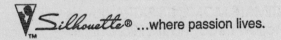